THE LITTLE CAKE SHOP BY THE SEA

LITTLE SHOP BY THE SEA SERIES

LIZZIE CHANTREE

lemon meringue

PUBLISHING

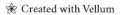 Created with Vellum

Dedicated to my beautiful friend Sara, who lit up a room when she smiled.
Our favourite place to sit and chat about our wonderful families, was a pretty little cupcake shop by the sea.
I miss you.
Always in my heart.

A LITTLE SHOP BY THE SEA SERIES.

BOOK 2

CHAPTER ONE

$\mathcal{F}$ern watched her birth parents hug each other and her stomach flipped over. She gripped the side of the table she was sitting at in the cake shop she ran beside a beautiful stretch of the Cornish coastline. She couldn't help noticing the surface needed a wipe and wished she wasn't so detail-driven in every single aspect of her life.

She bit the inside of her lip until she winced, then shoved a spoonful of the heavenly iced cake on her plate into her mouth to soothe the pain. The delicious burst of flavour made her salivate for more. The combination of coffee and caramel never ceased to make her sigh. She'd been creating masterpieces for years from the kitchen at the back of her little coffee shop – but she'd run it with her adoptive parents, Bill and Irene. Meeting her birth parents, Milly and James, had been both wonderful and traumatic all at once and she still hadn't quite recovered.

She was sure she'd aged ten years in the last six months, since her quiet world had been turned upside down and her serenity exploded. As far as she had known, her birth parents had died years ago… just after she was born. Now they were standing in front of her and hugging like lovesick teenagers. Could this day get any weirder or more uncomfortable?

She hadn't dreamed of this moment for years, unlike other adoptees she'd heard of. Being told that her mother had died in childbirth, and that Bill and Irene didn't know who her father was, had curtailed her questioning. Although she'd often wondered what her birth parents had been like, her adoptive parents had showered her with so much love and understanding that she'd never had the courage to ask for more information, for fear of breaking their hearts.

So Fern had taken the weight of her birth mother's passing onto her young shoulders and carried it with her. When friends at school had asked why her adoptive parents were older than most, she'd simply replied that she had been a gift to them, later in life.

Now she fully understood how true this statement was and it filled her belly with the fires of hell. Images of her kind and generous adoptive parents were now distorted, because they had lied to their only child, every single day.

Fern angrily brushed away a stray tear before anyone saw and looked around at the pretty café she'd created with her adoptive parents. It was small and personal and full of the scents of fresh-baked cupcakes and icing sugar. Fern was an award-winning baker and customers flocked to her little shop to taste her latest flavour combinations and delicious frothy coffees.

Fern's adoptive parents had made her the manager of the shop. They had bought the café and invested every penny they had to support her, but she'd never taken over owner-ship of the business. Their lives had been entwined with invisible ties that she'd never given a second thought to – until the day they were killed in a car accident. All of a sudden there had been a thousand decisions to be made. She'd loved the fact they had all worked together, but in reality she'd never taken full responsibility for anything and had just cruised along in her comfortable, and pretty happy, existence.

After the funeral she had learnt that the shop was now hers. More tears had flowed then. She'd sniffed and rubbed her tired eyes, hoping that she could make them proud and be an independent woman who was about to start to run her own life, but it turned out her adoptive parents were still caring for her beyond the grave. They'd given up everything for her and made their whole life about their daughter. She saw their kind faces in every carefully chosen teacup or brush of lovingly restored paintwork – but they'd lied to her too. They had kept her protected from the outside world, but she now understood it had been a way to keep her close and prevent her birth parents from finding her. Confusion filled her mind and made her head feel like it was stuffed full of marshmallows.

Even before she'd found out that her birth parents were alive, she'd needed to get away from the claustrophobic sympathy of her customers and had told an agent to sell the building and business as quickly as possible – it held too many memories. She'd built the café with her little family and without them, the building felt like a soulless shell. She could barely force herself to open the doors every morning. Then, exhausted, she'd thought of an idea to encourage a quick sale and had stupidly offered to help the new owners get used to managing the cupcake shop for six months while they settled in, giving her time to find her bearings, decide what she wanted to do with her life and come to terms with her loss. In her grief, she'd felt that being in the shop for just a few more months would ground her and make her feel closer to her adoptive parents and customers – but it just made the sadness worse.

She could barely pick up anything in the kitchen without

picturing her adoptive mother sitting watching her bake, or her dad cuddling her and sampling another slice of apple cake before declaring it the best he'd ever eaten. Tears sprung up and she grabbed a tissue and mopped them away, her thick wavy blond hair falling over her eyes and covering her flushed face. Never in her wildest imaginings had she thought that her 'dead' birth parents would find out what had happened, after searching for her for years, and swoop in to save her shop. It didn't even need saving! She was more than capable of making a mess of her life on her own.

She even had a sister now! She recalled how she'd stared out of the window of her childhood home, watching other children from across the street playing with their brothers and sisters in their gardens and wishing with her whole heart that she had a sibling too. She wouldn't even have minded if they'd squabbled, because in her young mind, having a blood relative meant they would always have your back and be by your side. They would chase the loneliness away. As she'd grown older and seen her friends fight with their brothers and sisters, she'd wondered if maybe she'd had the better deal, but she'd never shaken the isolation of being an only child. Fern had spoken to her new sister, Genie, for hours and hours last night and it felt like there was an invisible thread binding them together now. Genie hadn't been told she had a sister either until recently, so both girls were floundering together.

Fern had friends locally, but she was always working and had an 'unusual' boyfriend, which often hampered her plans. Going out and socialising hadn't been her priority. She'd worked so hard, trying to make her parents proud and to prove they'd made the right choice by adopting her. She hadn't even realised she'd been doing that until after they'd gone.

Now she had Milly and James, her birth parents, standing

in her café. It was like something out of a movie. She had a whole family she hadn't known about – and an evil grandmother who made her want to run for the hills, or at least sell the house she lived in now and move.

Fern quickly checked that everything was set up for the day's service and ducked down as Milly glanced her way, to check she was OK. She had a habit of doing this and to be honest it was taking a bit of getting used to. Fern closed the back door of the shop behind her and stepped out into the Cornish sunshine, trying to catch her breath. The garden behind the café was tiny, but it was bliss to sit on a little chair next to the delicate cast iron table and let the sun warm her skin as she turned her face to the sky.

She sat like that for a moment and then felt her breathing begin to regulate. Genie would be setting up her ice cream restaurant for the day and might have a few minutes to spare before she opened to the hordes of customers that poured into her premises on the seafront in Essex every single day. Fern had only known her younger sister, Genie, for a short while, but they had already become each other's greatest ally. Fern was in awe of all that Genie had achieved, if she was honest. She'd fought to save her family's heritage and refused to let her parents sell their failing ice cream business when they had rushed to Cornwall to be with Fern. They had tried to persuade Genie to move with them, to keep the family together, but she'd stayed put.

To be fair, Milly and James had kept Genie in the dark about the reason for their sudden move at first and Fern's heart broke for her, too. She must have felt like she'd been let down by the people she loved most in the world. But she'd bravely taken on a new business partner, Ada, and her restaurant was now flourishing.

Fern tapped Genie's name into her phone and smiled at the picture that came up. Genie's bright blue eyes shone and her long black hair whipped around her face in the sea breeze while she grinned at the camera. It had been taken the first time they had met, on the sandy beach opposite the ice cream bar. The sisters had bonded right from the start. Now Genie sold Fern's bigger cakes in her restaurant and Fern sold Genie's delicious ice cream flavours, too.

Fern held her breath and waited for Genie to answer, which she invariably did almost instantly, as she was always on the go and usually had her phone stuffed in her jeans pocket.

'Fern!' said Genie. 'How are you?' When Fern paused, Genie sighed. 'Have you told them yet?'

Fern rolled her eyes. Genie always seemed to know what she was thinking, which was weird when they'd spent most of their lives apart.

'How can I? Milly and James moved their whole life to be here with me in Cornwall, when they found out my mum and dad had died. I didn't even know they existed! I feel awful.' said Fern, her voice hushed so that they couldn't hear her, even though she knew they would be busy inside the shop. They were both very well practiced at owning a food business, as they'd formerly run Genie's little ice cream shop by the sea with James' parents. It seemed like a weird parallel universe to Fern and Genie, and was another reason why they related to each other so well.

'They'll be fine,' said Genie. 'They really wanted to move to a different part of the coast when this business started to fail and your café was an ideal investment, so they won't lose anything.'

'How can you be so reasonable, after what they put you through with your ice cream shop?' asked Fern. She couldn't help thinking about all the ways Genie was now linked to her life. Genie was stubborn, fiery, loyal and a brilliant business-woman. Fern was proud to know her, but also a teeny bit intimidated by her success. Genie had turned her parents' failing business into a successful foodie destination, with an ever-increasing clientele.

Genie spoke to someone in the background. Fern assumed it must be her smokin' hot waiter, Bailey. Genie had given him a chance when no one else would. Neither Genie nor Bailey had any formal qualifications, due to family circumstances, but both were savvy and organised. They shone with the customers, making them feel at home, and had loads of creative ideas. Genie had helped out in the family ice cream shop from a young age and Bailey had a small son, Liam, to provide for. Half of the female population on that shoreline came in either to see Bailey, or Cal, who was Genie's equally gorgeous boyfriend.

'Sorry,' said Genie. 'Bailey's just organising our takeaway service and little Liam is trying to build towers out of the cups. It's hard to scold a four-year-old when they are so cute,' she laughed, making Fern smile for the first time that day as she pictured Liam's chubby toddler cheeks and dark curly hair. He would be a heartbreaker when he grew up, with those piercing blue eyes that were older than his years.

Bailey was bringing Liam up with the help of his own parents and all four of them now lived in the flat above Genie's place. Bailey was on hand for the restaurant and Genie was putting him through night school, as he gradually stepped up to help run the place. Fern could tell that he was completely loyal to Genie. Fern pictured the guy she'd been dating, Brad, with his broad shoulders, angular jawline and sparkling, mischievous eyes and another big fat tear plopped onto her knee. She sniffed miserably. Brad was in her past.

'Liam's a complete cutie. I can't wait to see him again. You too,' she sighed.

'Tell them you're moving to Essex to be near me. They

can't argue with it. They did exactly the same thing to be near you,' said Genie.

Fern waited to hear the wobbly tone that she'd first heard in Genie's voice when they had found out about each other, but it wasn't there any more. She seemed to have come to terms with things. Evening after evening of discussing their lives and what had happened to them both had brought them closer. Now all Fern could think about was the premises that had just come up for sale along the coast from Genie's restaurant. It had room for Fern to grow her business and she could learn about her heritage there without Milly and James interfering. As much as she was growing to love them, she was still in shock about the way things had turned out.

Genie seemed like a life raft in a turbulent sea and Fern was going to swim towards her. After the way her 'boyfriend,' Brad, had treated her over the last few years, Genie had helped her see there might be a different way. Genie's own American boyfriend, Cal, might be feisty and a bit of a whirlwind, but Genie was a perfect match for him. They had shown Fern that the way Brad treated her wasn't in her best interests. So now she was ready to shake off the past and begin a new life – and that life involved setting up a completely new business on a different part of the coastline.

CHAPTER TWO

ern really wanted to sit on the slouchy couch at home and watch reality television for a few hours to ease her brain. It was a trick she'd used for years when her schedule got a bit tight, and she could feel her asthma flaring. The programmes distracted her. Her current favourites were Love Island and Married at First Sight, as there was such a lack of romance in her own life. She enjoyed seeing colourful lives and exciting locations on the screen. It made her happy to see others doing well, plus there was always so much drama and excitement that it lifted her mood, however grumpy she was feeling.

But what she was actually doing now was standing in the café's kitchen, making a mountain of cake for all her clients. She put a spoonful of the icing she was making into her mouth and almost went cross-eyed in sugary bliss. There was just the right amount of lemon to give it some zing. She made a mental list of the next day's tasks as she put the spoon in the sink. She knew she needed to get all her cake orders sent out before she began telling people she was relocating. The thought of their upset faces made her wince.

Many were regular customers who bought cakes throughout the year and she did care about them.

Most of her clients were local, as she wasn't a confident traveller, but now she would be situated miles away, running her very own bar and cupcake shop, with no backup plan in sight. Milly and James had helped her organise cake deliveries to Genie's shop, but now she'd be packing up and going to live near her new sister, leaving everything she'd ever known. Her hands shook a little. She dolloped some natural colour extract into the buttercream icing she was making, then cursed. She should only have added a tiny drop. She tried to fish some out, then gave up and slammed the bowl into the already full sink. She was usually a pristine cook with surfaces cleaned as she went, but today her bones felt like lead. She knew she needed to finish up and then approach Milly and James about her plans.

She ran the tap to begin washing up and then grabbed a clean bowl to finish icing the cake she was working on. It was a light lemon sponge, but the customer had wanted bright pink frosting and little crowns sitting atop, which Fern had made earlier in the day. They were setting in the fridge. Milly came into the kitchen and Fern couldn't help but smile. Milly had been working all day, but the branded apron she had tied at her waist didn't have a mark on it and her shoulder-length blonde hair looked like she'd just stepped out of a top salon.

Neither Genie nor Fern's hair was like their mum's. Genie had long black hair that she tamed with a hairband while working at her restaurant and Fern's wild blonde mop always managed to escape the clips she slid into the sides to hold it down. Fern guessed they must take after their dad, James, with his thick black hair. He always had it trimmed close to his neck, but it still managed to look a bit wild.

These people had bowled into her life not long ago and

explained they were her family – and Fern still hadn't quite recovered. They had left their busy lives, child and restaurant behind to rescue Fern, when she'd been at her lowest ebb and all alone.

Sometimes it made Fern stand stock-still in shock. Her adoptive parents had fed a web of lies to Fern throughout her whole life, and Milly and James hadn't known how to find her. When they were finally informed of Fern's whereabouts, due to the accident that had killed her adoptive parents, they had dropped everything and rushed to her aid. It had been like standing in the middle of a storm. The lid had been blown off her quiet life as soon as they had taken over ownership of the café, however kindly it had been meant. They had bought her business and had spent weeks bonding with her... before breaking the news that they were in fact related. Her world had then imploded – and now she was desperate to run away.

'You OK?' asked Milly. She sounded so like Genie that Fern had to pause for a moment and catch her breath. She quickly whipped up the butter cream but was using such force that Milly was frowning at her.

Fern blew some air up from her mouth to her hair, to try and get some rogue strands out of her eyes, before huffing and scraping them back into the hair slides once more. 'I need to finish this cake tonight. I'm running behind.'

Milly immediately grabbed the order book and her eyes expertly scanned the rows and columns. She frowned again and turned to Fern.

'This cake isn't due until Friday, and we don't seem to have many more orders booked in. What's going on? You usually have pages full of cake orders.'

Fern grimaced and started frosting the cake with the vivid icing. 'Can you grab the little crown decorations I've made, they're in the fridge?' she asked, stalling for time. She'd practiced what to say a thousand times but now the moment was here, her mouth was dry.

James came into the room, jangling the shop keys in his hand, but he paused and cocked his head to one side when he saw the two women staring at each other warily. 'What's up?' He looked to his wife for the answer.

She indicated Fern. 'I think Fern's about to tell us.'

Fern was still amazed by the fact that Milly always seemed able to sense her mood. James was oblivious, but he had a kind heart, and now had a concerned look on his face.

Fern quickly finished icing the cake and placed the delicate crowns on the top, before putting it in their specialised cake storage for delivery. She pulled out a seat at the staff table and they all followed suit, James' legs sticking out at one side as usual, which made Fern smile. She had got used to having them around and they tugged at her heartstrings, but she was fed up with being controlled by everyone. The handsome face of her ex-boyfriend, Brad, came to mind and she shook her head to get rid of the image. Milly's eyes were clouded with concern, so Fern put her hand on top of hers, to try and ease the worry.

'I'm moving to Essex,' she said simply.

'What?' said Milly, as James' jaw almost hit the floor. 'We have literally just sold up everything and moved here to be with you, after your... parents... passed away.'

Fern placed her hands in her lap and couldn't quite meet their eyes. She knew they would now be full of panic. *So much for her well-rehearsed speech!* They had sacrificed a lot to help her through a very difficult time. They had left their old ice cream shop behind – not to mention their other daughter, Genie.

'I never asked you to do that,' said Fern quietly. It was actually something she felt incredibly guilty about, even though she'd known nothing about it at the time.

Milly's eyes filled with tears and she sniffed and wiped her eyes on her white shirt, still not leaving a mark. *The wonders of waterproof mascara*, thought Fern fleetingly.

'Why are you moving to Essex?' asked James, but Fern could see he already knew that answer and he actually didn't look as upset as she'd thought he'd be.

'To be near Genie,' she said simply. James sat back with a huge sigh and crossed his arms over his wide chest, watching her.

'But we left Genie to be near you,' sniffed Milly, getting up to make them all a coffee, which seemed to be her answer to everything. Either the scent of the coffee beans or the activity with her hands seemed to help ease her thoughts. Fern was still learning about their personalities. Milly was vivacious and hard-working. James was quiet and dependable.

Fern turned her chair to face Milly. 'I know. I appreciate everything you've done and all you've given up for me, but my life has been tilted on its axis and I'm trying to find something to hold onto.'

'You can hold onto us,' said Milly quietly.

Fern tried to smile, but it ended up more of a grimace. 'I'm not quite ready for that yet... but I'm sure I will soon,' she said carefully, seeing Milly wince. 'I need to do something by myself this time. I'm sorry. I do understand what you've done for me and I'll never forget your kindness and generosity.' She lifted her gaze to Milly and her bottom lip trembled before she looked away and squeezed her eyes shut for a moment. She wrung her hands in her lap and felt tension fire across her shoulder blades. 'Genie's found a property down the road from the ice cream shop and it would be perfect for a cupcake and cocktail café. I've been wanting to experiment for ages, but couldn't risk Mum and Dad's investment in this cafe.'

Her eyes pleaded with them for understanding, when she was blowing their world apart. She flinched and took a steadying breath, as Milly came and sat down again with a thud.

'When I spoke to my mum and dad about the idea, they said it would confuse the clientele. They were probably right, as the average customer age here is much higher, although I'm pretty sure that Viv would enjoy a cocktail.' Fern pictured her favourite customer, who was full of life and enjoying every moment of her retirement.

Viv's recent penchant for bright purple leggings and big chunky trainers hadn't been missed by her other customers, who gossiped about her endlessly when she wasn't in earshot. Viv loved being the centre of attention and found the chat behind her back an absolute blast! *Did they think she was deaf as well as over the hill?* she'd often laugh. Fern adored the way she showed them all that age was just a number. Viv had more energy than Fern did, at well over twice her age.

James' face now held a pinched expression and Fern suddenly wondered if he and Milly had held Genie back from following her dreams. She made a mental note to ask her. They certainly hadn't done anything at the cake shop to suggest they were closed off from progress, but Fern did know the ice cream shop had been very run down when they'd sold it to Genie. She'd turned it around with her new business partner and a fresh outlook.

They all worked beautifully together here, and Fern did smile more often which, all things considered, was a bonus. But it was as if she'd stepped into a parallel universe, with her new parents now running the shop instead of her adoptive ones. It seemed she was just expected to be happy about this, and not have a mental breakdown at what the hell had been going on in the background of her life without her knowledge for so long.

'Genie found you a property?' gasped Milly, standing up again and almost knocking her chair over, new tears springing to her eyes, so James went to finish making the coffees, guiding her back to her seat like a small child.

Fern sipped the steaming coffee James soon placed in front of her and wondered when she'd start to think of them as 'Mum' and 'Dad', and not Milly and James. 'I have the money from the sale of this shop, now you own it. My parents' house sold last week.' She pulled a face, as she knew she should have shared this information too. 'It's too big for me on my own.' She took another sip of her coffee and let the caffeine fire her up with a little extra courage, warming her cold hands on the sides of the cup. 'I love that you two are here, but it brings a lot of complicated emotions and I need space to decide what I want from my life.'

Milly took her hand and then pulled her in for a hug. Fern loved that Milly and James were so affectionate, but she sometimes wondered if they were trying to make up for a lifetime of missed hugs each day. Plus her grandmother, Lucinda, kept popping into the café and it was driving them all nuts! She'd been a constant in Fern's life as her adoptive mother's slightly overbearing friend, but now she knew the truth about her – that they were related.

Fern wasn't at all sure how she felt about having a grandmother who was so manipulative. She'd managed to separate sixteen-year-old Milly and Fern, her firstborn, by saying James had deserted her. When James tried to find her, she'd told him that Milly had moved to her aunt's. He'd been sixteen too, so had only been able to come back once a year while his parents were on holiday. Lucinda was pretty intimidating and he'd believed her when she'd said Milly had moved on.

In the middle of all that, Lucinda had managed to keep Fern close by handing her granddaughter over to her childless friend as soon as she was born. There had never been a formal adoption and Milly had been kept in the dark about her baby's new home, so she had moved away as soon as she was able and had met James again a few years later. Fern had been a secret she'd been too ashamed to tell anyone about. She'd told Fern that she felt she hadn't fought back hard enough and had allowed her mother to tear them apart.

The way Milly managed not to scream at her mother every day was testament to her being such a devoted mum and daughter. Fern knew Milly had been pushed to her limits by Lucinda. Now her grandmother kept popping in every day, as if nothing had happened, and it was making Fern's nerves jump. Lucinda seemed to think she'd done them all a favour by bringing them back together, as if the last thirty-odd years had never happened.

Brad piling on the pressure to keep their three-year relationship a secret had also been too much. She got it, he was famous, but he managed to be 'papped' with various other women and that seemed to be ok. He constantly told her that they were starlets his management company wanted him to be seen out with, and assured her it was all platonic.

But, since her mum and dad had died, it was as if the veil had lifted and she suddenly saw what her parents had seen... Brad was using her and was never going to change. They had liked him – he was charming! But her mum had never quite relaxed in his company and the very few times they had met, her dad had questioned him on his intentions and Brad had easily ducked the subject and turned the conversation around. Her dad had let it slide, but Fern knew they didn't quite approve, even though Brad was a rich, famous movie star. They were more impressed by one of her cakes than by Brad.

She didn't know how Milly or James would feel about him, but she got the impression they wouldn't swoon at his feet either. Genie was already mentioning kicking him in the balls for the way he'd treated her sister, so Fern imagined feistiness must be a family trait. She hoped it was one she learnt soon. Having Milly, James and Genie around her had given Fern the strength to finally leave him behind. To leave everything she held dear behind, in fact. Brad was her past, Genie, and the new adventure with her little cupcake café, was her future.

CHAPTER THREE

*M*illy had been pacing the little café floor all day. James glanced her way again and she stopped, realising she might be scaring their customers off. Viv, who was a regular from before they had bought the café, smiled at Milly in sympathy as she took the latte from James and brought it over to her. Today, Viv was wearing leggings with purple flowers all over them with a bright pink T-shirt, which was making Milly's brain ache.

Viv had been a good friend to Fern's adoptive parents, Bill and Irene, and was one of the few people who understood Irene's actions in taking on a friend's granddaughter in difficult circumstances. Nothing had been official, Viv had learned. They'd brought Fern up as their own, but lived in fear of her being taken away from them. When Milly and James had arrived looking for their birth daughter, Viv had told them she was almost glad that her friends weren't there to feel that pain.

'I'm sure Irene would have grown to love you and you'd have all been one big happy family,' said Viv to Milly, looking around to make sure there was no one else listening. It was an unusually quiet day as the weather had turned windy and wet, so only the brave, like Viv, had ventured out. She refused to conform by wearing drab colours to suit the weather, though – her orange cardigan was firmly placed on her knees.

Milly shivered, pulled out a chair and signalled to James to make her a coffee, which he did without a word, his face glum. 'That would never have happened. There's no way we would have met. If they hadn't had the accident, my mum, Lucinda, wouldn't have told us where Fern was. The lies were too ingrained.' Tears of frustration sprung to Milly's eyes and Viv patted her shoulder as James brought over three coffees and sat down too.

'You'd have found her somehow,' said James. Milly gave him a watery smile.

'I would have loved to have met Bill and Irene to say thank you. We're so grateful to them for looking after Fern the way they did. Her life was full of love. It's a shame they felt the need to hide what had happened.'

Anger flashed across Viv's face and Milly frowned. 'That was down to your mother too. Lucinda has a lot to answer for. She kept Irene feeling vulnerable about you finding out and seeking custody of Fern. It made her very paranoid. I never knew quite what was going on at first, but I suspected that Lucinda had some sort of hold over Irene. I would never have imagined it was something to do with Fern, until Irene broke down and told me.' She sipped her coffee and sighed, sitting back in her chair and regarding Milly and James' downcast faces. 'No wonder you moved away,' she said thoughtfully.

'I'm sorry for what Irene went through,' said Milly, hanging her head so that her hair swung over her face. James brushed it aside and lifted her chin.

'You didn't do anything wrong,' James told her. 'You were

young and we made mistakes. You trusted your mum implic-itly and were guided by her. In fact, we all were!' he said forcefully, making Viv's eyes twinkle.

'Look,' Viv soothed them both. 'You have Fern in your life now and you're all together. Irene would be happy that you're here for her now. She'd have hated for Fern to be lonely. She's led a very sheltered life.'

Milly sniffed and rubbed her tired eyes. 'She's moving to Essex.'

Viv's eyebrows shot up into her hairline and Milly laughed at last. 'See. We can still surprise you. She loves the café and I know she's growing to love us, but I think we pushed too hard by buying this place. We should have just sent a formal letter introducing ourselves, or something. That way she could have refused to meet us. I didn't give her that chance as I was so desperate to see her again.'

Milly took a sip of her coffee and rolled her shoulders, glancing up as a young couple burst through the door, laughing and brushing rain from their coats. James jumped up to help them. 'We panicked when the accident happened and Mum finally told us where Fern was. She said this place would be sold to developers and Fern would have a double loss.'

'That woman is pure evil,' said Viv, face like thunder.

'In her warped mind, she's helping everyone and she can't understand the fuss,' said Milly.

'Helping, or controlling?' Viv turned and smiled at the excited chatter of the couple as they bent their heads over the menu James had just handed them.

Milly couldn't help but smile too. She and James had been just as excited about life once. 'Fern should have kept the café, but she was grieving and wanted to let it go. Now she'll eventually inherit it from us, along with Genie, but in hindsight, we should have given her time to catch her breath, without swooping in thinking we were saving her. She's a grown woman and is still the manager of the business she's built from scratch – just with a different set of parents running it. Not even the better version,' said Milly sadly. She stirred her tall glass of coffee and her shoulders drooped.

'She's glad you're here,' said Viv, kindly, finally pulling on her orange jumper and making Milly blink at the strong colour.

'So much so that she's running away.'

'Not running away. Finding some breathing space. She's had people telling her what to do her whole life. Maybe it's good to see her taking control for once?'

Milly thought of her other daughter, Genie, and how feisty and brave she was to stay at home and fight for her heritage, when Milly and James had been determined to start again in another part of the country. She nibbled on her lip and wondered if it was in their genes, that spirit.

She would always feel guilty about the fact that Genie had chosen to stay behind when they packed up and left, but it had turned out well. The business was flourishing thanks to her creative ideas, she had a new business partner in Ada, and was dating Ada's gorgeous grandson, Cal. Cal was now working in London a lot and Milly knew Genie missed him, but hopefully their relationship was strong enough to overcome any obstacles thrown their way. Milly felt the loss of their friends at the ice cream bar in Essex. She hadn't told James, but she had already been thinking of how to split their time between their two children.

The bell above the door jangled. Milly cringed as her mother, Lucinda, walked in, and shook her umbrella out all over the floor. Then she looked up to see who was in the café. Her eyes lit on Milly with Viv. Her laser stare made

Milly jump up and offer Viv an awkward smile of apology as she quickly grabbed her pen to take the young couple's food order. James sighed and grabbed a mop to clean the floor as Lucinda walked over to Viv. Milly grinned at how quickly Viv was suddenly glugging down that piping hot coffee.

CHAPTER FOUR

*F*ern was energised after a day off work away from the café, but knew she'd have to face Milly and James soon. She shouldn't just drop a bombshell like that and then run away – but that was what she was probably going to do. She'd made an offer on the shop Genie had sent details across for, without even seeing it in person! She knew people might say she was reacting to grief, but she didn't think so. Her stomach was buzzing with possibilities, finally, and the fog in her brain was lifting. She didn't have to stay stuck in a rut for the sake of a man, or hide herself away to mourn. She would never forget her parents and was worth more than playing second fiddle to a man like Brad. Life was too short to wallow – and she finally had a backbone growing where Brad was concerned.

The warmth of the sun caressed her face and tension floated away. The beach was still looking slick after yesterday's rainfall, but it would soon be full of families making the most of the brighter weather. She waved to the young couple who had recently opened a sweet trolley cart that they walked all the way along the beach every day. Its vibrant pop of colour and eye-catching branding made children drag their parents to it for a sugar rush or an ice lolly. The tall palm trees that lined the beaches offered shade during hotter months, while flower baskets overflowing with blooms lined the walkways in the summer. It was a beautiful place to live, Fern would miss walking here every day. But she pictured her new shop, nestled into a sandy cove and sitting proudly at the end of a row of artisan shops, and smiled to herself. *She could do this.*

Noticing the café was already open, she walked in and called hello to Milly, who was organising the cutlery. Milly smiled and came over to give her a warm hug. Fern was getting used to her friendly nature and she leant in. Milly finally let her go and kissed her cheek in greeting. 'Good day yesterday?' she asked breezily, but Fern could instantly feel an undercurrent to her words. 'You managed to avoid a visit from your grandmother, which is always a bonus,' she joked.

Fern grinned and put the back of her hand to her brow theatrically, in relief. James popped his head out of the kitchen and came over to hug her too, kissing the top of her head. Her heart broke a little at how much she would miss them. They had given her so much support and unconditional love. Not many people would uproot their whole lives to find a daughter they'd never met. Leaving another daughter behind must have been devastating too.

'Make us a coffee, before the world and his wife descend upon us,' Milly said jokily to James. He was definitely the maestro when it came to coffee and he'd fallen in love with the big machine Fern had bought. He spent hours tinkering with the row of buttons along the front, brewing different types of coffee to find the ultimate blend, even though it was near perfect anyway. He smiled and went to start up the machine.

'Are you sure?' asked Milly.

place there to call home,' said James, staring out of the front window in thought, probably picturing the huge old house they owned near the ice cream shop in Essex, a little further up the road and facing the sea. 'We were getting stagnant there, we refused to accept change. The place needed Genie's vision and talent to bring it back to life. You and this business have given us a second chance too.'

He held his breath as if he was bursting to say something taboo. 'I do miss home though,' he blurted out quickly and then flushed red and wouldn't look at Milly in case she thumped him.

Fern thought it was telling that he didn't call the flat they lived in here, above their café, home. Her mind whirred with exciting possibilities.

'Let me find my way in the new town – and then why don't you come 'home' too? Do you have to stay here?' Her eyes twinkled with mischief. She didn't miss the longing in James' face either, as his head snapped up to listen intently.

'There isn't a business for us there,' said Milly. 'Plus we've just invested in this place.'

Fern looked around her little shop, every detail etched onto her brain. She adored the café and had put blood, sweat and tears into making it perfect, but it was time to move on. 'Sell up and find a new adventure. You've been here for a while now – and there is no one to say how long you have to stay for.'

'It's something to think about, Milly,' said James, his voice hopeful. 'We could even get in a manager for this place. Fern could send her cakes, the way Genie sends her ice cream, or we could hire someone locally to make them to Fern's recipes.' He glanced at Fern and she mock fainted and then laughed. He held his hands up. 'You aren't easily replaced, I'm just talking through some options out loud.'

'Not that you've thought about this a million times before,' said Milly dryly.

James' cheeks flushed and he hid his face behind his coffee.

'Seriously, James! I thought you liked it here?' fumed Milly.

'I love the café and most of the locals. Just not all of them...' he said.

Fern pictured Lucinda's pinched face and couldn't help but snort into her coffee. Milly had to laugh too.

Fern glanced at the clock on the wall and got up, clearing their cups away. 'Come on, you two. This place won't run itself. We've got a lot to think about and, if you do decide to hire a manager, we need to make sure the café is as organised as possible. Will you tell Lucinda about your change of plans?'

'No!' came the reply in unison, as they all picked up their aprons and got ready to open the café for the day.

CHAPTER FIVE

$\mathcal{F}$ern sat on her new terrace with her feet propped on an upturned bucket. The wooden decking shone from being mopped a few hours earlier and the cleaning fluid left a lemony scent in the early evening air. The breathtaking view of the coast from her new home was incredible. Deep blue skies, glistening water and there wasn't a cloud in sight. There were miles of sandy shores to explore. She smiled at a woman who was walking her dog on the beach, laughing as he jumped in and out of the sea spray. Then he shook himself dry right by her, making her hop about to avoid him.

Fern took a deep breath and tried to steady her nerves. Leaving her previous life had happened quickly, once the paperwork had been signed on her old house. She knew that Milly and James were still reeling now that she'd gone. She ached for parts of that life and missed daily hugs from Milly, but knew something had needed to change. There hadn't been a leaving party full of friends for her, just a few sad goodbyes from Viv and her regulars who had mostly asked her not to go, or begged her for cake recipes. Viv had worn the brightest outfit ever in Fern's honour and it was now scored onto her brain. It had almost hurt to look at her, though Viv's cheerful insistence that Fern was doing the right thing had helped keep the tears firmly at bay until she was back in her house and could sob to her heart's content.

Now Fern looked further down the glorious beach to where Genie's little ice cream shop sat, and finally felt a genuine smile lift her face. Genie was a whirlwind and her energy was infectious. It was a comfort to know that her sister was nearby. Genie's business partner, Ada, had been a good friend to Fern too, although she seemed to spend much of her time with their grandad, Gus, these days. It was still weird for Fern to think that she now had new parents, a sister, a grandmother and two grandads! Growing up, she hadn't spent much time with the couple she now knew to be her maternal grandparents, Lucinda and Edward, but they had always been a part of her life. She'd never been to their home, but Lucinda had visited regularly and was her mother's friend – or so Fern had thought.

Fern frowned when she recalled how naïve she'd been, thinking of Lucinda as a slightly overbearing friend of her adoptive parents. She was there for birthdays and had popped by with gifts at Christmas, but Fern had never understood the connection until now. There had always been an undercurrent of tension when Lucinda visited which Fern had felt but never been able to fathom.

Fern had assumed Lucinda was a bit lonely and didn't have grandchildren of her own to shower with gifts. Little had she known *she* was Lucinda's grandchild – or one of them! Edward had stayed in the background and hadn't got involved. Fern wondered if he even cared? He'd certainly not welcomed her into the family the way James' father, Gus, had. Edward had been polite, but it was almost as if the whole mess embarrassed him which, to be fair, it probably had. Gus, by contrast, had whooped in delight and had almost cuddled the air out of her, when they'd met. She'd had to rely on Genie and Ada to tell him to stop.

Genie had said not to worry about Edward and that Gus could be grumpy too, but he seemed to always be smiling to Fern. For the first few days when she'd arrived, he'd turn up every day with misty eyes and tell her she looked like her paternal grandmother, who had sadly passed away some time ago. Apparently she was the one who had originally set up the ice cream shop and her flavours had brought custom from miles around. Genie was now just as popular and Fern hoped her new cupcake and cocktails venture would bring in custom too, and make the grandmother she'd never meet proud. She was learning just how long her family had been living along this gorgeous stretch of coast and she found herself yearning to be part of that history.

She missed the routine of walking to her old café in the mornings and opening up the shop with Milly and James, but she was also enjoying the freedom from their hovering parental presence for a moment. She wasn't confident enough in their love for her yet. She knew they meant well, but they had lied to her, unlike Genie. Milly and James had bought the café, and then only told her who they were weeks afterwards. She understood it must have been terrifying for them to uproot their whole lives for a lost child, but her mind was muddled about that. Lucinda had lied and so had her mum and dad. Her memories of them were now tarred by that. Some evenings she raged to the sky, telling them how much they'd hurt her by not trusting her with the huge secret that her birth parents were alive.

She sighed and closed her eyes. It was definitely time for a fresh start. She knew she could have chosen anywhere in the world, but she wasn't quite brave enough for that yet.

Genie mentioning that a shop was for sale down the coast had been like a gift from the gods.

Fern's new shop almost had its own beach, as it was beside a small sandy cove with huge boulders round the edges that people could sit on. A row of boats was often moored to the far side, attached to a jetty that was sturdier than it looked.

Yes, she now owned the property, at the edge of a tiny town that had a cobbled street running through the centre, called Main Street. Most of the fisherman's cottages had been converted into artisan shops, each with different-coloured pastel front doors. Most of the doorways had hanging baskets, with trailing flowers adding further splashes of colour. It was truly charming.

Her building, right next to the cove, was made up of two shops with two flats above, with side and rear access to the beach. With the sale of the Cornish café to Milly and James and the money from the house she'd grown up in, she had been able to grab the sizeable property as soon as it came up for sale. Genie had heard whispers from the previous owner that he was keen to sell and she had swooped in and set the contracts up for her sister. Fern had an idea that Genie would have bought it herself if Fern hadn't, which had made the decision easier for her. If Genie thought it was a hot property, so did she.

Fern just had to settle her nerves and stop being such a wuss about living in a new area. She hadn't thought much about the fact that she'd barely been out of her hometown before, and had never travelled abroad. But now she wondered if her adoptive parents had discouraged the idea, in case they got found out for not having formal adoption certificates and the authorities put Fern into care.

Now her mum and dad would never be caught out. They wouldn't have to face up to her, or Milly and James, and in a way she was thankful that they wouldn't suffer that pain.

This new coastline was where her paternal grandparents and James had grown up, so the area was part of her heritage. But Cornwall, where her old café was, was actually in her blood too. She'd always felt a bit lost when it came to roots, but Milly had been born in Cornwall. Fern hadn't realised she had grown up in the same spot as her birth mother. Knowing that might have made her more comfortable, but there had always been a part of her missing. She'd sometimes stared at her face in the mirror and wondered if she'd ever meet anyone who looked just like her. Her adoptive parents had both had very fine dark hair, until they grew older, but Fern's hair was thick and fair. They'd had big brown eyes but Fern's were a greeny-blue. They were both small-framed, whereas Fern had felt like she'd never stop growing as a child.

She sat further back into her deckchair and tried not to look over her shoulder at the flat next door, but it was impossible. She wondered what Jessie, her new tenant, thought of her plans to open up the back wall and create a seating area beside the beach.

She hadn't planned on becoming a landlord, she'd actively shied away from that kind of responsibility with the old shop, but now her adoptive parents were gone, she knew she had to grow up.

It was weird how she and Genie had followed such similar paths. Fern's ex Brad was a celebrity, and so was Genie's boyfriend, Cal. Cal was a dream, though, whereas Brad had been a nightmare. He'd undermined her, made her keep their relationship a secret, and then got a glossy new toy who helped him market his new movie, which had flopped, incidentally. Fern hadn't been able to face seeing it, where she had usually rushed to the cinema and enjoyed the secret of knowing she could actually touch Brad's skin and make him smile in person. Now she would rather forget the whole relationship ever happened. In fact Brad acted like it never had! It was mortifying.

She pulled up the blanket on the side of the chair and snuggled into it. The last few weeks had taken their toll on her and she hadn't been eating properly. She loved Genie's gorgeous curves and felt cross with herself for being lovesick over someone who didn't actually care. Jessie could have been a tonic for that, with his bronzed, taut body and sexy eyes, but his moody demeanour made her even more agitated.

The news about Milly and James being her parents had pushed Fern over the edge. She had decided she would be strong and end the relationship with Brad, but then when she'd tentatively told him, he'd begun wooing her and flattering her already tiny ego, albeit in her house and out of sight of prying eyes. Then he had turned up one evening and made love to her and then, when they were snuggling together on her couch in her living room, he got up and announced it would be better if they were just friends. Just friends! They'd just spent two hours rolling around naked, after he'd convinced her not to dump him!

Brad had never spent that much time in bed with her, so she should have sussed something dodgy was going on. What a loser. He'd just wanted the upper hand. Her usually quite calm persona had dived for cover and an enraged wild woman had taken her place. She'd screamed, thrown things and he'd made a hasty retreat. She hadn't heard a thing from him since.

It had pretty much sealed her fate about the move, though. She had been dithering, but suddenly her blood was full of ice. She already loved Milly and James and, in her sensible mind, she knew it wasn't their fault that she was so full of grief and anger. But them being around had made her pine for Bill and Irene and she knew she had to get away.

The terrace she was currently sitting on was above her new shop and the surfboard business next door, which she also owned – well, the bricks and mortar, anyway. Jessie owned the business itself and she was now his landlord. She lived in one of the two flats above the shops and Jessie had the other – which had come as a bit of a shock, as she was actively avoiding attractive men. Especially ones as gorgeous as Jessie.

She'd put plant pots on the shared deck between the flats to try and create some sort of barrier and ward off the pheromones wafting around, but Jessie had wandered out there in his boxer shorts the previous evening. She'd jumped up after hearing someone crash and turn the air blue with swearwords outside her lounge window. He was hopping around and holding his foot, his muscled chest glistening in the moonlight. She'd tried not to stare... but she wasn't dead!

She had kindly offered to check over his hurt foot, and she had explained that it was her property and she was trying to make sure he had his rightful space as her tenant, but that just seemed to enrage him further. Then he'd shouted at her for being stupid and putting pots where you couldn't see them. Now she looked at the rearranged pots, which stood like sentries along the side wall, and she winced. He'd been right. He had said caustically that he had always shared the terrace with Harry, the last owner.

Fern had sighed. But then the new temper she seemed to have acquired had surfaced, and she'd told him that was about to change and he'd better get used to it. She'd had just about enough of bossy men. She hadn't moved miles away from one, to have to deal with another on a daily basis. Jessie might be her sitting tenant, running the surf shop next door to her new café, but she owned both his flat and his shop and he could shove off somewhere else if he thought he could tell her what to do.

Fern smiled to herself and wished she'd been able to tell Brad where to go a long time ago. She could see how he'd used her now, keeping her a secret as if he was embarrassed about her, or as if she wasn't famous enough to be seen out with. She was an entrepreneur with her own business and she didn't need a man to validate her. She wondered fleetingly if she could buy some sort of a sign from the internet that said that, to remind herself if she ever wavered and tried to call Brad. She'd wiped him from her phone – but his number was etched on her brain, so blocking him was only symbolic. He hadn't tried to call her, but then why would he? She was insignificant to him. Her lip wobbled so she gritted her teeth and stared out at the darkening skyline.

Now she'd moved away from her birth parents, she could see what Milly and James had been trying to do. Well, Milly anyway. James was just following her lead, apparently. He hadn't known he had another child, born years before Genie. He must have been shocked and hurt at the lies he'd been told, but then he'd moved to the other end of the country to help Fern out, without question. How his relationship with Milly had survived her revelation, she didn't know, but she was sure Genie would fill her in, at some point.

Fern got the vibe that Genie was missing her boyfriend, Cal. He was one of the good ones as far as Fern was concerned, but even they had had a shaky start, it seemed. Now he was incredibly busy with his new job as a chef on daytime television and Genie's ice cream shop was bursting at the seams with customers. His profile was already sky high, but Genie's was growing too, as her ice cream recipes became more and more popular. She'd been featured in glossy magazines and Fern didn't think it would be long before someone realised what a great team she and Cal would make on a programme. Viewers would love them, but perhaps Cal's bosses didn't want a good-looking man like him to lose female viewers by having a red hot, successful girlfriend. That had been Brad's running excuse for years. How she'd fallen for that line, she would never know, as she was neither of those things. Brad's fans would adore him whoever he dated. She'd realised that it was more about his own perception of his image than anyone else's issues.

She bit her lip and hoped she'd made the right choices. She certainly wasn't someone that lived in the moment. Most of her time was meticulously planned to the nearest minute. Brad made her want to try harder to shine, mainly to make him notice her more, but instead he'd pushed her to her emotional limits. He hadn't bothered to console her over the loss of her parents, or even send her flowers. She had just shrivelled a bit further inside her shell and hidden in her childhood bedroom licking her wounds whenever Brad ignored her.

She hadn't been ready to leave the building she'd grown up in, but Milly and James suddenly turning up nearby had made her place of comfort feel alien to her. Her adoptive parents had been gently encouraging her to take the reins of the cake shop, for years. Pathetically, she'd wanted to be able to drop everything and go to Brad if he called her. She'd put him above her parents and her business. Maybe if she hadn't, they'd have been sunning themselves on a beach and wouldn't have died so suddenly in a car crash on their way to a supplier meeting. Her eyes squeezed shut and she bit back the bile in her throat. She'd got used to the guilt – but she'd never told anyone it was her fault they'd died.

She'd also never quite fitted in with the local community, as no one had filled her in on the details of her heritage. She now knew she had been born in Cornwall, but the Essex coast somehow felt like home. She was gradually unwinding, but perhaps that was just because she was taking strength from her younger sister and was inspired by the choices she'd made in adversity. If Genie could make a success of things on her own, without the help of any parents or even friends, other than Ada, then so could Fern.

She didn't need a rich, sexy boyfriend to make her feel worthy. She would make something of her own life and, although the deposit on the shops had come from her inheritance, she'd been as much a part of the old café's success as anyone. Her cakes had been the impetus to finally bring customers flooding through the door. Could she bring some of that family magic with flavours to her new venture, and make her innovative idea of cupcakes and cocktails together a perfect mix?

If only she could stop picturing her new neighbour half-naked and concentrate on herself for long enough, she'd be able to reach a work-life balance. She puffed out her cheeks and vowed that she'd never let an overbearing man dictate her routine or her self-worth, ever again.

CHAPTER SIX

*F*ern glanced towards the open door of the café and ran her hands through her thick hair, reminding herself that she needed to get it cut or she'd end up looking like a scarecrow and scaring potential customers. The shop was a mess outside, but the inside definitely had potential.

Her café was sitting on a corner plot right beside the sea, with worn red bricks and big windows that had seen better days. She could picture it with shiny new floor-to-ceiling windows that slid open and a kiosk at the front, leading out onto the cobbled shopping street. The back of the property led straight to the beach via a walkway, and there was room for seating all the way round the side and to the back. The shop wasn't huge, but when used properly the outside space would transform it. She was also thinking ahead about placing a cocktail cart outside in the evenings to offer cupcakes and cocktails to passing trade. She didn't want to offer evening meals, but was happy to entice people in with her mouth-watering desserts and pair them with delicious drinks. She just needed a bit more oomph to get started with everything, instead of wallowing in self-pity.

She had already ordered a cart online and hoped it wouldn't be too much of an eyesore when it arrived. It looked like it needed a lot of work, which was probably why it was so cheap. She could picture it painted in a soft grey and lined with sparkling vintage glasses and spirits to temp passing trade. She wanted to keep the current side kiosk as a cake display, as it might entice new customers strolling past. She didn't want a single person to be able to go by without coming over to peer through the glass. She knew her cupcakes were good enough to make people stop in their tracks.

They were decadent, prettily finished and sprinkled with real fruit and handmade adornments. The tiny iced sprinkles she made herself were part of her branding and history. People used to come to her old shop just to see if she'd made miniature stars, crowns or hearts that week. She had fleetingly thought of boxing them up to sell, but that would take up too much of her time. Besides, she'd rather her customers sat down and had a cup of frothy coffee with their cakes, rather than make their own at home.

Genie stuck her head round the door, her dark hair falling across her face, reminding Fern so much of James' cheeky grin and sparkling blue eyes. You couldn't help but smile at the sight of Genie. She always wore beautiful colours and textures with delicate patterns that usually referenced her ice cream shop. Today it was strawberries. She looked fresh and energetic, which was the exact opposite of how Fern felt.

Genie came and sat next to her, sitting cross-legged on the floor. 'You OK?' She leant in and pulled Fern towards her for a hug, which Fern sank into gratefully. She had been missing human contact but was loathe to admit that fact to anyone, as she was the one who had run away.

Fern then put her head in her hands. 'What have I done?' She peeped through her fingers at the mess. There were two buckets full of broken old crockery, left over from the previous business, by one wall and half an oyster shell was propping up the leg of one of the tables.

'You've made the right choice,' affirmed Genie. She looked around at the upturned chairs lying around and layers of dust that had accumulated over the last few months. 'OK, it doesn't look great now. But this used to be a popular coffee shop. Then word got round that the service was lacking.' She looked over her shoulder as if to check that no one could overhear her, even though they were alone. 'Mr Aldous,' she paused for dramatic effect. 'That was the previous owner... Well, he just seemed to have lost interest. It kind of reminded me of how my place was before I took it over. Mum and Dad were snowed under with bills and couldn't see how to update things, however much I told them I could help.' She shrugged and gazed around. 'You've taken control of your own life. A bad reputation is there for changing. You're rebranding, starting afresh and this business is yours, not your parents'... *our* parents!'

Fern sensed that Genie was still a bit resentful about what Milly and James had done, leaving her in the lurch, however well-intentioned it was at the time. She got up and Fern admired the fitted jean shorts she was wearing and the pretty blouse that was knotted at her waist. It had tiny daisies as well as strawberries dotted all over it. Fern had seen photos of Genie's run-down ice cream shop before she'd found her own confidence and wished she could get some of Genie's focus by osmosis – or whatever it was that helped you get energy from something else.

Genie began picking up chairs and putting them into two

piles. Fern noted one pile had dents or cracks and the other was useable. 'Can the broken ones be fixed?' asked Fern, ever the businesswoman. Genie grinned and stuck out her tongue, then grabbed two chairs and put them into a third pile.

'These can be donated to Granddad,' laughed Genie. 'He will probably make a trellis or something out of them. A wonky trellis.' Gus had a workshop in the tiny back garden behind Genie's ice cream shop and made all kinds of projects in there. His blossoming relationship with Ada had been a surprise to them all, especially Genie, but everyone was happy for them and Gus was finally smiling again after the loss of his wife some years ago. Fern felt sad for a moment that she had never met her grandmother, but the family she already had was a bit overwhelming at times, so she put that emotion away for now.

Fern giggled. 'Hasn't Ada put a stop to his inventions and projects?' Fern pictured Gus' handsome face, thick grey hair and twinkly eyes. Genie said he laughed more since he'd met Ada, even though they drove each other nuts. Ada was a neat freak and Gus was such a messy man. Neither had expected to fall in love ever again, but they seemed to make each other happy.

Genie pulled a pen and small pad from her back pocket and waved it in the air. 'Right,' she said. Her long dark hair fell over her face and she took a hairband from her pocket to tie it into a high ponytail. Fern admired how self-confident her sister was. She couldn't match the image before her with the things she'd heard about a frightened girl, who had fought her parents to make her business survive. 'We should write a list of what we want to do…. what you need to do,' Genie continued. 'Sorry! I get all enthused and tend to take over. My staff are always telling me how bossy I am.'

Fern smiled. 'Your staff love you and you juggle them all

and their lifestyles. You let Bailey go to college and look after his son, you employ lots of kids at university in their holidays, and you even let your mum and dad come and interfere when they visit,' joked Fern.

'*Our* mum and dad,' corrected Genie, tutting. 'I let them think they're interfering and then ignore them.' She threw back her head and laughed. 'They haven't really visited much, but knowing Mum she'll have the cake shop in Cornwall sold and will be back causing havoc here before we know it.' Genie busied herself with a dusting cloth after delivering that bombshell.

Fern winced. 'They won't leave that shop so soon, will they? I know they said they would, but I didn't think they meant it. They love the café in Cornwall.'

Genie came over and took her hand. 'It's time. They went there for you. If you aren't there, they certainly won't stay near our 'evil' grandma, Lucinda.' Genie pulled a dastardly face and bared her teeth, making Fern laugh. 'Will it kill you if they sell it?'

Fern thought for a moment, but the stabbing feeling she'd expected to feel in her heart wasn't there. She had nothing to go back to Cornwall for. Her friends had drifted away because Brad was all consuming and refused to let her confide in anyone about their relationship. In the end it had been easier to turn their offers down until they'd stopped asking. She'd been lonely when he wasn't there, but the slivers of hope he'd given her about a future together had been enough to focus her mind on him. Looking back it was very clever and manipulative, but she'd been too clouded by love to see what he was doing.

He'd tried to ring her in the past few days, after months of silence. She knew that he liked having her at his beck and call and was probably shocked she hadn't responded. He didn't know where she was and there was no one there to tell him.

He wouldn't approach Milly and James, knowing who they were. She'd broken down and told him about them over a year ago now. He'd encouraged her to talk about it and been unusually kind and thoughtful. Fern rolled her eyes. He was a good actor and had made her believe in him for years. What an idiot.

'Shouldn't you be at work?' she asked her sister.

'I've taken the day off to help you,' said Genie simply, not meeting her gaze.

'Day off? You never take a day off!'

'Today I do,' Genie said firmly. Tears almost sprung into Fern's eyes and she squeezed her lids shut quickly and blinked them back. She knew how busy her sister was and she pulled her into a big hug and kissed her cheek.

'You're the best.'

Jessie strolled past the front window, which looked out onto Main Street. The shop was sandwiched between the seafront and a row of creative businesses. Fern loved the eclectic mix of crafts, designers and artists she saw milling around. She felt so lucky to have the small kiosk area at the front of her new café. Perfect for cakes and coffees on the go. Maybe the other business owners would become regular customers too? The kiosk had an awning above it, to keep customers dry and out of the sun. There was one at the side and rear too, but they all needed to come down and be scrubbed, which made Fern tired to even think about. Her arms already ached from cleaning the beautiful original parquet floor. Luckily the awnings were plain bluish grey and didn't have logos on them, or she'd have to have replaced them too.

'Wowzers! Jessie is looking sexy today!' joked Genie, nudging Fern in the ribs and watching her sister with hawk-like eyes. Fern had spent the last few nights on the phone to Genie, growling and complaining about him being such a grumpy and unapproachable man. She knew he had a problem with her, but he didn't have to be so forthright about it!

'How well do you know him?' Fern wasn't sure how she felt about her sister and tenant getting along, when she couldn't stand him. She wanted Genie on her side, so they could complain about him together.

'He's made some customised surfboards for Cal and his friends, so I know know him fairly well. I've spoken to him quite a few times when he's come into the ice cream shop, but I'm usually working and can't stop. Plus he's always got a bevvy of women pawing over him, trying to catch his attention.' Genie mock swooned and mopped her brow with a nearby napkin. 'It's the blond surfer dude look, all those sexy muscles and the nonchalant air! He literally doesn't notice the women who drool over him. My staff fight over serving his table,' giggled Genie as Fern pouted. 'He's always polite, though. Not the bear with a sore head that he is with you. Perhaps he's just miffed that he missed out on buying the shop?'

'That's his problem. He shouldn't have gone abroad for so long and left his business behind.'

Genie gave Fern a hard stare. 'Don't be unfair. You know full well that he was working on a custom build, for a very rich client. I told you about it. He can't turn down work like that. It helps his reputation spread and they offered him free board and travel. He's an artist.'

Fern sniffed and ignored her. It was still his fault for not regularly checking on his lease or the shop's status. The old boy who owned the building probably couldn't stand Jessie. *She could understand why.* To Fern, the timings seemed weird, as if Mr Aldous had waited for Jessie to be away and then put the property up for sale, knowing full well it would be snapped up in days. It was prime real estate, even in its run-down state.

As if reading her mind, Genie mused. 'I wonder what Jessie did to annoy Harry – Mr Aldous – so badly that he sold the shop from under him? Not that I'm complaining, as he basically asked me if I knew anyone who'd be interested.' She frowned and then sneezed as she brushed some dust from the skirting board. 'I was pretty shocked. I know him quite well, as he often pops in for dinner and makes a point of stopping by for a chat. I assume it's because he's lonely in the evenings. He gets on really well with all of the café owners along our strip of beach.' She frowned and tilted her head to one side in thought. 'I wonder if that was his plan? Maybe he knew I'd snap it up, as we're so busy at the ice cream shop. He's such a kind man. Used to be a bit of a heart breaker in his day, so I've heard. He never married, though.'

'Children?'

'Not that I know of. He never mentions them. I don't think he likes to talk about his past unless it's about the café. He loves talking about that!' she laughed. 'I was shocked when he sold to you so quickly, but he said the shop was too much for him and he wanted to sell to another food business.'

'I wonder why?' mused Fern. 'Your place has regenerated the parade you're in. Maybe he was hoping you'd do the same here?' It was Genie's turn to blush.

'Everyone has played their part. They all work super hard.'

'But they've followed your lead and asked you for help. I know how much you do for them all, Genie. You send them to branding specialists and help them with marketing and interior design.'

Genie brushed that aside. 'I just like helping people. I'm

helping you!' Genie's cheeks were still a bit pink and they both laughed.

'OK. I'll stop embarrassing you now and I'm grateful for any help you can offer me too, although I'll be using my own branding and experience from the last shop. When I left, I set Milly and James up with a new supplier.'

'Mum and Dad,' corrected Genie on autopilot and Fern ignored her again. She sighed and rubbed her temples with her hands.

'Well, if they do sell up, they can promote it as a going concern, the way I sold it to them. It ought to be snapped up, and that's not me being big-headed. We had a regular customer base.'

Now Fern began really wiping down the glass on the front of the beautifully crafted food display cabinets. They were one thing she wouldn't be changing. The serving area was in an L-shape and made up the main part of the café. Everything was at waist height so the proprietor could see the whole shop and every customer from most places behind the counters. The coffee machines could be installed along the back walls, which had fitted cupboards for crockery, plates and sundries. All she needed to do was paint them to make them fresh and attractive again.

The main work would be in replacing the windows and updating the tables and seating area. Fern hated sitting at a restaurant and getting a painful backside from an uncomfortable chair, so comfortable seating was her priority. She would be ordering cushions for the existing chairs and adding plush armchairs in gorgeous fabrics as well. She wanted to create an air of comfort and luxury, but with quirky twists that befitted the coast and artistic surroundings.

She'd already approached the owner of the gallery along the road and offered to display her work behind the counter too. The canvases had vivid splashes of wave and expanses of sky and suited the coastal vibe perfectly. Fern loved plants, too, so she had already envisioned pots of leafy plants everywhere as well. Fern's mind slid back to Jessie falling over the flower pots on the deck and her first glimpse of his glistening, naked chest. She blinked furiously to clear the image.

'Anyway, you've already got a delicious man at home,' Fern nudged Genie in the ribs, making her jump and cover herself in a layer of dust. 'You don't need a man with an attitude like Jessie's.'

'Who said I was looking for me?' grinned Genie. 'Plus Cal has more attitude than anyone I know,' she sighed and pushed herself up to sit on one of the little round tables that she'd dragged out of the store room.

'You can be as feisty as the best of them,' said Fern. 'Everything OK with you and Cal?' She didn't like the frown on Genie's face, or the way she was suddenly staring at her feet. Her sister did not look the epitome of relationship bliss.

'He's working away a lot and although we knew it would happen, it's harder than we thought. I miss waking up with him every day and it's making me grumpy.'

Fern smothered a laugh. Ada had told her how Genie used to kick plant pots when she was angry and how she'd once almost broken a toe. She hadn't realised that a simple vessel for holding flowers could cause so much trouble! She quickly walked to the store cupboard to pull out the industrial hoover she'd hired to make the shop a bit more presentable for the builders who would begin work the next day. There wasn't too much point cleaning when it would all be ruined again, but a girl had standards and it stopped her moping around, interfering in the love life of her sister or thinking about blond surfer dudes with attitude.

CHAPTER SEVEN

$\mathcal{M}$illy hoped they'd made the right decision. They had decided to put the Cornwall shop up for sale as a going concern, as soon as possible. James was ecstatic, so she had an inkling that he hadn't wanted to leave Essex in the first place. Now they had no business to return to, but their children had shown them that change was good, and they were willing to try something new.

Genie's was now packed to the rafters with customers and although it stung Milly that they hadn't seen the potential of the place, she and James were glad Genie had. Milly felt pride glow in her stomach and was actually secretly pleased Fern had fled to be near her sister. If she hadn't, their parents would have been torn between both coasts and children. Plus, Lucinda lived nearby and Milly could only put up with her mother for so long. The cake café was a testament to Fern's baking skill, but it pretty much ran itself with the few staff they had, and Milly admitted to James that morning that she was bored and anxious at the same time. Her mother brought tension and Milly needed a fresh challenge that was about her and James, and not everyone else.

She smiled finally, as she watched her husband chat to a customer. He was in his element here, but was desperate to get home to Genie, Fern and his dad, Gus. She had opened the computer that morning and seen that he'd been looking up kite surfing schools and food carts for selling hotdogs on the beach. He had no clue how to kite surf and he'd complain about his arthritis if he had to push a cart along the beach, if that was even possible with so much sand!

Milly had had enough drama recently to last a lifetime and was content to live a quiet life. She might even become a lady who lunched. She grinned and her eyes sparkled. She knew she'd be bored in about a nanosecond and would start interfering in her girls' lives. Luckily she and James hadn't sold their house and as Gus had now moved in with Ada, they could rent the annexe next to the main house to a lodger and make a small income from that. Genie was living in a flat with Cal, in the same building as Ada and Gus. Ada had the penthouse apartment with stunning views along the coast. Genie and Cal's flat was far more modest, but it still had floor-to-ceiling windows overlooking the sea and was a far cry from the room Genie had grown up in, which she'd crammed with cookery books and posters of her favourite pop stars.

Milly tilted her head towards the kitchen and James finished his conversation and followed her in, looking enquiringly at his wife. He'd seemed more youthful of late and she knew he was excited for a new adventure. 'We could run our old house as a bed and breakfast,' she said thoughtfully. 'It has four good sized bedrooms and even though the building is quite old, it has charm…'

James' eyes went wide as if he'd just been electrocuted, then he grinned, tilting his head from side to side as if thinking. Then he grabbed her face and kissed her right on the lips, making her heart beat faster, as she stepped back with a grin.

'Brilliant idea!' He gazed around their kitchen. 'It's lovely here, but it's not home, especially now Fern has left. It feels like its soul has gone. I was thinking of new skills I could learn for a venture back home.'

'Like kite surfing or selling hotdogs?' she asked innocently.

He burst out laughing. 'Did I leave the computer open this morning? I was racking my brain for ideas.'

Milly laughed and he hugged her. She loved the feel of his arms around her and was so grateful that they had got over the bumps in their journey. He'd always been her rock and she should have trusted him to understand about Fern a long time ago. Instead, she'd kept her teenage pregnancy a secret. She pictured her mum's pinched face and her equilibrium burst. Her shoulders sagged and James seemed to sense the change in her mood.

'It's my mum's fault for causing this problem in the first place. Now both our girls are in Essex and we're in Cornwall.' They heard the bell above the door chime and James gave her a quick peck on the nose as she went to see who it was. Hearing her mother's high-pitched tone made her wince, but James gently eased her out front as he'd dealt with her mother last time and it took a while to recover mentally from each meeting.

Lucinda was talking to another customer, but looked up as Milly moved nearer. James ducked back into the kitchen to fill a food order and Milly cursed under her breath. The café sale couldn't go through quickly enough for her, and she wouldn't be sorry to have half the country between her and her mother again.

Lucinda made herself comfortable at a table near the

window, where she could spot anyone she wanted to terrorise, thought Milly unkindly. Lucinda's grey hair was immaculately set as usual and she was wearing tailored trousers and a taupe jumper with a round neck. She looked like she meant business. She asked Milly to sit with her and Milly darted a glance around for an escape route, but there was none without scaring her other customers. She sat down heavily and waited.

'Where is Fern?' asked her mother.

The bell above the door jingled and a handsome man with thick black hair and a chiselled jawline came in on his own. He was casually dressed in dark jeans and a crisp white shirt, with the sleeves rolled up to his elbows, but he didn't have a hair out of place and even his sunglasses were perfectly perched on his head. He was dazzling. Most of the men locally were a bit windswept after a stroll on the beach. This man glanced around and then found himself a table. Milly frowned. A few people were gawping at him and she squinted too. He looked familiar, but she couldn't think where from.

'Fern has gone to visit Genie,' said Milly, turning her attention back to her mother and noticing two of her waitresses were already at the table to take the man's order. She'd have to talk to them about that. They had set tables to work on.

'You scared her away?' said Lucinda in a scandalised tone. Milly held her breath for a moment to control the anger that always bubbled inside when her mother spoke.

Milly pushed out of her seat as James arrived with Lucinda's usual order of tea in a teapot and an iced cupcake with buttercream frosting. 'Yes, mother, *we* scared her away.'

James rolled his eyes but said nothing. The gentleman who had just arrived caught Milly's eye and she went over to see how she could help, ignoring her mother's loud tutting.

'Can I help you with anything else?' she asked politely,

trying not to stare at his perfectly white teeth. She noticed he'd already had his drinks order delivered. How speedy her staff could be when they wanted to!

He leant in confidingly and the fragrance of his after-shave wafted around her. It was spicy and inviting. No wonder half of her clientele, as well as the staff, were suddenly primping themselves, or mock fainting over tables. 'I'm looking for Fern,' he said, his voice low so no one else could hear.

'Um... she's not here,' said Milly, wondering what he wanted with her daughter, but the hairs on the back of her neck stood up. Fern's decision to leave so suddenly had bothered Milly and her mum spidey-sense was telling her part of the reason was sitting right in front of her. Her hackles raised. She saw James watching them and smiled reassuringly at him.

'Could we speak privately?' the man asked, looking towards the kitchens at the back of the shop as if he was familiar with them.

'Uh... OK, I guess,' said Milly, as he got up and brought his mug of tea with him. Milly scooched her gawping staff into the café to look after their customers and led the man into the staffroom. James followed protectively and stood by the door as Milly sat down, the man following suit. Lucinda pushed past James and sat next to Brad, making him jump.

'Lucinda,' warned James. 'I think this might be a private conversation.'

'Oh pfft,' said Lucinda. 'Brad and Fern have been dating for years, haven't you dear?'

Brad's mouth fell open, but then he laughed. 'I knew we couldn't keep anything a secret from you, Lucinda. Fern often speaks about you.' She gave Milly a smug look until Milly's steely glare made her cough slightly and stop showing off.

Another thing my mother hasn't told me, thought Milly, her blood boiling. 'If you're dating Fern, why didn't she mention it?'

Brad looked uncomfortable suddenly. 'We decided to keep it below the radar. My job is...' he puffed out his chest and gave them what she supposed was a winning smile. Lucinda simpered next to him. 'I'm an actor and my bosses are very strict about who I date in public.' He smiled at James as if that made everything OK. James didn't smile back and Brad's own grin faltered. Lucinda patted Brad's leg.

Her mum might be star-struck, but Milly and James were used to famous boyfriends, as Genie's boyfriend Cal was a famous chef and his gran Ada used to be a Hollywood film star. Lucinda looked disappointed in her, but then that was nothing new. Milly could now remember seeing Brad in a recent movie and could understand why his presence in the shop had created waves with her staff.

'You've been here before?'

It was Brad's turn to stutter. 'Only at night. Fern thought it better that way.'

I bet she did... not, thought Milly, grinding her teeth and thinking of Fern sitting alone at night while her 'boyfriend' was papped out with other women.

'I had my phone stolen last week and I haven't been able to get in touch with Fern,' he continued, 'so I thought I'd pop in to see her. She'd hardly be avoiding me,' he laughed at his own joke and checked his audience, who didn't seem to be smiling.

James was about to speak, but Milly interrupted. 'She's gone on holiday for a couple of weeks with her sister. Probably too busy sunning herself and sipping sangrias to check her phone. Do you want me to give her your new number when she calls? She usually rings from whichever hotel she's holed up in. She's quite the independent woman,' she said. He paused for a fraction too long, then caught himself and beamed a megawatt smile her way. He got up, going over to shake James' hand. He turned and handed Milly a business card and gave her a quick kiss on the cheek. She smiled but it didn't reach her eyes.

'Let her know I'm missing her,' Brad said as he left the room, put a ten pound note on the table for the drink and left the building with a quick wave to Lucinda who was almost back at her table and clearly loving the fact he'd singled her out. No one spoke for a few seconds, and you could hear the fridges humming loudly. Then chatter broke out and a few people rushed to the window to watch Brad jump into a waiting car and head off at speed along the coastal road.

Milly gave her mother a scathing look and stomped back into the staff room, James following suit. They stood staring at each other and she immediately grabbed the phone and tapped out Fern's phone number, waiting for the call to connect.

CHAPTER EIGHT

*F*ern put down her phone and rubbed her temples. This was just what she didn't need. She was thankful to Milly and James, but now she'd had to quickly explain about Brad and ask them not to say where she was. The texts from Brad were becoming more insistent and cajoling. She was being a silly emotional woman, who'd overthought their last conversation and misunderstood his intention, apparently. Of course he wanted to be with her, he was now saying. Ugh!

Milly hadn't asked any questions, she'd just listened, which was comforting. Fern had expected them to shout at her for being such a sap, or for not confiding in them about her ex-boyfriend's celebrity status. Funnily enough, Milly hadn't even mentioned that, but she must have recognised him, everyone did. Genie looked up in question, but didn't pry.

'Brad's been looking for me at the other café in Cornwall. He never goes there in daylight! He must be desperate,' she said sarcastically.

Genie bit back some rude words, then continued. 'He's

probably after a booty call,' she said through tight lips. 'The git.' She growled protectively, making Fern smile. It was good to finally have someone she could confide in about Brad. She got the feeling she could talk to Milly about him too. Neither had judged her, or told her she was a loser.

'Brad wouldn't usually turn up at the café during the day. He is always working. What's he playing at? Anyone could have recognised him.'

'Maybe he's missing you?' said Genie, gently. 'And he might be a git, but you must have liked something about him. You dated for ages.'

Fern thought for a moment, then dismissed the idea that Brad might actually miss her company. 'Brad could have any number of women. His last film was a flop, but the media circus around it blamed another poor sod, and Brad came out as the worthy hero who dragged it into passable viewing. He was awful in it, but he's got hard-core fans who'll never desert him.'

Genie rolled her eyes and scrubbed harder at a small stain on one of the tables, almost rubbing off the surface.

'He's definitely up to something,' said Fern. She wrinkled her nose, as if she'd just smelt something out of date. She squirted some of the fruity air freshener she was using to clear the air then blinked as it stung her eyes.

'Maybe he's building up to a grand declaration of love and has found out he can't live without you? You were together for ages, so he must have really liked you, you idiot,' Genie scolded. 'More film stars in the family,' she mused dreamily, before Fern nudged her hip. 'Ouch!' What was that for? Ada's Hollywood past means we get to meet loads of interesting people and Cal's work in television brings more. But I'm happy with my customers and their exciting lives, let alone a room full of A-list celebrities. It was enough of a shock to find out that Ada had such a glamorous past,' she said quickly before carrying on with her whirlwind of information. Fern listened in anticipation, but a niggling thought lodged itself between her shoulder blades. She'd have to delve into that later. For now, she was enjoying the excitement in her sister's voice. She loved Genie's dramatics.

Genie's eyes glittered and she took a deep breath, as if she'd need it to get all her words out. 'Della from down the road breeds rare miniature pigs and dresses them up like princesses. She's got a huge following on social media. People pay big bucks to have photos with the pigs in her allotment shed. She's decorated it like a castle,' she laughed, holding her tummy as she giggled. 'She's probably more famous than Cal, Brad and Ada, but she wears a blonde wig and glasses to meet clients and in photos, so no one knows it's her! The locals think it's hilarious.' Genie rocked back and forth in mirth and Fern couldn't help but join in.

'Bob from the next road up comes in every night for dinner. He's sixty-nine and smokes like a chimney. During the day he's a voiceover actor for audio books for those big swoony publishers. He portrays sexy young hunks, as his voice is so husky.' Now Genie's shoulders bobbed up and down as she spoke and tears escaped while she laughed. She dried her eyes and looked at her sister with a smile. 'Sorry. I got a bit carried away. What I mean to say is, maybe Brad's changed?'

'I doubt it,' said Fern with conviction. 'There's something else going on. Anyway, how are you and Cal?' she asked, deflecting more questions. Genie obligingly let the other topic slide.

'It was bliss… it still is,' said Genie, not too convincingly. 'But he spends most of his time in London. He's famous again and that brings its own problems.'

Fern winced as she knew this only too well, or would have if Brad had ever admitted to knowing her over their three year relationship. It was mortifying that she'd gone along with it for so long. She'd been in a bubble of love, or lust! The parallels between her and Genie were scary, but up to now Genie had flourished where she had failed. Fern certainly didn't want a man in the spotlight, it was exhausting. She could see the pain her sister was in, and it was worrying.

'Do you want to talk about it?' asked Fern.

'Not really,' sighed Genie. 'I'm hoping it all works itself out. Plus he's coming home again soon and can make it up to me.' She grinned suddenly and her eyes filled with mischief.

Fern giggled and then pictured Jessie. 'About Jessie...'

'You seem to be thinking about him a lot,' observed Genie, poking her in the ribs and making her jump.

Fern stuck her tongue out at her sister. 'He's my sitting tenant. You conveniently forgot to mention him when you told me how beautiful this shop could be and how much potential it had! I'll admit it's perfect for me,' she looked around. 'Or it will be when it's been renovated. I'm putting sliding doors to the side and back to open the whole area up. Jessie will hate me even more as it will mean more building work, but I've already had three quotes and someone is booked in to start on Monday.'

'Wow! There's you pretending to be confused and really you've already started with your plans. Come on. I bet you've got it all drawn out. I know how organised you are.' Genie slapped her pen and paper on the tabletop and then grabbed the bag she'd dumped by the door. 'I asked my new kitchen staff to make us some sandwiches and my mouth is already watering. My new chef is a miracle from heaven,' she said with a theatrical gesture. 'When Cal left, I decided to take on a full-time chef and Suze rocked up one day saying she was looking for a job and had heard about the place. She's fitted in perfectly.' She looked at the sandwiches and smacked her lips in anticipation.

'We don't get any of the screaming and stress you some-times assume comes with a busy kitchen. Suze works with zen charm and she even leaves scraps out for the pigeon family that live in Grandad's shed.'

Fern chuckled as she'd heard all about the feisty pigeon that lived in the shed behind the ice cream bar. Apparently their granddad Gus had made her a pigeon house with a little ledge for her to sun herself on.

'About Jessie?' asked Fern again, knowing full well that her sister was stalling for time and probably had her escape route planned already. 'You know, the tenant I wasn't expecting?'

Genie shrugged and looked at the door, chewing on her lip. 'Jessie is a bit of a star locally, for his art.'

She glanced over the plans that Fern had spread out over the counter. Fern hoped that Genie could see her vision in the prettily drawn out shop layout. It was functional, would be profitable as far as table layout was concerned and also made the most of the aspect out to sea. There was room for seating all around the outside of the shop, without visitors to the area or locals bumping into it. Fern explained that the shop owned some of the space outside, but Mr Aldous had never utilised it. She envisioned Jessie's face when he learnt there would be customers sunning themselves outside his back window – but to be fair, the view for them would be great in every direction! Genie had mentioned in passing that she'd heard on the grapevine that Jessie often painted his boards half-naked! As if that wasn't prime gossip.

Genie told her she loved the plans. 'Plus, Jessie's gorgeous and you've been too pre-occupied with past relationships to take care of your current love life. I know you weren't expecting a tenant, but I did go over the lease carefully with

Ada and our lawyers. Jessie always pays on time and his shop is stunning. He won't be any trouble. We're so lucky that Harry clearly hates him and sold the shop to you instead,' she joked. 'Did I mention that Jessie's hot?'

Fern raised her eyebrows but said nothing. A picture of Brad's dark hair and chiselled features flashed into Fern's mind and she firmly shut it out again. She was a sucker for big blue eyes. Brad had only had to stare her way and she'd been a goner. The image switched to Jessie's angry blue eyes and she gritted her teeth and decided she had to change her type.

'Genie!' she admonished, half laughing at her sister's cheek. 'You only have a love life because a hunk hid in your kitchen and refused to go away when you told him to! Your friends tell me you're a workaholic.'

'Well that seems to run in the family,' said Genie, ignoring the jibe. She took in all Fern's carefully laid out plans. 'For all of the protesting, you certainly understand food businesses. We can't let a few sexy men derail us from world domination in this corner of the cake and ice cream universe.' They both burst out laughing.

'I can smell food,' said Fern as her stomach rumbled. Genie grinned and handed her one of the sandwiches. It was layered with ham, salad, sun-dried tomatoes and the tiniest slivers of apple between delicious thick slices of homemade bread. 'Oh wow!' Fern sighed with bliss between mouthfuls.

They sat in silence and gave the food the concentration it deserved, then Fern decided that she needed some answers and this was as good a time as any. 'Did you ever dream of having siblings?' she asked, whilst nibbling on the side of her sandwich. It was the one topic they had steered clear of and Fern wasn't quite sure why. She'd always wanted a sibling, but her parents' ages would have stopped them adopting again even if they had tried. They hadn't gone through the proper channels with her – her grandmother had given her away like a prize pig.

Genie paused and gazed out at the serene sea, not showing the storm that was probably raging underneath. Neither of them had been left unscathed by their parents.

'I always felt as if something was missing,' mused Genie. 'Maybe because I could sense something, with Mum. She often spoke about how precious siblings were, but she hates her own sister.' Genie grinned suddenly and her whole face lit up with mischief. 'Have you met aunty Serena yet?'

Genie's haughty tone made Fern almost choke on her sandwich so she quickly gulped it down and took a swig from her water bottle. Genie was so funny. She could imitate most accents, but also loved her own Essex twang. Fern knew she was fiercely proud of the little stretch of coastline where she'd been brought up.

Fern dabbed her mouth with the paper napkin the food had been wrapped in and recalled Genie speaking about her aunt… their aunt! 'No. I haven't had that pleasure yet, thank goodness. She sounds like a carbon copy of Gran!' she joked.

'You're lucky!' said Genie, her eyes wide. 'She's an absolute horror. She's younger than Mum and thinks I'm irresponsible for not going to Cornwall and supporting my family, when they were the ones who deserted me! Plus, Mum and her sister don't get on anyway, so why does she care?' She rolled her eyes and shook her head, her long dark hair falling around her shoulders. Fern's own thick blonde hair was a similar colour to Milly's. Fern was taller than Genie and they had often stood side by side comparing features in the time they had known each other. Genie was more like James' side of the family, while Fern was more Milly and Lucinda, which made her pull a face and Genie roll around laughing.

'Back to my annoying tenant…' Fern said. Genie paused

and Fern could imagine her brain working at full speed as she dodged Fern's question and spoke about Milly's side of the family again. Fern was still intrigued about the family dynamics and listened avidly.

Genie obviously decided not to touch on the subject of the pain their gran had caused them all. Instead she joked, 'Aunt Serena is a pleasure you have to prepare yourself for – for months in advance. You have to brush your hair until it's like fine silk,' Genie smoothed her hair over her shoulder and looked demurely at Fern. 'And you have to only eat food that is green as everything else will poison your brain. Even her house is painted green. She thinks its zen, but the neighbours hate her as it's electric green and it gives them all a headache.'

Fern giggled, then frowned as she pictured a house the colour of mushy peas. 'But on the subject of my moody but good to look at tenant…'

Genie wouldn't meet her eye and threw the last scraps of her sandwich into her mouth, chewing thoughtfully for a moment. 'You saw the contract. You signed it!'

'Yes, of course I did. But it said he was a very happy tenant who'd been here for years. That he had a long-established business and was no bother. I pictured a middle-aged carpenter.'

'I didn't have the time to worry about details,' said Genie, brushing a speck of dirt from her arm. 'For some reason Harry said it had to be rushed through. He said he was intending to sell up and had his eye on a flat to rent, so he needed to move quickly to secure it.'

'I guessed he was retiring?' said Fern.

'Kind of. He loves working and just wants a smaller space where he can spend more time with his hobbies, apparently. He's an incredible chef, but he said he's worn out and he didn't have the energy to rejuvenate his place, like I did with mine. It's why he spoke to me, I suppose,' she shrugged.

'Wow!' said Fern. 'That was so lucky when you think about it.'

'It was!' Genie got up and twirled around in excitement for a moment, then looked a bit dizzy and sat on another of the tables until she noticed Fern's disapproving stare. She slid her backside onto a chair and gazed thoughtfully out to watch the waves lapping at the shore through the side windows.

'I assumed you'd checked everything over for us. That was my own stupid fault,' Fern added, rubbing her bottom lip and making her mouth sore.

'I did!' said Genie. 'Of course I did... but I thought you could just kick him out if he annoyed you,' she joked, making Fern smile at last. 'Harry said he was the ideal tenant. Plus if the shop doesn't work out, I'll buy it from you, so you don't need to worry. I want you to succeed.'

Fern's mouth dropped open. 'The ice cream business is doing that well?' Now she looked around the open plan space and visualised it with big sliding doors on all sides and her eyes sparkled with pride. 'If I can do only half as well, then I'll be happy here,' she said realising it was true.

Genie shrugged. 'In the evenings, the restaurant gets booked up weeks in advance and we've had to allow only walk ins during the day to stop upsetting people. Plus the takeaway service and deliveries are working a treat. I'm shipping our ice cream brand to other stores, after it worked so well with your cake shop in Cornwall.' Her eyes sparkled with new challenges. 'It means working on building my brand, but word seems to keep spreading. I'm not complaining,' she sighed, rubbing her back and rolling her shoulders.

Fern frowned and sighed too.

'Look,' said Genie. 'You've had a lot going on, what with new parents popping up in your life and Brad going AWOL, before seeming to decide he wants you back again. It's not surprising you wanted a change and jumped into this. Maybe it's just what you need? A hot surfer dude and loads of sexy locals to distract your mind,' she winked, making Fern roll her eyes.

Fern started searching under the counter for some more cleaning supplies that she'd shoved in there the day before. 'Brad doesn't want me back and Jessie isn't a help. He's a pain in my butt.'

Genie snorted and took the cleaning cloth that Fern held out to her. She grabbed a bottle of spray and began to wipe down surfaces, more gently this time.

'He told me in no uncertain terms that he's not happy that I bought the lease 'from under him" said Fern. 'He didn't even mention you! But you organised it so it's half your fault.'

'I bet you'd like to be "under him" in a different sense,' cackled Genie and Fern gave her her first older sister look, to shut her up. Genie blatantly pretended she hadn't seen for a moment and then doubled over laughing, just as Jessie himself strolled past again. His hair was mussed up from running his hands through it, probably when thinking about his new landlady, thought Fern grumpily. How did he manage to look so good even when he was frowning and clearly in a hurry to get somewhere? She brushed her fingers through her own hair, but they got stuck halfway and she hastily pulled them out.

'He told me he wanted to buy the lease but Harry never hinted that the place was for sale. They were good mates apparently, so Jessie is double fuming. It's a bit confusing – if we can believe anything Jessie says.' Fern scrubbed at a particularly grubby stain while she was talking and was pleased to see it disappear. 'Maybe his feelings are actually hurt?' she said generously.

'That's his own fault for being out of the country!' said Genie. 'How could we realise that he didn't know about it?

He should have been on top of it,' she smiled again and Fern couldn't help but join in. For once she was going to embrace good fortune and not duck out of its way. She suddenly pictured Jessie's clear blue eyes and taut leg muscles as he stomped up the stairs to the flat and then shook her head to clear the image.

'You were thinking about him then, weren't you?' asked Genie, and Fern swiped the cleaning cloth through the air and swatted her backside, making her yelp and get back to cleaning.

'He probably was on top of someone,' grumbled Fern, making Genie smile to herself and Fern rub the counters even harder. 'Have you seen the number of cute surfer chicks who congregate outside his shop? It's ridiculous!'

'Great for business though,' said Genie. 'They can all come in and buy delicious cupcakes while they drool at him over the new balustrading I was going to tell you about.' She slid her phone out of her jean shorts' pocket and scrolled to the right page. Fern came round and looked at the images, seeing immediately how they could work with her planned outside space.

'It will stop him complaining your customers are blocking his doorways or intruding on his artwork.'

'He already hates me!' complained Fern, brushing moisture from her top lip and trying to tame her hair out of her face, with two hair slides from her pocket.

'Then we need to make him adore you,' winked Genie, but Fern rolled her eyes, as that was never going to happen, and went to check on her supplies list.

CHAPTER NINE

*G*enie tidied away the remnants of their lunch and looked around the new shop. It was already taking shape and she could see Fern's vision for the place. Fern was still muttering that she didn't care about her annoying new neighbour and his growly ways. 'Plus, we're his landlords, so he has to play nice.'

Genie didn't mention the fact that Harry had given them the shop for a cut-down price as a sweetener to entice them to take it over fast. Property prices might not be as high as in Cornwall, but this little corner of heaven could be a tourist hotspot. Currently it was full of the art crowd, and Genie had noticed more and more tourists visiting the little galleries and tutting that there wasn't a decent place to sit for a coffee. Since Harry's café had that musty unloved feel, people hadn't liked to venture inside too often and she couldn't blame them. The takeaway service from the side window had probably kept him afloat. The same thing had happened to her parent's ice cream shop before she'd taken over. It was rundown and unappealing. Working in food service was exhausting – but it could be exhilarating at the same time.

She was addicted to it, and could see her sister had the same passion.

Harry was a regular at Genie's ice cream bar. She hadn't mentioned it to Fern, but she'd told him about her sister's award-winning cakes and how much business they would bring to the local area if she ever relocated. Harry was a big part of the community and loved seeing his own bit of shore-line gradually shrug off its cobwebs and begin to sparkle. Genie knew that he didn't have the energy to do the same himself. These shops and flats were absolute gems, though, and Genie had been desperate to entice her sister to live closer. They had spent most of their lives apart, and she'd fought so hard to save her own business that she couldn't abandon it and move to Cornwall. Plus their gran lived there, and that was enough to scare most people into staying away. Lucinda did have a big group of friends, but Genie and Milly had never quite worked out how, as she was caustic to her own family.

'Mum told me that Gran's been terrorising the local women's group for years, although she has nothing to show off about, as she would never praise Mum or Dad. Even Aunty Serena hasn't done anything well enough to meet Gran's standards, even though she runs yoga retreats and classes that are really popular. Serena might be a misery, but in front of her own customers she's amazing, apparently.' Genie thought for a moment. 'Maybe it's Gran that makes her nasty! Aunty Serena can't be that awful and run a company that makes people relaxed and happy, surely?' her brow creased and she thought back. Had she ever seen her aunt without her grandma? Surely that was weird?

'You might be right,' mused Fern. 'Maybe Lucinda tries to control her too, and it makes her angry whenever she sees you all, as you can get away from her and she can't?'

'She must be seething now Mum and Dad are coming

back,' Genie winced and pulled a face at blurting out the news.

Fern's head whipped up. 'So they are definitely coming back soon? What about the shop?' Genie looked away and started fussing with the cleaning products. 'Genie?'

'I'm sorry.' Genie hung her head and then gazed at Fern from under her lashes. 'They only went there for you and if you aren't there, then there's nothing for them. Dad's so homesick for us, and for Grandad. Even Mum wants to move back. They love the café you created with Bill and Irene, but without you it's not the same.'

'They've only been there for just over a year,' said Fern sadly. Genie could tell she hated the thought of her shop being sold, but in fairness it had already been sold to Milly and James before that. Fern had been the one to jokingly suggest they move back, but she probably hadn't expected it to happen so quickly. But it was time to move on. Genie went over and hugged her sister. It sometimes still felt so weird to think that she had a sister. She thought back to the phone calls she'd had with her mum and how much she talked about their old restaurant and her friends here. Milly loved this seafront and Genie could tell she was unhappy in Cornwall, even though she loved the coastline and customers. Genie hadn't been surprised that her mum and dad were moving back home as soon as possible.

Thank goodness they hadn't sold the house. Apparently they already had a possible tenant for Grandad's old annexe to the side of their big house overlooking the seafront. It seemed a lifetime ago that Genie had lived there, when in reality it was a matter of years. Their grandad Gus was happy with Ada and it didn't look like he'd ever move back. He still tinkered in the shed in the small garden at the back of her ice cream shop when he needed to get away from the calm space of Ada's penthouse flat to his own messy kingdom.

Her grandparents had started this whole tradition of food shops on the seafront with some friends, who had run the businesses alongside Genie's little ice cream shop. Genie had inherited her grandmother's skill with flavours, and Fern had too, judging by the way she whipped up cakes that were as light as air. Between them, Genie was determined that their brands would become household names. Hers was already becoming better known outside their town and she fielded new enquiries daily.

Moving to scribble some ideas on her notepad, she pulled her sister to her side and they began to sort through what was useable and what they would need to buy for the grand opening of the little cupcake shop by the sea. Genie was hoping that they would call it 'Fern's', the same way her ice cream shop was called 'Genie's'. It had taken Ada a while to persuade her to rebrand, but it had been the right decision. Genie grinned at the dust that had settled on her sister's shoulders and the dark smudge on her nose. Fern really had no idea of how strikingly pretty she was. She had glowing skin and beautiful greeny-blue eyes with the same sooty black lashes as Genie. They both had curves, although Fern was taller than Genie. It had taken Genie a while to become comfortable in her own skin and she could see the same thing gradually happening to her sister.

Fern's long blonde hair was thick and had a slight wave, like the sea, although she favoured adding pretty clips to the sides of her hair to keep it out of her face. It made her look young and carefree. If only that was they way they felt, after their parents' revelations, she mused. She picked up one of the old menus and felt suddenly sad that the world wouldn't be able to sample Harry's food any more. In its heyday this shop had been buzzing, apparently. Her mum and dad had said it was a treasure on the seafront, but like others along the parade, it needed some love and attention lavished on it to bring back its sparkle. Genie straightened her shoulders and hoped that Fern would be the one to do it. Genie would get right behind her and support her all the way. She would try not to be bossy and take over, but she was not about to let this business fail. She wouldn't let her sister flee back to the other side of the country without a fight.

CHAPTER TEN

*J*essie banged his wood-working equipment down on his workbench and slammed a cupboard shut. His mouth was set in a grim line. For an easy-going, sunny kind of guy, he really wanted to stamp his feet and yell at someone. Preferably his new landlady, or landladies, as he now knew Genie was in on the scam too. Somehow he'd managed to go abroad to work and come back to find the building – and his shop – had new owners. The site had been sold from right under him. It was a kick in the ribs.

Genie knew him and how much he loved this building, although he had to admit that he'd never mentioned wanting to expand. Her ice cream restaurant was always buzzing with customers and if more of that happened next door, then bang went his quiet life. Harry had run a simple business where Jessie could pop in for a quiet coffee. The place had been old fashioned and felt unloved, so customers had drifted away, but it wasn't because of the food or coffee. It had just needed a lick of paint and some elbow grease. He'd offered to help often enough, but Harry had always brushed his offers aside.

The timings of the sale were a nightmare and he still couldn't work out what had happened. A few weeks previously, he'd received a call from a very well-known celebrity who'd bought two of his customised surf boards. The figure to make them alone had been incredible, but he'd also been offered travel and board to bring them over personally and then spend a month teaching the guy how to use them. The celebrity had already been a good surfer, so it hadn't exactly been taxing, and Jessie had enjoyed every minute and made loads of new contacts, but he'd had to leave his assistant running the show. And then he'd come back to a new landlady!

He didn't know what irked him the most, the fact that Fern was so pretty and he kept thinking about her, or the fact that she was already changing things, like moving the plant pots around on their shared terrace on the first floor outside their flats. He'd often sat there with Harry and enjoyed a few beers. Now he'd have to get dressed every time he went outside, and watch what he said and did. What would she think if he brought women home? He scoffed at that notion, as he'd been too busy with work to date anyone lately. Now his ex, Khloe, kept turning up outside his shop and was making him uncomfortable after he'd cooled things off. Women were nothing but trouble! He'd thought Genie was his friend. But she obviously put business before friendship. He'd remember that.

He could look around for new premises, but it wasn't that he needed more space. He just loved the building and had wanted to own it if it was available. He didn't like the uncertainty of renting. Harry had been pretty easy, to be fair, but it was the sea views and the closeness to the shoreline that really sold this little corner of paradise. Jessie could literally step out of his door and be in the sea in five minutes.

He'd be the first to admit that the building was in

desperate need of some tender loving care, but he quite enjoyed its rustic charm. The front of the building had serving windows onto the little shopping street and the back had double doors practically onto the beach. Upstairs the two flats were mirror images of each other, with one big bedroom, a small kitchen and open lounge area with a sofa bed. The big sliding doors leading out to the wide roof terrace gave stunning views across the sea. It was prime real estate and he was livid that it had landed in Fern's hands and not his own.

When she'd first shown up, he'd been bowled over by the sight of her. She had lashings of silky blonde hair, sea green eyes and long, long tanned legs, as well as some pretty spectacular curves. Then she'd shattered his wandering mind and salivating mouth by sticking her hand out and introducing herself as his new landlady. He'd come crashing back to reality and had been lost for words, before getting angry. He wasn't proud of himself, but it was a big change to his otherwise quiet life. He'd almost broken his neck on those stupid plant pots.

Fern was annoyingly alluring and she kept wandering around in tiny little jean shorts that showed off her legs and T-shirts that she tied loosely in a knot at her waist, giving glimpses of her midriff with the movement of her hips. It was distracting and it made him keep eyeing the windows in case she walked past.

He wasn't a teenager and he'd seen an attractive woman before, so he didn't know why his eyes kept searching her out. She wasn't his usual type, an easy-going surfer chick, either. She was tall and had those freckles dotted over her nose... not that he'd really noticed. She had a graceful way of moving, as if she was completely unselfconscious and had no idea of her charms either. He'd noticed lots of builders turning up to quote for jobs and they hung around for ages.

He'd had to growl at a few to move them on and it wasn't helping. He felt like a bear with a sore head. His life had changed in an instant from chilled and fun, to angsty and annoying.

The memory of Fern, in a little strappy top and shorts nightwear set, while she hung some bikinis out to dry on the clothes horse she'd assembled in one corner made his blood flow faster in his veins, but he shut that emotion down. He definitely didn't want to fall for another woman who lived nearby. He'd started to care for Khloe, who had regularly visited his shop, but she'd become obsessive and now turned up at all times of day and night, often with friends in tow. They'd only dated for a few months, but he'd been so busy with work that he'd barely seen her. When she'd stormed into the shop while he was with clients, demanding his time and energy, he'd apologised to his customers and tried to make her happy. The problem was that the more attention he'd given her, the more she wanted. She'd hooked up with other men to make him jealous and it had emotionally exhausted him in the end. He hadn't been able to tell where the lies ended and the truth began.

He'd finished the relationship, if you could call it that when it had been such a train wreck, just before he'd left to work in America. He'd heard she was dating another guy and rather than make him jealous, it had been the final blow to the tenuous thread that had kept him coming back for more. He'd trusted her, but now he was incredibly wary and in no rush to jump back into the dating game.

Once he'd gone to America to work, she'd barraged him with hundreds of texts and calls saying she missed him, but the week before he'd left and he'd ended things, she had ghosted him, as if that might make him more interested. It had the opposite effect. Khloe made him feel like he'd been run over by a bus. Even when he had tried his hardest, nothing was ever good enough – his job, his home, his attentiveness. He'd liked her, but the more she'd smothered him, the more he felt like he couldn't breathe and needed space.

He'd seen Genie go into the shop that morning and he'd tried not to call her over for a chat or an explanation of her sister's actions. She was actually a lot of fun and he had met Cal quite a few times. He'd popped into the surf shop and was now a customer. Jessie had wondered if he should drop Cal a text and ask him what the hell had happened to his lease, but he discarded that idea pretty quickly. He didn't know Cal well enough and as a celebrity, he probably had an assistant dealing with any calls from unknowns anyway. Maybe he should go to Genie's ice cream shop for dinner one night soon and try and suss out what the hell was going on? He certainly felt like he'd been played, but he couldn't put his finger on how, or why.

He looked up as two regular customers entered the shop. A genuine smile lifted his face. This was what his life was about – satisfied customers. He decided that distracting landladies and confusing old landlords would have to wait, but at some point he was determined to find out what the hell had happened while he was abroad. What hold could those two innocent-looking sisters have over a vulnerable pensioner like Harry, to sweep in and steal the shop right from under Jessie's nose?

CHAPTER ELEVEN

he number of builders seemed to be multiplying. They'd arrived early and Fern had scrambled to rub sleep from her eyes and throw on some clothes. She'd grabbed soft grey jogging bottoms and a fitted white T-shirt and had added some diamanté hair slides to her hair to keep it out of her eyes, which made her look about five. She'd stuck her tongue out at her reflection and grabbed comfortable shoes, mentally reminding herself to buy some simpler hair adornments.

Now she was standing where the windows had been and the butterflies in her stomach were back. It was a total mess! Jessie had walked past and ignored both her and the building work, and then come back to ask if the changes would affect his shop. She'd had to bite her tongue. She had knocked on his door several times to try and discuss the ongoing structural work, but he'd been out all week. She'd have happily discussed the plans with him, if he'd ever bothered to be around. She'd smiled sweetly and told him about the new layout, which he'd digested quietly, then nodded his head and left her to it, leaving a waft of citrus from his aftershave that made her hungry, but she wasn't quite sure what for.

Genie arrived, with the huge carton of milk Fern had asked her for. She had just made what felt like millionth cup of tea for the men and women installing the windows. Genie held the carton up to show her sister and then stepped over some rubble to put it in the fridge. Fern plastered on her brightest smile and tried to hide her exhaustion. She blamed Jessie for making her toss and turn in bed at night, worrying about what he would think of the plans.

She beckoned Genie over to sit at the little table she'd set up in the kitchen. Every other surface seemed to be covered in dust sheets and machinery at the moment and this felt like the safest place to be. She'd made a few batches of cupcakes in her own small kitchen upstairs the previous evening and was gratified to see them being hoovered up by the workers. The latest plate had mere crumbs left. At least she could use this time to product test and then ask which were firm favourites. If they loved them enough, the builders might return as customers with partners and friends. It was an exciting thought.

'These builders might become customers,' Genie remarked, then saw Fern's expression. 'Ah, that's the plan. I'm glad you've got it all in hand.' She pressed her fingers into the crumbs they'd left and tasted a bit of frosted icing. 'Mmm. Fresh lemon rind? Do I get free samples too?'

Fern grinned and went to the fridge where she'd hidden three extra cupcakes. She shoved one to the back of the plate and picked up two. That final innocent-looking cupcake was being saved for Jessie. She was going to pop by later with it as a peace offering. It might not look like much, but the caramel and liqueur laced buttercream, and the tiny apple and cinnamon bites in the sponge, would hopefully make their mark and he would understand a bit more about what she was doing. This had been her bestselling recipe in Cornwall and hundreds of happy customers had attested to its worth.

Genie took her lemon frosted cupcake reverently and bit into it, signing with bliss. 'Oh my! This is almost orgasmic.'

'Genie!' laughed Fern, wondering if she should rename it, then shaking that idea off.

'It's so good. Is it alcoholic?'

'Just a tiny bit. It has a dash of Limoncello in the batter. It's something I've been thinking about. I'm going to offer cocktails in the evening with cocktail-themed cakes. Maybe just one or two days a week. What do you think?'

Genie took another mouthful and sighed in bliss, her eyes closing for a moment as if she was at absolute peace. 'Great idea. And you could eventually offer a cake and cocktail delivery service to people having picnics on the beach.'

Fern thought for a moment, picturing how that could work, and smiled. 'Maybe, one day. For now I want to get this place ready and find some actual customers.'

It was shocking how quickly the shop was starting to take shape. The builders were happy and so was she. Fern smiled and briefly responded to one of the women who was helping to fit the windows, as she stuck her head round the door to ask Fern something. Fern could finally see her vision for the place coming together before her eyes. It was fun to be around a group of people again. She'd missed chatting to her café customers. She tried not to think about the fact that she longed for her customers more than her friends, but she'd been a solitary child with older adoptive parents, and Brad had pretty much destroyed any other friendships she'd had by always expecting her to be free. She hated cancelling on anyone, so it was easier not to arrange anything in the first place. She thought of her old customer, Viv, with her bright clothes and warm smile. Fern was glad they still spoke on the phone and shared text messages. Maybe Viv might even visit one day and then she could meet Cal, Gus and Ada. She'd fit right in with them all.

Her body yearned for Brad, but her mind pushed back, reminding her that she was better off without him. He'd been smooth and sophisticated, but everything had been on his terms. It hadn't occurred to her to question his motives or ask him to change his plans. He was a busy superstar and she was an unknown who worked in a café. She'd never thought about how busy she was herself, as the manager of a popular venue, or what her own needs might be. Working in food service was demanding, both physically and emotionally.

She'd simply looked into his big blue eyes and become a simmering pool of lust. He'd just had to text her and she'd move heaven and earth to be by his side. *What an idiot!* she fumed to herself. Thank goodness moving away had broken that spell. Her ego was bruised, but she'd get over it. Her heart wasn't as battered as she'd thought it would be. She had sobbed into her pillow many times, but the further away from Brad's influence she was, the more she found that she actually felt free of the burden of secrecy.

She looked around at her new domain and smiled. Brad was in the past and the changes she'd made to the shop were like seeing a butterfly emerge from a chrysalis. It was as if the shop had been sleeping under a layer of dust, but was shaking itself off and coming back to life.

One of the builders walked past and blushed when he saw her. She smiled at him kindly. He looked to be a few years younger than her, so was probably in his early to mid-twenties, and every time he saw her he went bright red! She hoped she didn't make him nervous, but she was starting to enjoy being noticed for once. She might even learn how to flirt. Genie seemed like a natural when she was around Cal and it was about time Fern took notes. She hadn't looked at another man in years, but she smiled suddenly and decided to enjoy herself.

She watched as Jessie left the building by the back door of his shop. He went to sit on the sand after stopping to say a quick hello to one of the builders, who she'd heard he knew from school. She tried not to stare, but she often found herself scanning the pavement outside to see if he was around. It was an annoying habit and she chided herself for being so weak. The last thing she needed was another man in her life, even if he was as toned and lithe as Jessie. Not that she'd really noticed...

Her phone pinged with another text and she glanced down. It was from Brad. She swiped to delete it before going to look for the blushing builder.

CHAPTER TWELVE

That evening, Fern was sitting outside on the terrace by her flat and rubbing her sore shoulders, which wasn't an easy feat when her arms ached too. Jessie stepped out onto the deck with a beer in hand and then stopped suddenly when he saw her, as if deciding if it would be too rude to run back indoors and hide. She flushed and tried not to stare at his tanned, muscled legs and bare feet. He turned around and went back inside and she sighed and stretched her legs out, catching the last few rays of the late afternoon sun, trying to shrug off the sting of humiliation at being hated so much that her tenant despised the sight of her.

She jolted in surprise when a beer was handed to her and she looked up to see Jessie pull a chair over next to hers and stare out to sea, sipping his beer. She took a taste of the cooling liquid, letting it soothe her parched throat. She tilted her head slightly to be able to look at his brooding profile. He had slight stubble and his thick blond hair was swept back off his handsome face.

'Thanks for the beer,' she said simply, a bit at a loss for

what else to say and wondering if it would be rude to move back a little, as her thigh was almost touching his and she could feel the heat from his skin. Both of them were hot and sweaty from a hard day's work and she wished she'd bothered to shower before slumping down on the deck in exhaustion. Thank goodness she hadn't put her pyjamas on. It was so quiet that she had assumed he was out.

He turned and gently smiled at her, his eyes alight with mischief. She was taken aback as she'd never seen a genuine smile from him before. 'You're welcome. You look how I feel,' he joked.

She grinned. 'That bad, huh?'

His gaze slid over her face and body and she felt her skin grow warmer.

'You look fine, but I've seen how hard you've been working. You need to take care of your muscles, or you'll burn out.'

I'll burn up if you keep staring at my legs, thought Fern, trying not to wriggle in her seat at his open assessment of her body. They'd bumped into each other a few times and been a bit more civil lately, so she was hoping they could call some sort of truce. He might actually like her, if he bothered to get to know her.

She rolled her neck and rubbed her shoulders again. 'I didn't realise how hard fitting out a shop this size would be. My last café was much smaller. Plus it was already a modern coffee shop, they had just missed the mark with their chef. He frightened the customers half to death with his weird jokes and then almost killed them with his food. The owners were too scared to sack him so they sold up!'

Jessie spluttered, as he had just taken a mouthful of beer, and laughed heartily. Fern liked the sound. 'Weren't you scared he'd expect a job with the new owner?'

'No. I ran a cake shop and he was a meat and two veg

man,' she giggled. 'He thought cakes were 'arty farty' – his words – and a waste of time. Plus he was a local bodybuilder and he said I'd make him fat,' she laughed at the memory. He had towered over her, even though she thought of herself as pretty lanky. 'He said I'd never make a go of it, but we were full to capacity most days,' she smiled at the image she conjured up of their lovely customers and how they had raved about her baking skills. She hoped Milly and James had found a buyer who would follow the tradition. They'd be crazy not to keep the business the same.

'Why did you leave if it was such a good business?' he asked and she drew in a sharp intake of breath. 'Sorry. I don't mean to pry. It's not as if we're bosom buddies.' She looked at her chest in confusion and he laughed. 'Haven't you heard of that term? Close friends.'

Fern burst out laughing and Jessie joined in. She looked into his eyes and made a decision. He'd given her a tiny opening for friendship and she could push him away or let him in. She was so used to mistrusting people, after Brad and all his tricks, but it might be nice to have a neighbour that she actually spoke to about real things, not just trivialities. She was an honest person and having to keep her relationship a secret when people had asked her before had made her anxious.

'My adoptive parents died in an accident and my birth family came to rescue me,' she explained. She smiled when his mouth hung open and she pushed herself up to stand over him. 'I think we need cake for this.'

She walked into the kitchen and brought back two slices of the spice-infused coffee and walnut cake she'd made that morning to feed the workers, plus the lone caramel and apple cupcake she'd saved especially for him. A couple of the builders had asked for takeaway boxes to take a piece of walnut cake home. She handed him a slice and he took it and smelt the heavenly buttery scent of the sponge. He tasted a mouthful and made a kind of purring in his throat as he stuffed in another huge forkful. She laughed and sat back down with her plate on her lap. Her bones ached and she wasn't sure how much to confide in a complete stranger, but for some reason she felt compelled to share her story, perhaps hoping it might soften him towards her a little. She wasn't an awful person and hadn't purposefully set out to own his shop.

She was fed up with the loneliness that often crept into her evenings. It was nice to talk to someone about a topic that wasn't building work. She'd decided over the last few days that perhaps he wasn't as bad as she'd first thought and maybe even that he had had a rough deal from Harry. No wonder he'd been upset with her buying the shop, when he'd been here for years and she was new to the area. She wanted him to trust her if they were going to be working side by side in their respective shops – and living next door to each other.

'I'm sorry about your parents,' said Jessie, eyeing up the cupcake, so she laughed and placed it on his plate. 'Did you know you were adopted?'

Fern stared out to sea and watched a little sailboat drift across her vision. 'I think I always knew. They never hid it from me, but they told me my birth mother had died in childbirth and my father was absent, which were lies.' Jessie put his empty plate down and took her hand in his. She didn't flinch and just stared at their linked hands for a moment. 'Genie's my sister, but I'm guessing you already know that. I hadn't met her until just over a year ago, so I wanted to be near her. It was a big shock for both of us.'

'Didn't she know about you either?'

Fern shook her head, letting her hair cover her face a little. She couldn't bear to see anyone's pity. Jessie let go of her hand and nudged her plate, so that she ate something. The sugary forkful of nut and coffee broke her reverie and she smiled at him.

'That's understandable,' he said. 'Do you have other siblings?'

'Not that I know of,' she laughed suddenly, making him grin. 'I was bought up as an only child and I dreamed of a brother or sister. Now I have Genie, but both my birth family and adoptive family lied to me, so who knows what else is hidden away.'

When Jessie frowned, she took another forkful of cake and chewed it thoughtfully. 'My birth grandmother basically gave me to her friends and didn't tell my real parents where I was. I grew up thinking she was just a close family friend.' She looked at Jessie's shocked face and smiled sadly. 'I don't know why I'm telling you this, when we don't even like each other.'

His lip quirked up at her honesty and he took another sip of beer. 'I like you,' he said quietly. 'I was just upset you beat me to the building. I've been here for a long time. But maybe you need to be near your family more than I need the space.'

'When my birth parents finally found out what had happened, they bought my cake shop in Cornwall to help me out. I lost it a bit after my adoptive parents died, and couldn't run the café on my own. I wanted to get rid of any memories of happy times, so I put it on the market. Then my real grandmother called my birth parents and told them that she'd always known where I was and that I lived just down the road from her. She asked them to come and save me and the business.'

Jessie was lost for words for a moment. Then he said, 'Bloody hell! That must have been life-changing for them. Two shocks at once. Bravo to them for dropping everything to be with you. But what was your grandmother thinking?'

'She's evil,' said Fern vehemently. 'It's why my birth mum moved away in the first place. My grandmother – Lucinda – kept my parents apart when I was born. They would have kept me if she hadn't interfered.' She put her hand to her mouth. She had shared far too much. The beer on a mostly empty stomach had made her mind a bit foggy. 'Sorry. I probably shouldn't have said that.'

'So she's why you moved away? But what about your parents and the café?' he jumped up and asked her to wait while he brought more beers, but then came out with a bottle of red wine and two glasses. 'I think we need something a bit stronger.' He handed her a glass and sat back down, resting his hand on her shoulder as he did so and making her feel confused at his sudden kindness.

'I feel awful,' she admitted. 'It was all too much, losing Mum and Dad and then Milly and James arriving like the cavalry.'

'Milly and James! Blimey, of course. I hadn't put two and two together. I hadn't thought about them as they moved away a while ago. I heard it was all rather sudden.'

'To rescue their lost child,' she said sadly. 'Now the ungrateful child has run away to be near her sister and they are left with the evil grandmother.'

'What a nightmare! But surely they're happy with the business though? Genie mentioned they'd bought a successful café on a different coast. Your café?'

'That's right. They're brilliant with the customers, but they can't stand Lucinda. It's hard for them to reconcile what she's done to us all. If I hadn't been there, they would never have moved. Now they're stuck there, at least for a little while longer,' she said gloomily.

'Will they sell up now you're not there?

'That's the plan. They are thinking about how it could work and already have a few ideas in motion. I think James would love to come back, Milly too, actually. They miss Genie like crazy and it must have ripped their hearts in two to have to leave one child for another. It was all a bit suffocating for me, though, as I was trying to come to terms with what happened to my adoptive parents. I had to get away. I feel like I can breathe here.' She pictured her asthma inhalers and realised that she hadn't needed them nearly as much since she'd moved here. 'When this shop came up, the timing couldn't have been better.'

'What about a boyfriend or partner,' asked Jessie, casually. 'Did you leave them behind too?' Fern almost choked on her wine and he gently patted her back, running his hand up and down to soothe her, before dropping it back in his lap.

'Um. I was seeing a guy called Brad for a long time, but he wanted to keep it secret for various reasons and it became too much for me.'

Jessie frowned. 'Why would he want to keep a relationship with a beautiful woman a secret? Was he married?'

Fern gasped again and put her wine firmly down on the floor beside her.

'No.' She waited while she caught her breath and digested the fact that he'd called her beautiful. 'He was just a self-centred idiot. He's in the public eye and was more interested in his image.'

Jessie still looked confused, so she brushed over the subject. 'He had to be seen out with glamorous starlets. I wasn't up to par.'

Jessie almost snarled and stood up, starting to pace up and down. 'What an idiot! Well, his loss is someone else's gain.'

'I'm happy on my own. In fact I'm enjoying not having to worry about him at all. It's liberating! I've moved away, he doesn't know where I am and I have a new business that I'm building myself.'

Jessie rubbed his forehead and stood looking at her. 'Does that cake have magical powers that makes you share your innermost secrets with strangers?' he joked, and she flushed.

'Sorry. I think it might have been the beer, not the cake,' she said.

'Don't be sorry! I'm glad. I'm not usually a miserable git and I hated seeing you upset because of me. I've been trying to work out a way to say sorry.'

Fern smiled and felt some butterflies start to swirl around her stomach. 'It was my fault too. I should have been more understanding about all the changes I'm making. I am trying to improve things, and not destroy the history of the building.'

'I can see that,' he said generously, as the shop was currently a pretty big mess of dust and rubble.

As the evening wore on and the sun dipped below the horizon, Fern realised that it had been a relaxed and happy few hours. They had got on well, which had surprised her. Jessie had grudgingly admitted that her ideas for the cake shop were good and jokingly asked if she needed a cake tester to try out recipes on.

Stars started sparkling in the night sky and she hugged her knees up to her chest and bit her lip to stop herself crying. 'I miss my adoptive parents – Mum and Dad,' she said quietly, as a big fat tear dolloped onto her knee and she brushed it away. Jessie got up to fetch a blanket from her lounge and tucked it around her shoulders. He stared up at the night sky before hunching down in front of her and staring into her eyes. 'I bet they are looking down and smiling at what you've achieved,' he said, then took his seat next to her and poured her the last of the wine.

CHAPTER THIRTEEN

*T*he next morning she sat on the edge of her bath in the tiny bathroom, holding her head in her hands. Why on earth she'd spilled so much personal information, she had no idea. She'd basically told a complete stranger her life story. What an idiot! She shook her head to clear the picture of Jessie's suntanned face smiling at her, his eyes locked with hers. After her emotional show of tears, she'd hastily got up and said she needed her beauty sleep, then kicked herself for sounding so vain.

As the days passed, she gradually forgot about it and decided to hold her head up high and pretend their evening together had never happened. The tears she'd shed for her adoptive parents seemed to have had a cathartic effect – despite the fact she'd spent months crying into her pillow at home before that. Now some of the dark clouds of gloom seemed to be lifting. She let the warmth of the early summer sun invigorate her skin.

Since that night, Jessie had been kinder, though. He'd brought over a bottle of sparkling wine one evening and they'd shared chips on the terrace another night, so perhaps they could be civil after all. He had also told her a bit about his life, saying he was local to the area and that his parents lived further along the coast. He'd been obsessed with art and the sea from a young age and she'd been able to agree that the coast was in her heart too.

She wiped another layer of dust from the new doors she'd had made for the huge cabinets that ran along the back of the shop. They were too beautiful to overlook. The kiosk area inside was almost ready, with fresh glass on the chilled counter that led to outside and the front of the shop. There was space for glass cake stands, bowls of confectionary and cupcakes galore in that section. She intended to have a weekly theme and everything in that window would be frosted, iced, baked, sugared or set to perfection. The main café area now had a serving counter along the centre with a gap towards the kiosk end, so staff could access the kitchen and kiosk. The freshly cleaned awnings for the outside were arriving in the next day or so and would have 'Fern's' written on them in gorgeous scrolling letters, with a cupcake and a cocktail glass outline at the end. That would make the restaurant feel more official.

People had been popping in to say hello and they hadn't made her feel like an outsider at all, although to be fair she was a local – just one who had been born somewhere else. James had been born in a tiny house along the little coastal path she'd found the night before. She'd also stood outside the house Genie had grown up in, and had looked in awe at the double-fronted façade and the climbing roses that grew up and around the front door. Genie had told her the small building at the front of the house was an annexe and was where their granddad Gus had lived before he moved in with Ada.

Currently the big house was rented out to a couple with four dogs and she often saw them coming and going as she walked up to meet Genie in the evenings. It was great to stretch her legs after a long day amongst the builders and sometimes she treated herself to dinner in Genie's café. She tried not to let her legs take her there every night, or Genie would know she hadn't made any friends yet. A young woman had applied for a waitressing job the day before, and one of the builders had mentioned that his sister was looking for part time work around the school run, so hopefully she might meet a few other people that way.

Genie had introduced her to the other café owners along her strip of shops and to her group of friends, some of whom Fern had warmed too, others not so much. Genie's old school friends were a bit sharp for her taste. Then she tutted to herself, as who was she to say anything about anyone? Genie's friends had been nothing but nice to Fern. She just got the feeling they weren't that supportive of her sister's work ethic. Then she shrugged. Not everyone was as food or business-obsessed as her own family seemed to be. They probably worked hard and then spent their evenings at wild parties with their other flamboyant and interesting friends. She fleetingly pictured the photo she'd seen of Brad and a supermodel going into a film premiere a few days previously, his hand curled round her waist, her face turned to smile up at him, making Fern's stomach contract and her eyes sting. She sniffed and started stacking boxes in the cupboards that would need to be taken out again when the build was finished.

She spent the rest of the day sorting out the new stock of glasses, cups, plates, plus endless boxes of cutlery, but finally things seemed to be coming together. The phoenix was rising from the ashes and the café was starting to feel like a shop again, and not a building site. She looked up as a blonde woman with a short spiky pixie haircut and big green eyes wandered in, looking around. She caught sight of Fern and waved.

'Hi. I'm Allison. Genie told me to pop in to chat to you about your branding.'

Fern wished she'd remembered to change, as Allison was wearing a cute patterned blouse and knee length black denim skirt. She looked business-like but casual in a creative sort of way. Fern held out her hand as Allison approached and she indicated for them to sit at one of the café tables.

'Of course! Genie mentioned you might pop by if you found a space in your diary. Time got away with me,' Fern said.

'This place looks amazing!' said Allison and Fern instantly warmed to her frank style, plus she was gazing round in awe. Fern hadn't taken the time to actually appreciate how much work she'd done, as there was still a huge list of jobs to do.

Allison jumped up and asked for a tour of the place and Fern was only too happy to show off her new baby. Fern led Allison through to the kitchens and showed her the state-of-the-art ovens and pristine preparation areas and cold store, plus her cute little office, which still had the original floorboards. Then she opened up all the folding doors to the front and side of the shop to the beach and let the sea breeze flow through. Allison stood back, admiring everything. 'I love the natural wood, the leafy green plants you've got ready to dot around and the fact that there is glass everywhere. The setup is beautiful. The serving area to the shopping street hasn't changed, but the rest looks like you've waved your magic wand in here. It was a bit dreary before. I think Mr Aldous didn't have the energy to update. His cakes were amazing, though.'

'You know him?'

'Oh yes. His produce used to draw people from miles around, but lately it was getting quieter and quieter. Maybe that's why he sold to you? Another cake shop fits in perfectly. I work with most of the shops and artists in this street,' she said, waving her arm in the direction of Main Street, the cobbled path that ran along one side of the shop.

'Mr Aldous was a legend in his day. A bit of a heartbreaker too, so I'm told,' Allison laughed and twirled around. 'Sorry! I love seeing creativity come to life but I should be trying to impress you with my design skills. Genie mentioned you might need flyers, business cards, menus and loyalty cards to match your logo?'

'The logo you designed!' Fern laughed. 'I was thrilled when I saw what you made from my very basic sketches. Sorry I couldn't get to the last meeting.'

Allison laughed. 'Genie always has enough ideas to keep me busy for months, so it was nice to work on another project. Plus I pretty much copied your original sketch. It was very detailed.'

Fern grinned. Allison's energy was infectious, even though she was so tired. Every part of her body ached and her jaw was sore from smiling at passers by. People kept popping in to enquire about the new shop and she felt like she always had to have her game face on. It was great, now, to relax and laugh with someone her own age. Allison looked to be in her mid to late twenties, so they might have other things in common.

Allison spread some paperwork with new ideas on the table and Fern made them coffee, grabbed a cupcake each from the chiller as she'd forgotten to have lunch, and they pored over the designs for the next hour. Allison was suitably excited to taste the cupcake and loved the drink, too. She promised to bring her friends and family to the café.

'I've bought a food cart for outside,' said Fern, conversationally. 'You know, one of those old fashioned ones with big wheels and an awning, so I can have a cocktail bar and alcoholic cake stand at night.' She looked outside and could picture it standing proudly there – after it had been stripped, painted and she'd employed a sign writer to brand it, she sighed. 'It's arriving soon and I'm going to match it to the natural wood and blue/greys of the rest of the shop. I might add a pop of gold here and there too.'

'Sounds incredible!' said Allison. 'It'll be great for the local shops if they do a late night opening and the surfer dudes and gals will be able to get a drink after an afternoon of surfing. There's a shower on the beach, so they can shake the sand off first,' she joked. 'There are so many beautiful people going in and out of that shop,' she nodded her head towards Jessie's place. 'It's ridiculous. Lucky you for bagging this spot. Plus Jessie's pretty gorgeous too. Women hang around outside the surf shop, just to catch a glimpse of him.'

Fern's stomach began to hurt all of a sudden and she wasn't sure why.

'That will be good for business then,' she said brightly. 'Is Jessie your type?'

Allison laughed heartily at that. 'I think he's most people's type, but my new boyfriend might not like to hear that.' She flushed, then grinned. 'I only met him a month ago, but things are going well.'

'Oh. How exciting! How did you meet?'

'He's an artist,' said Allison, her voice becoming light and wistful. 'He's got a shop just up the road. I have a lot of graphics customers on Main Street, so I'm here quite often. We've been circling round each other for a while.'

Fern recalled a tall, shaven-haired man with a kind face and big biceps that were always covered in paint. She'd spoken to him a few times and admired his work, which was made with cement and acrylic washes.

'I think I know who you mean. Lucky girl!' said Fern,

genuinely happy for her. Not every man was as unreliable as Brad.

Allison put down the papers she'd been showing Fern and tilted her head to one side. 'How about you? Is Jessie your type?'

'Oh… um,' faltered Fern, who suddenly decided that a few crumbs from their cupcakes needed brushing from the table. 'I've just come out of a long-term relationship, so I'm off men at the moment.'

'Shame! You won't be short of offers, the way you look, and with your shop being next to a popular surf destination.'

Fern looked down at her black fitted jeans and soft grey marl T-shirt that skimmed her curves. She certainly wasn't anything like a cute surfer chick – more washed-out old hen. Her jeans flowed over her proportions and made it easy to do her job without worrying about flashing her backside to anyone while she stocked the shelves.

'I'm not sure surfer boys are going to be interested in a twenty-nine-year-old woman who usually has cake in her hair.'

They both laughed and Allison asked if Fern had thought about uniforms. So far they had compiled a list of necessities and it would be good to have something to make the staff stand out.

'I was thinking of black short-sleeved cotton T-shirts or blouses and then jeans, shorts, or trousers on the bottom half,' said Fern. 'The shirts could have the logo in light blue and gold on the right-hand side of the chest. I might even get matching blue aprons that tie at the waist. What do you think?'

Allison thought for a moment before speaking. 'It's a great idea. The black will stand out against the wood and soft blues and greys of the painted woodwork and glass. If you went for a blue or grey uniform, it might blend in too much.'

'OK. Can you do the designs for those too, then?' asked Fern.

'Of course,' smiled Allison as she drank the last of her coffee and prepared to leave. 'Are you having an opening night?'

'I guess so,' said Fern, chewing on her bottom lip. 'Genie kept trying to organise it, but at first I couldn't see who to invite! Now lots of people pop by and I agree it's a good way to let customers know who I am.'

'Genie said you had a café in Cornwall. What made you move here?' asked Allison.

Fern was still a bit raw from confiding in Jessie, but she yearned for a female friend. 'I broke up with my ex and I needed somewhere to lick my wounds,' she said honestly.

Allison leaned in and gave her a swift hug of solidarity. 'You'll love it here. You definitely made the right decision. And when your heart starts to heal, there is always a shop full of sexy surfer dudes next door to distract your mind and fill your days,' she sighed dreamily and then burst out laughing so that Fern couldn't help but follow suit. It felt good to be able to joke about the heartbreak she'd suffered. She thanked Allison and showed her out, with the promise of including her in the launch plans.

CHAPTER FOURTEEN

*F*ern pushed her hair out of her eyes and grinned when she noticed one of the builders glancing her way appreciatively. The shop was looking good, they were in the final stages of sorting out suppliers and the beautiful soft grey awning now hung in pride of place on the front of the café. Harry had popped by to admire it, and although she'd been gripped with worry the whole previous evening about how he would take the changes, he was clearly very pleased and kept patting her hand. She thought he had a tear in his eye at one point, but it had probably been dust.

Having the building team around had been flirty and fun, but they would be leaving that evening and she would have to begin to fend for herself. She offered Harry one of her cupcakes. He reverently placed the plate down on the table she'd guided him to, as if she'd just handed him a treasured gift. He breathed in the scent of the spiced fruit, took a taste from the side of the delicate cupcake with a little of the buttercream frosting and then looked at her with his eyes shining. 'You really are a sublime baker, Fern. This reminds me of walking into this shop all those years ago and asking for a job.'

'You didn't always own the place?' Fern assumed he'd been the owner forever and hadn't thought that he might have been an employee.

'Not at all. I worked here as a teenager and for many years after that. That was how I learnt how to run every inch of the place. The original owner, Mr Frost, must have seen something in me, because he took me under his wing and taught me everything he knew. He didn't have children of his own and could see I was eager to learn. He rented the shop from a local landlord and adored this place.'

'Do you have children?' asked Fern, and then gasped and put her hand over her mouth. 'I'm so sorry! That's none of my business.'

Mr Aldous laughed. It was a deep and throaty sound and it made her smile. 'Not at all, my dear. I was never that lucky. I dedicated myself to building the business and eventually it became mine. That was a very proud day. My customers all feel like my children.'

'I can imagine,' said Fern. 'That's how I feel. I used to run a café with my parents, but when they died, I needed to get away. This is a fresh start for me. I hope I do you proud.'

She felt her eyes mist over and she really did want to make him happy, for some reason. He was almost ingrained into the place and would be a hard act to follow, even though the eatery had become run down. It had just been too much for one person to run. She would need a small army of staff if the cafe became as popular as Genie's place was. Living onsite made the commute much easier though, she grinned suddenly, sniffing and turning away before Mr Aldous saw her soppiness.

'Have you met Jessie yet?' Mr Aldous asked.

'Um... yes,' said Fern, taking his empty plate and placing

it behind the counter, returning with two cups of tea. She sat down opposite him and glanced around to make sure the building team were finishing off in the kitchen. 'He's a character,' she said with false gaiety.

Mr Aldous looked at her carefully, his deep brown eyes not leaving hers. 'He's a good lad. I know he's upset about the shop and he's certainly told me how he feels,' he laughed suddenly and she couldn't help but join in, even though she wasn't quite sure what was so funny. 'I probably should have offered him the shop first, but I'm a spontaneous kind of person and when I decide something, I go with it,' his eyes were sparkling and he suddenly looked years younger. 'Jessie was away and I was feeling lonely and not sure how to make the shop work again, so I went to Genie's restaurant for dinner. I heard her saying how much she'd love to find the perfect café for her new sister and the solution came to me!' He leant back and his chair almost tipped. She was just about to spring up to catch him, but he was a nimble sort and settled back down again.

'So you know about my connection to Milly and James?' She blushed. *Did everyone know her family business?*

His cheeks flushed too and he grimaced. 'Sorry. I don't always think before I speak. It's a close community here and of course we look out for our own,' he sighed and gazed out of the new windows at the beautifully framed sea. 'Everyone was upset when Milly and James left as we didn't know why they had gone, but Genie has made a great success of the ice cream restaurant and they come back to visit her, so it's not all bad. Plus now there's you.'

Fern frowned. 'Me?'

'You've rejuvenated this area. I'm too old to run the place any more, but it's coming back to life and that's because of you. Your roots are in this area and we are all happy to have you back.'

Fern felt tears fill her eyes and she brushed them away with a napkin that was on the table.

'Thank you. I've been worried how the locals will take an outsider settling here, so that means a lot.'

Harry took her hand kindly and patted it again. 'You are certainly not an outsider,' he said forcefully and Fern's eyebrows shot up into her hairline. She quite liked this feisty side of Harry. 'Plus I overheard Genie say that Milly and James are coming back because of you,' he said with wink. 'So it's a double win for all of us. Opening a bed and breakfast in their old house? Well I never would have imagined that!'

Fern burst out laughing. 'Is nothing a secret around here?'

Harry grinned at her and got up, taking his cup and walking into the kitchen to wash it, as if he'd never been away. 'Nope,' he called behind him and she grinned as she got up and tucked the chairs neatly back under the table. He bid her goodbye.

Suddenly she was enjoying herself. Perhaps she could build a new life here. She looked up to see the blushing builder walk by and admired his strong arms and fitted T-shirt. Maybe her dormant libido might even wake up and she could go on a few dates. The men she'd seen so far in this area were beyond gorgeous. A surf shop next door did help, she admitted, smiling to herself as she dusted down the paintwork again. It was like window-shopping in reverse, where all of the delicious goods were outside of the glass and she was shut indoors. Maybe she'd keep those windows open and a few sexy men might wander her way. A girl could dream.

CHAPTER FIFTEEN

*J*essie glanced up when he heard movement outside. He tried not to think about how alert he was to every sound from the flat next door now. He saw Fern walk to the end of the terrace to take in the view and he couldn't help but appreciate what he was seeing, too. Her shapely curves enticed him and her sweet smile and fiery nature intrigued him. He could see a lot of similarities with Genie's personality, even though Fern seemed to think they were worlds apart. The fact that her stupid ex-boyfriend had hurt her so badly made him grind his teeth in annoyance, when it shouldn't have been any of his business. The guy was a douchebag if he thought he could treat a woman that way.

Jessie had been brought up to respect others and he expected the same in return. This Brad guy had obviously hoodwinked Fern, as the woman standing in front of him surely wouldn't put up with that kind of behaviour? She'd certainly told Jessie often enough in the past few months how annoying and opinionated he was. A smile tugged at his lips as he watched her tilt her head from side to side. He'd seen her do this many times now and he wondered what she was thinking about when she scanned the horizon. His stomach lurched suddenly when he thought that maybe she was wondering where Brad was. He squelched that thought quickly. They had come to an uneasy truce, but the time they'd spent together a few nights ago had changed everything. He had finally come out of the red mist he had been feeling and could see her ideas were sound. It made sense to keep the coffee shop to the same usage and it would bring in customers from miles around – all good business-wise for his surf shop.

He'd got used to Harry's quiet comings and goings and actually felt bad that he'd had a 'heated discussion' with the old man. Jessie still didn't agree with the way the shop had been sold from under him, but it was Harry's right to do what he liked with it. Seeing him pop in regularly to chat to Fern and spotting how much happier he looked these days, Jessie grudgingly admitted Harry had done the right thing.

Harry had explained that when Jessie was away, he'd panicked and suddenly decided the shop was too much for him. He didn't have the energy to change it and although he did wonder if Jessie might be thinking about expanding his shop, it was a conversation that Harry had avoided, as he wanted to see the shop continue as a café but in fresh hands. He didn't have children to pass it on to, but he liked the idea of coming in as a customer and enjoying his retirement. His thinking was that without the café, the little parade of shops and businesses might lose customers. He was probably right, however annoying that was to admit. Jessie still felt a bit uneasy about it, though, as if there was something Harry wasn't telling him.

Fern turned and saw him and he tried to think of a way not to be caught staring like a letch, but gave in and went to say hello. She was wearing cute little shorts in the colour of seaweed that sat snugly on her hips and thighs and a pretty blue T-shirt, the colour of the evening sea. She had delicate silver loops in her ears and barely any make up. She had sooty lashes like Genie and natural beauty. Her skin was golden from the sun and she looked like she'd risen up from the sea to claim her victim. A weird sort of pain flitted through his heart. He caught his breath at the sight of her and fumbled over his words as he spoke.

'You look like a siren in the evening light,' he said gently, making her flush. She brushed her golden hair out of her eyes and frowned as if to see if he was making fun of her. 'Sorry, I was just watching you admiring the view and when you turned round, you kind of fitted in with the landscape.'

She glanced down at her clothes and brushed some sand away from her knee. 'Ever the artist,' she joked. 'Is it because I'm covered in sand?' she laughed, clearly hiding her embarrassment. He could have kicked himself for thinking artistically, in terms of pictures. It was something he'd always done and why he did the job he did. Everything was colour and light to him.

'No, it's because you look beautiful,' he said simply, making her flush again and her eyes go wide in surprise. He wished he'd been nicer to her before so she didn't think he was playing her now. The evening sun shone on her skin and the confusion in her eyes made a punch of lust hit his chest. She really had no idea how gorgeous she was. She had soft curves and an easy smile and he found he didn't like the way so many of the workmen were still hanging around on their breaks and after work. And now his customers had started coming in and commenting about the beautiful new blonde next door! His mood hadn't improved with that. She wasn't his woman, but after what she'd confided about her past and Brad, he did feel some kind of loyalty to her. They were gradually feeling their way to becoming friends and he felt protective about her and didn't want lecherous males in her vicinity. Not that she'd thank him for it. He knew from his dealings with her that she was perfectly capable of telling them to get lost herself. He paused suddenly, realising that perhaps she would like the attention from one or two of those men – and just like that his bad mood was back.

'Uh... thank you. I think,' she smiled at him and her eyes crinkled at the corners. 'I never know if we're fighting or becoming friends,' she shrugged suddenly. 'It's not like you to pay me a compliment.'

Jessie grabbed two beers from the cooler he often left outside on the deck in the evenings and opened them, moving forward to hand one to her.

'We must stop meeting like this,' she joked, then became more sombre. 'I'd like us to become friends. It's exhausting fighting with people.'

Jessie sighed and sat down heavily in the deckchair outside his back door. Fern grabbed her own chair and put it next to his, sitting down with him. He pictured his ex, Khloe, and the row they'd had earlier that day. She'd screamed at him for not paying her enough attention, though they weren't even dating any more. She'd come into the shop with two male friends who had then annoyed her by asking him about buying new surf boards. She'd been furious with them too.

'More arguments with Khloe?' Fern asked casually, seemingly sensing his change in mood.

Jessie stared out to sea, the way Fern had earlier. It really did ease his mind and cool him down, although Fern's knee being so close to his own brought the temperature up a notch or two again. 'She's escalated the arguments now. She's started bringing guys into the shop to make me jealous. Today she got angry when they wanted to buy some stock.'

Fern almost spat out her beer and laughed. He liked the

sound. Having her around was actually pretty nice. Plus she baked and the scent from her flat each day was incredible. He'd managed to bat his eyelashes at her a few times and filch a cupcake or two. Fern brushed her legs with her hands and he couldn't help follow the movement before coughing and carrying on. His eyes seemed to follow her around of their own volition.

'She was the one who caused the break-up. She was seeing someone else. Now she seems to think it's her life's purpose to get me back or cause me no end of hassle. Having your café next door will probably mean she spends half her life in there waiting for me.' He looked at the floor dejectedly and she patted his shoulder in sympathy.

'Great for me though,' she joked, grinning suddenly, her eyes sparkling with mischief. 'Extra customers, and the guys she drags in might be cute. It will brighten up my day.' She was on a roll now and he could see she thought she was really funny. He poked her gently in the ribs and she yelped and scooched her chair back, laughing.

'My pain is your gain?' he asked incredulously, wishing she hadn't moved further away.

'Yep!' she smiled again. 'Look, why don't we go over my plans for the shop properly before opening day? You can tell me if anything might bother you and, although I will most probably ignore you, I might consider your ideas.'

She jumped up and came back with a roll of paper and a plate with two frosted cupcakes. He'd be the size of a boat at this rate, but he couldn't seem to resist Fern or her cakes. He knew she wasn't interested in him. Her ex, Brad, had put paid to that, but she seemed to be warming to him and he enjoyed her company.

He hadn't realised how much he'd come to rely on the odd evening chat with Harry over a beer. He was too tired after work to socialise much, but a beer and the incredible view they had often restored his energy. He missed the old guy.

Now he got up to help Fern unroll the floor plans and they spent the next hour talking about her ideas and then ordering a pizza because they were both too tired to cook. Sitting watching the sun set over the horizon, with good company and food, meant Jessie didn't feel so bad about prolonging the evening and drawing out further details about Fern's life and family. She'd had a rocky ride, but perhaps when she got used to the area and the people, she might to decide to put down roots here. She was fun to have as a neighbour and now he'd got used to the chaos next door and seen the final plans, he was happier than he'd been in a while. Maybe both he and Fern could find someone to love again?

Fern had confided that she missed her adoptive parents and told him a bit more about her past. He'd grudgingly admitted that her ideas for the café were good, and apologised for taking his annoyance at Harry's antics out on her. When she'd finally said goodnight, he'd sat for a while longer, staring out at the moonlit sky and feeling that his new neighbour was going to change things for all of them somehow.

CHAPTER SIXTEEN

*F*ern heard whistling from next door and realised Jessie must be in his flat too. She'd popped up to make lunch now that the shop was almost ready and was taking a breather from the hard work.

Weirdly, they had gotten into a routine and she had even made Jessie sandwiches too for a few days, before she'd realised how domestic that was and stopped. It had started after he'd snaffled a sandwich she'd left out on the deck and she'd had to tell him off about it. He'd hung his head and apologised, but hadn't looked that sorry. She knew he'd been working flat out on a commission board, so he probably hadn't had time to eat. It was still stealing, though! The next day, he'd left a little dusky pink rose pot plant where the sandwich had been. He still joked about how much she must love plant pots after the tripping up in boxer shorts incident, the night they'd argued. Somehow it had broken the ice and they were now rubbing along together as people who shared some of their living space.

He stuck his head through her open double patio doors and called out to her. 'You making sandwiches?'

'You do realise you'll have to pay for these once the shop opens,' she laughed, grabbing the bread and slicing into it to make another cheese and spiced chutney doorstop. He picked up the chutney jar and sniffed it, sighing happily.

'I will. Did you make this? It smells incredible.' She grinned in thanks and brushed some dust off his nose.

'Bringing your work home again?' she joked.

He rubbed his nose with the back of his hand, his eyes sparkling. 'No different to you,' he inclined his head towards the chutney and gently wiped a dash of it from her cheek with the pad of his thumb. She gasped and tried to move back but she was wedged between the kitchen counter and him. Her eyes went wide and for a second she thought he might kiss her, but then the moment was gone and he'd moved away to look at the racks of cupcakes she'd just pulled out of the oven. He sniffed the air appreciatively. 'This place always smells heavenly. If you leave a window open when you're cooking, then my stomach starts grumbling in protest.'

She looked at his fitted T-shirt stretched across taut abs and then had to turn away to start filing his sandwich. Her mouth was suddenly salivating – and not just for the food. She hadn't had a relationship for a while, and just being near a man seemed to set her off these days. Although it hadn't happened with any of the builders, or the admittedly gorgeous surfer guys who were always hanging round outside Jessie's shop. One or two had said hello and eyed her appreciatively, but she'd begun getting more and more voice messages and texts from Brad and she was feeling confused.

Brad's texts were sweet and cajoling and she did miss being in his arms. He had been a useless boyfriend, but was still a sizzling date. She'd never been bored in his company and she missed having fun. Not that they had ever gone to the cinema or out to eat together. They had stayed in and watched movies or spent the evenings with their limbs entwined and their bodies slick with sweat. Brad didn't disappoint in that department, but that was all the relationship had been and in the end she had felt used. The thought of an actual date with another man both terrified and thrilled her. Maybe she'd try it sometime. Genie's boyfriend Cal was bound to know some interesting men, and maybe Jessie had some single friends? She looked at him and grinned and he seemed immediately suspicious.

'What are you after?' he asked. 'You have that look on your face, like the one when you asked me to climb up onto the roof to check the skylight as you don't like heights, or to empty the bins because you're cooking and can't touch them.'

'I do ask you to do nice things, too. Plus I feed you constantly,' she protested, laughing. 'I hate taking out the bins.'

He laughed too and quirked his eyebrow, waiting to hear what she wanted.

'You know I told you that Brad never took me on dates?'

'Um… yes. What of it?'

'Well I was thinking that I ought to get back out on the dating scene. Brad's texting me a lot and trying to find me, so maybe if I went out now and again I'd feel stronger about looking at the messages.'

Jessie frowned and his gaze pierced her. 'Does he hassle you?'

Fern held out her hand to touch his arm to stop that train of thought. 'No. He just wants to meet me. I'm not ready for that, but a few local guys have asked for my number and I thought a friend of a friend might be a better place to start.' Jessie didn't look too sure, but he did tilt his head and look at her, as if assessing if she was mentally stable or not. 'I promise I won't eat with my hands or swear at them,' she joked feebly, a bit uncomfortable now. She'd though he'd love the idea. She knew he didn't like Brad.

'You swear at me,' he said, deadpan.

'Only because you steal my food and keep moving my plant pots so I fall over them.'

'That's payback,' he smiled suddenly, a light going on in his eyes. He narrowed them and then seemed brighter. 'I think I have just the man. He's sporty, independent and local.'

Fern's stomach swirled suddenly. Maybe this wasn't such a good idea!

CHAPTER SEVENTEEN

*F*ern loved seeing her shop come back to life. She spent most of her days baking and organising deliveries. She had employed a young woman who'd popped in with her CV. She was starting work the next week. Genie was pushing ahead with the launch day plans and Fern found she didn't have time to feel lonely, or to pine for Brad. In fact she barely thought of him until another message dropped in. They were less sweet nothings now, and more insistent that she respond. He'd been back to the old café a few times and she could tell that Milly was quite enjoying making him suffer. She'd giggled when they'd spoken the previous evening and Milly had told Fern she'd sent Brad off to get some supplies for her, since he kept popping in and said he wanted to 'help' Fern.

Brad had probably been fuming, but he'd done it, much to Fern's surprise. James had told her off for being hard on the guy, but Milly wouldn't give an inch. He had hurt her daughter, therefore he was a charlatan, Milly's own words. Fern smiled and a warm sensation unfurled in her stomach. Her adoptive mum had always looked out for her, and Fern missed her dreadfully. Milly's mothering was different, more direct, but still fiercely protective and loyal. Brad didn't stand a chance. Fern could learn a thing or two from these woman and keep Brad away. He'd offered to take her to dinner in his last text, but if he found out how far away she was, he'd probably give up. No way was he travelling halfway down the country for a date with his ex. Maybe she should tell him and he'd leave her alone, but she kept putting that off. She wasn't sure why. She hoped she didn't want him back, but was too busy to analyse her feelings for the man she'd loved for three years.

She watched a young couple stroll past the side window and look into the display shelf, before linking hands again and wandering towards the artisan shops. It was great to see potential customers go by. It would be a matter of days before her racks would be packed full with sweet confections and she hoped every single person passing would stop. She'd devised a low sugar cake batter for any customers who might be diabetic, and had vegan specials, too. Her café menu was simple and effective, with firm favourites, like carrot cake and Victoria sponge, but also daily specials like raspberry delight and chocolate heaven. Then the evening menu would be alcoholic cake pops and cocktails. She had also thought about occasionally hiring a local band or a singer. She wanted to support other local creatives, but was mindful of her neighbours. Luckily most of the surrounding area was beach or shops, so it should work out fine.

She locked up the shop and popped her nose around Jessie's door. She hadn't actually stepped inside yet as he was always busy, but today the shop was clear. He looked up from a board he was working on in the back room and smiled when he saw her, beckoning her inside.

She walked over to him, nerves suddenly hitting her body as she stared at his latest board design in awe. It was stunning, with waves splashing around the edges and a shark looming menacingly at one side. Another board propped up against the wall had an underwater scene with a giant octopus swimming towards the surface and a tiny unsuspecting boat.

'They're works of art!' she gasped. 'How can you sell these? They belong in a gallery,' she said, running her hand along the smooth surface of the sleek wood and enjoying the warm feel. He stood watching her and she flushed under his gaze. 'Don't they get damaged when people use them?' she mumbled, forgetting that she'd come in to ask if he wanted to join her for dinner.

'No,' he smiled, linking his arm casually around her shoulders and making her skin fire up at his touch. 'They're built to last.'

She turned to face him and his arm slipped to her waist. 'How did you get into it?' She tried not to move too much as she liked the feel of his arm around her.

'I've always been drawn to the sea,' he said. 'I loved painting as a child and started dabbling in designs, putting them on boards as I got older, then I started to build my own custom boards for fun. Customers flocked and it seemed mad not to combine the things I love.'

'Makes sense,' she mused, breaking contact and walking around the shop, picking up one or two gift items and then poking through the racks of beautifully designed surfwear that Jessie also stocked. The worn natural wood walls and handmade metal racks blended seamlessly with the theme. It was a surfer's paradise and she could see why he was so popular. Not just because he had a reputation as the local dreamboat either. This shop was seriously sexy. She turned as the little bell above the door jangled and someone came in. It was a beautiful girl with piercing blue eyes and long blonde hair slicked back into a sleek ponytail. She was wearing a cute little sundress that skimmed her slim body and she was smiling brightly until she caught sight of Fern, then her smile slipped away and a scowl replaced it. She looked Fern up and down. Fern felt herself standing taller and straightening her shoulders, tension zipping up her spine. What the hell was her problem?

Fern raised her eyebrows in question to Jessie but he just shrugged and avoided her gaze, which put her immediately on edge. Fern quickly made her excuses to leave as a couple of other customers came in. She sidestepped the angry woman and gave her a friendly smile anyway. She didn't want to upset potential customers, however threatened they were by the presence of another female. So much for girl power, she scoffed as she left the shop. Outside, she felt the sun hit her face and warm her skin after the cool interior of Jessie's place. The fresh scent of the salty sea spray that was always in the air and the sound of the waves lapping against the shore lifted her mood. Plus, she had a blind date to look forward to.

She was happy she and Jessie had become friends, but wasn't quite sure how she felt now that Jessie was back with his girlfriend Khloe – assuming that was who the woman was. But who else would behave like that?

Fern decided that maybe she was a bit territorial over Jessie's friendship now, as if he came with the building! She laughed at herself and decided she needed a day off and to get out more. Her friends could have other friends. She just wished she had that option. Maybe the date with Jessie's delicious friend would open up new doors for her. If he was hot, that was. Knowing Jessie he'd set her up with someone Mr Aldous's age, for a laugh. He was still arranging the plant pots like an assault course, and often stole her cupcakes. She now had five little rose plants by way of apology, but he still thought it was hilarious! She'd have to start getting her own back somehow. Her eyes narrowed as she thought of evil ways to make him suffer for her own entertainment, like he had. They'd end up with a whole deck full of little roses in planters if they kept this up.

She heard the shop bell chime and the woman she'd just seen in Jessie's shop strode out, before turning and calling back that she'd see him that evening. Fern puffed out her cheeks.

She unlocked her café and sighed with bliss at the scent of sugar and coffee, a perfect combination as far as she was concerned. She walked over to the back window to look out at the beach view and mentally ticked off the list of jobs she needed to do before launch day. Most were in hand, but she would have to start baking enough stock to fill the shelves soon and that would bring the shop to life. She'd already offered free sample platters of tasty bites of cake to passers-by and they had been well received. The two most popular flavours had been her salted caramel cupcakes with tiny chunks of fudge in the batter and her light as air, lemon meringue cupcakes, with a lemon curd filling and a toasted meringue frosting.

She heard the ping of a text arriving. She had given in one night and spoken to Brad on the phone, but the old gnawing pain in her chest had come back and she'd realised again he wasn't good for her. He hadn't taken the news well, but had left her alone until now. She glanced at her phone, which she'd left on one of the tables, and rolled her eyes when she saw it was from Jessie. He was reminding her about the date he'd set up for the following day. She was finally having a day off work, but suddenly her pulse was racing and she was sure she'd rather stay within the familiarity of her café. She couldn't get hurt there. After Brad, she wasn't sure if she was ready to date someone new.

She gazed at the children running along the shoreline and

watched the smiles on their faces and the sunlight dancing across the water and a grin began to pull at her own lips. The new Fern wasn't scared of a few dates with new guys. She'd moved halfway across the country to begin afresh, without any friends nearby other than Genie, Ada and Cal. They were all such busy people, but they made time for her, so she could take a day off and enjoy good company and a new vista.

She straightened one of the chairs and ran her hand over the cool wood surface of one of her round tables. She pictured them set with sparkling glasses and vintage teapots and teacups. She'd already organised stacks of beautiful pale blue napkins and blue plates in a soft hue that was almost iridescent. They had tiny waves splashing around the edges and looked as though they had just been dipped into the sea. When she sat a napkin and a cupcake on top of them, they looked delicious and so pretty. She wondered if she should have a range of cakes with sugar or biscuit sand on them, and perhaps even some starfish decorations to adorn them. She hurried to grab a pen before the idea faded, just as Mr Aldous stepped through the door. He looked around in approval at the recent changes.

'Hi Harry,' said Fern, quickly jotting down her ideas in a notebook. Genie had a thousand scraps of paper with ideas written on in her restaurant, but the sight set Fern's teeth on edge and made her want to reach for her asthma inhaler or start tidying them up. She straightened her notebook and put it away tidily, turning to welcome her visitor.

'I was passing and thought I'd stop by to say hello,' said Harry.

'It's lovely to see you,' said Fern. 'But I was wondering if you'd like to come back later and join me for dinner?'

CHAPTER EIGHTEEN

Fern stirred the water so that the spaghetti would cook evenly and checked the Bolognese she'd prepared was simmering. She'd tried to mask the disappointment that had overcome her when she'd overheard Jessie and his girlfriend talking about their date. He'd told Fern it was over ages ago, but perhaps he'd been missing Khloe. Fern winced. Then the doorbell chimed and she glanced around to make sure everything was tidy and rushed to answer the door.

Harry held out a bunch of wildflowers to her and she took them and inhaled the scent of the daisies and pretty blue cornflowers. They were tied with a satin ribbon. She drew him inside and went to find a vase. No one ever bought her flowers these days, but she had kept one of her mum's favourite vases and she carefully filled it with water in the sink. She arranged the blooms to her satisfaction and tuned to smile at him. 'Thank you for these, Harry,' she smiled at him.

'Thank you for inviting me to dinner,' he bowed theatrically. 'It's not often that a beautiful young woman invites me to her abode these days,' he joked, lightening the atmosphere, as Fern was mightily nervous for some reason. He was wearing a white cotton shirt that was rolled up to the elbows and a pair of dark green linen trousers. He looked quite dashing and she was glad she'd decided to ask him to dinner instead of Jessie. Her shoulders relaxed and she felt some of the day's tension float away. She really should stop worrying about Jessie and his relationship status and concentrate on her own. For now, she'd settle for a good meal with a friendly face.

'I've set up a little table outside. Jessie and I eat there sometimes,' she ignored the sudden glint in his eyes and lifted the lid of the saucepan to release some steam. 'Why don't you wander around and see if you approve of the changes I've made, while I serve the dinner up. You OK with pasta Bolognese?'

Harry smacked his lips in pleasure. 'My favourite! It gets boring cooking for yourself, so I don't always bother.'

'You must eat properly,' Fern scolded gently, then put her hand over her mouth and laughed. 'Sorry! I can be a bit bossy and tend to try and organise everyone's lives into straight lines. I'm trying to be a bit more laid back.'

Harry laughed and glanced around the little flat. 'I don't mind a lovely young person fussing over me. Jessie used to do it all the time.'

Fern brought the two plates of steaming pasta to the table and Harry followed. She'd already placed a big ice bucket by her chair with wine and soft drinks inside and a water jug and glasses were on the table. They sat down and took a moment to enjoy the stunning view of the sea and horizon as the sun began to dip and the sky turned a hazy blue grey. A few people were enjoying the early evening warmth and were strolling on the beach in front of the café. One small dog was sitting on its backside and refusing to walk any further, so its owner had to turn round and pick it up. Fern could see from the dog's happy face that this was not the first time this had happened.

'Do you miss living here?' she asked.

Harry took a deep breath and sighed. 'I do and I don't. It was a big responsibility and my passion had gone. You might not understand that, with such drive for your café.'

Fern ate a forkful of the Bolognaise, enjoying the tangy sauce hitting her taste buds, and thought about what he'd said. He made appreciative noises as he began to eat and they grinned at each other. 'It's as if we haven't eaten all day,' she laughed.

'Well, have you?' he asked, cocking his head to one side.

'Not yet,' she conceded. 'I was making batches of cakes to fill the shop for the launch and forgot.'

'I know how distracting baking can be,' he nodded in understanding. 'You must eat though,' he scolded, mirroring her earlier accusation and they both giggled like school-children. 'This meal is delicious. Thank you for inviting me. You must have had a thousand more interesting people to have asked.'

Fern felt her skin grow warm. If only! 'I wanted to invite you,' she said honestly. He really intrigued her and had a wealth of knowledge about the locals and what they liked. Plus he was a local baking legend. 'You're fascinating and I love hearing about when you ran the shop. It sounds like it was the centre of the community.'

Harry finished the last mouthful of his Bolognese and patted his stomach appreciatively. 'It was a popular venue. It will be again. People used to drive for miles for one of my cakes and now they will do that for you.'

'I hope so,' said Fern, pouring them both a glass of rich red wine. It glistened in the evening light and they clinked glasses, toasting each other.

'To you and your successful new café,' said Harry.

'And to you for creating the cake shop and customer base in the first place,' she said in return, making his cheeks flush this time.

'I know what you mean about burning out,' confided Fern suddenly. 'I adored my other cake shop, but after my parents died, the heart and soul of the place seemed to have disappeared with them.'

'What about when Milly and James arrived?' he asked. Fern still flinched at the fact that everyone locally knew her private business. Thank goodness she'd never mentioned Brad. He'd be over the gossip tannoy within seconds.

She sipped her wine, enjoying the zing of berries and grape on her tongue and mulling over the mixed-up thoughts in her mind. 'They're amazing,' she said truthfully. 'They swooped in like guardian angels, even though they had to leave the most important part of their own lives behind. It cost them a lot emotionally, as you probably already know,' she sighed, seeing sympathy in his eyes. 'Now I've deserted them.'

'I'm sure they're happy that you are happy,' soothed Harry, taking her hand and patting it gently before taking a sip of his own wine.

'But they could have stayed here and thrived,' said Fern, her lips wobbling suddenly. She'd not really discussed this in depth with anyone other than Genie. She'd touched on it with Jessie, but they were still finding their way.

Harry looked at her and shook his head. 'They weren't thriving, Fern... they were surviving. They were in a rut and needed change. Genie tried to tell them, but they wouldn't listen,' he said. 'I overheard her offer them new ideas time and time again. They were a bit like me, hanging on to this shop, and memories, for too long. The place needed new life and customers, a fresh mind and ideas. They were stagnating here. It may have hurt them temporarily, but it helped them in the end.' He looked at her gravely and she could tell that what he spoke was the truth.

'But they had to move away from their family.'

'Don't they also have family in Cornwall?' he asked. 'Plus you were there and needed them. Most parents would move heaven and earth for their child.'

Tears filled Fern's eyes and she quickly brushed them away. 'I feel like I've let them down.'

Harry got up and gave her a hug, then picked up the plates and took them into the kitchen to wash them up. 'Ever the restaurateur,' he joked, as she got up and followed him. He turned her to face him and placed his hands on her shoulders so she couldn't look away. 'Meeting you is the best thing that has happened to them, alongside having Genie. It may have shaken the family up, but it's been a blessing. They'll be back here in a flash, don't you worry. They still have that house on the hill, so they always intended to come back one day. Now you can all be together, so you've actually done them a favour.'

Fern burst out laughing and then sniffed and wiped her tears away. Harry spotted the cake stand full of cupcakes and he turned back with puppy dog eyes. 'Yes,' she laughed, 'that's dessert. I'm hoping your discerning taste buds can help me decide on some upcoming weekly specials.'

She picked up a cake with shimmering gold frosting. 'This one has a secret caramel centre and chopped nuts inside.' She pointed to a second one with buttercup yellow icing and white chocolate sprinkles. 'This one is lemon and white chocolate, but with a hit of Limoncello.'

Harry grabbed that one and bit into it, sighing in bliss, making Fern grin suddenly. She had four other flavours she wanted him to try, but she hadn't even had time to mention those yet. 'Let's take them to the table and we can try them all. Maybe a sample though, and not every cake,' she said as Harry popped the last mouthful between his lips.

'That was incredible!' he said as he followed her out. Fern flushed at the compliment. She was used to people liking her cakes, but from Harry it felt extra special.

'Do you want coffee or more wine?' she asked.

'Let's stick to the wine for now and maybe we might need coffee later, if all of these are alcoholic,' he joked, sniffing the air and appreciating the scent of the sponges.

'I'm going to open one or two evenings a week to serve alcoholic cake pops and cocktails,' said Fern. 'That's what the new cart is for.' Fern pictured her newly painted and branded drinks and cupcake cart and her heart swelled with pride. It had been a lot of work and hours of sanding and polishing, but the end result was worth it. Jessie had even leant her some of his power tools and helped her get it ready for painting. She'd had to make him more sandwiches as payback, as he'd refused her first offer of financial reimbursement for his time. The cart now stood proudly outside the beach area of her shop and had a brand-new zip-up cover and locking system for overnight. Not that she'd leave alcohol out there, but it meant they could store plates and glasses on both the internal and external shelves.

'Great idea. Although I wondered why you needed that, with enough floor space already. You've made much better use of the outside space, and the new windows make the inside roomier too.'

'It makes it easier for people sitting on the beach to wander over and order at the cart, without filling up the café, or becoming intrusive to people sitting at the tables and enjoying the sea view.'

'Smart girl,' said Harry. Fern felt a warm fuzzy feeling unfurl inside her and realised how much she'd missed having her adoptive mum and dad to talk things over with. She bit back more tears and smiled at Harry.

They both watched a woman stroll past with a dog the size of a small horse and then turned back to each other in amazement.

After a moment, Fern piped up. 'You didn't answer earlier when I asked about missing Jessie,' she said.

Harry avoided eye contact for a minute and then nibbled on a mocha cupcake with expresso frosting, before declaring it the winner. 'If I'm being honest, I was worried about becoming too reliant on Jessie. I heard him arguing with his girlfriend,' said Harry, before sighing. 'She screamed at him that he spent all of his time with the pensioner next door,' he said. 'She had a point. We did spend a lot of time together and I almost felt like he was my grandson. But it wasn't my place to keep him from the people he loved.'

Fern winced. She really liked how close Jessie and Harry were, but then she'd come in and ruined it all. Plus, love? Jessie had never mentioned being in love with the blonde bombshell.

Harry was looking longingly at one of the light and airy Margarita cupcakes with lime zest on the frosting, left on the plate. 'Try it!' laughed Fern. He bit into it and sighed happily. *For a slight man, he could certainly pack away some food*, she grinned to herself.

Harry dabbed the cake crumbs from his mouth with a napkin. 'I felt I needed to give Jessie his life back. I was clearly crowding him.' He gazed at the now inky blue sky and they watched a shooting star whiz across their vision and then disappear. 'I also wanted to keep the cake shop alive to bring customers to all the businesses on the street, the way it did in my heyday. My cafe was the only coffee shop along here. If I closed my premises and the place became part of Jessie's surf shop or something else, it might drive customers further up the coast,' he paused and looked around them. 'The other shops here are too small to be food businesses, except the pub – and Charley who owns it only likes cooking fry-ups. The shops are perfect for artisans and other creative businesses,' he said, glancing at the roof of the pub that you could just see over the top of the tiny shops, from their elevated vantage point. 'Was Charley upset about your cocktail cart?' he asked Fern.

Fern grinned at the memory of that conversation. 'No. He was relieved! He said he keeps getting asked for 'poncey cocktails' and hates serving them. He's a craft beer kind of guy. He said that those types of drinks don't fit with his ethos of a good bottle of wine or a pint. I don't serve either of those, so he's happy.'

Harry heaved a sigh of relief and she grinned at his clear friendship with the other business owners along the street. 'I was worried how he'd take it,' he admitted. 'I didn't serve alcohol for that reason. Plus I always enjoyed a beer in the pub after a busy day on my feet,' he grinned suddenly, his eyes sparkling with mischief.

'I can see what you were trying to do by selling the shop to another café business,' said Fern.

'I stomped around for a bit after hearing that argument between Jessie and his girlfriend, and I felt old and useless for a while,' he admitted. 'I even sulked.'

When Fern burst out laughing at his candour, he laughed too. 'In the end I decided I wanted to rejuvenate this little corner of paradise, like Genie had done further along the coast. So I put my coat on one evening and stalked up there to ask her advice. I'm not too proud to take it, even at my age,' he admitted.

'What did she say?' Fern was agog to hear the rest of this story. She glanced at the open windows to both her own and Jessie's bedroom and heaved a sigh of relief that he was out with the apparent love of his life, so wouldn't be able to listen in on her conversation with Harry. At the same time, she made a mental note to tell him off for leaving the window open while he was out.

Harry leaned in conspiratorially, but then spoke at the same volume, so she had to jump back in her seat and rub her ear. 'I didn't get a chance to ask her. She was talking to a customer and said she was looking for a shop for her sister who was an award-winning baker. I couldn't believe my luck. I sat there all night plotting my move. All of my ideas came together, but I wasn't sure how to implement them. When Jessie got the call to see his famous client in the States, I took my chance and spoke to Genie about the shop, knowing she'd want to act quickly to persuade you to come here.'

Fern sat back in shock. Harry looked bashful for a moment, but then held his head up with pride. 'Sorry if it was calculated. I knew Jessie probably would have liked to expand his business and take over my premises, but it would have killed a lot of the custom on Main Street – and he'd never have had a love life. He'd have had to work all the hours, like I did,' he said sadly. 'I couldn't tell him that, though.' This time it was Fern who took Harry's hand and patted it.

'I think we need that coffee. Maybe with a shot of Amaretto,' she said, getting up and taking the cake stand with her before Harry ate another cake and was sick. What a night of revelations.

~

*J*essie paused as he heard Fern move back into the flat and drew in a sharp breath. He'd only been home for thirty minutes and hadn't meant to eavesdrop, but he'd had an awful evening with Khloe. He'd tried to calm her down and reason with her, but she'd yelled at him for not wanting to be in a relationship for a full two hours and he was emotionally wrung out. He'd stepped inside the sanctuary of his flat without turning the lights on, and then heard Fern and Harry outside. It lifted his spirits and he'd been wondering whether he should join them, when he'd heard their conversation. It was like another punch to the guts. Khloe had not only caused him aggro for months of his life, but she'd also managed to ruin the perfect set-up he'd had with Harry and make the poor man feel so guilty he'd had to pack up and leave to give Jessie and Khloe space. There wasn't enough room in the world to get a safe distance from that woman. She was a menace.

When he calmed down, he supposed he did actually agree that the area needed a coffee shop, but it still stung. Hearing Harry talk about being eternally single and working every hour had made him stop short too. Jessie had assumed the guy loved his work and wasn't interested in a family. Women turned up asking after him often enough. The man sure wasn't celibate. Maybe he'd felt he could never pursue his love life, due to the demands of his job? Jessie had to concede it might be good for Harry to be free of the shop, but he popped back often enough. Perhaps he was regretting his choices? Who the hell knew?

It was all a bit of a mess, but he didn't have time to dwell on what Harry and Fern had spoken about. His friend Wes had called him just before he got home and backed out of tomorrow's date with Fern. Jessie knew she'd booked a rare day off and cursed himself for getting involved. He grabbed a beer from the fridge and slumped into bed without bothering to turn the lights on. He could hear Fern and Harry happily chatting still, but they'd obviously gone back into the flat. He needed his beauty sleep to come up with a way to let Fern down gently the next day. He knew how important getting back into the dating scene was for her, so he cursed and drank some more beer, before sloping into the shower and turning it on full blast.

CHAPTER NINETEEN

*J*essie picked up his car keys and took one last look around the flat. He'd already seen Fern go onto the deck and then back inside again. She was wearing a cute short sundress with little flowers dotted all over it and her newly tanned legs had made his mouth water.

His palms started to sweat and he brushed his thick hair out of his eyes. He'd shaved his morning stubble and ironed a smartish dark blue T-shirt and put on a crisp pair of jeans. His usual workwear of shorts and a surfing T-shirt wouldn't suffice today.

Fern was going to be mad when he told her the date was cancelled, so he'd needed to man up and find a solution. The one he'd come up with might not appeal to her, but he'd got staff in for the day and intended to make the most of every minute away from the shop. He'd got his swim shorts and a couple of towels in his bag and had told her to pack a bikini. She'd not looked too happy at that, but originally his mate Wes had been planning to take her to a beach along the coast that was lined with palm trees and had white sandy shores.

Jessie wasn't big on organising dates, he was more of a spontaneous guy, but Wes was a science professor and a busy man, and he meticulously planned every minute of his day.

They'd been friends since junior school, so Jessie had known there must be a valid reason for Wes to back out – apparently his ex-wife had finally decided to let him spend the day with her again. Jessie now understood very clearly that Wes wasn't over her and all their chats about his new single life had been masking pain. His heartbreak was the original reason why Jessie had thought of him as a good match for Fern. They could have begun to heal each other, or at least had some fun along the way. Now that Wes was out of the picture, Jessie didn't have time to analyse why he had such a spring in his step or why he'd caught himself whistling a tune he'd heard on the radio earlier that morning.

He opened the doors out onto the deck and then turned and locked the door behind him, giving himself a moment to formulate a battle plan. He wished he wasn't about to squash the bright hopeful smile on Fern's beautiful sun-kissed face. A few of her freckles were showing in the sunlight. Her lips were slicked with a glossy soft pink lipstick and her hair was pinned back at the sides with two pretty silver slides that left the rest of her hair trailing across her back. She looked edible and far too eager for this date.

Hi Jessie,' she said brightly as he approached. 'Shouldn't you be at work? Where's Wes?' Jessie leaned in to hug her, buying a moment to put off the inevitable, but then her perfume hit his senses and he was struck mute while his body fought not to respond to the floral, oh so sexy scent. Wes would have been a goner within seconds. He stood back and admired her outfit.

'I've got a rare day off. You look great, by the way.'

Fern's skin flushed and she began twiddling with her hair. 'Um… thanks.'

She slung her beach bag over her shoulder and looked around, presumably for her elusive date. She stopped and noted his jeans and T-shirt and tilted her head to one side, taking in his appearance. It made him sweat a little and want to fidget.

'You look good too. Where are you going on your day off? I've never known you to have one before. You're a workaholic,' she joked.

'Spoken like one who knows,' he quipped back, grinning at her and wishing he could just grab her hand and lead her off for a day of debauchery. He could easily imagine lying in a little sand-covered bay all day with Fern in a tiny bikini. He coughed and squared his shoulders. 'Wes can't make it.'

Fern's face fell and his insides pulled tighter in discomfort. He knew how important this date was and he hated to see her hurt. 'I'm really sorry. His ex-wife decided last night that she suddenly wanted a reconciliation with him. I didn't know that was what he was hoping for, or I'd never have set this up. They've been separated for almost a year.'

Fern blushed and she hastily started to move away from him towards the deck stairs to the beach. 'Uh... no problem. I'll just go for a walk along the beach and then get back to the café.'

Jessie caught hold of her arm gently and stopped her. 'Hey, wait a minute. Did you not just comment on my freshly-washed jeans and ironed T-shirt?' Fern stopped and looked him up and down in confusion. 'I never take a day off, as you so rightly stated, so I thought we could go along the coast and have a relaxing day together?'

Fern frowned and didn't look too sure. 'But then we'll both waste a day off.'

'Thanks!' he laughed.

'Oh!' Fern covered her mouth with her hand and her eyes watered. She took a steadying breath. 'I didn't mean it like that. It's just that, won't your girlfriend have a problem with you spending the day with me?'

'Girlfriend?' It was Jessie's turn to frown.

'Khloe? The woman who was scowling at me in your shop? Blonde, beautiful, and a bit scary if I'm being honest,' she looked at him from under her eyelashes and he sighed and took her hand.

'She's my ex, as I told you.'

'But... last night...'

'Last night was two hours of her telling me how useless I am, after asking me why I'm not chasing after her. Khloe enjoys dramatics. She's only interested in me because I'm not interested.'

Fern slowly ran her eyes over his earnest face and he felt his skin grow warm. 'When we were dating, she was playing the field. I'm a one woman man and I expect the same from my partner.'

Fern nodded and then bit her lip and seemed to be thinking about his offer. He'd never had to try this hard for a friendship date before. Even though he did fancy the friend, he finally admitted to himself. 'I don't want to waste your day off,' said Fern, backing away.

'I heard what Harry said to you last night,' he said in desperation, running his hands through his hair and mussing it all up. She stopped moving and her mouth dropped open in shock. 'I wasn't eavesdropping... I got in from seeing Khloe and heard Harry mention my name while I was lying in bed in the dark.'

'Oh no,' said Fern. 'I'm so sorry! I was going to tell you off for leaving the window open while you were out,' she cursed under her breath. 'We weren't talking about you really, but rather why Harry sold up in a hurry.'

'It's OK. It's better that I found out that way than assuming I'd done something wrong. At least this way I understand his motives. Khloe's caused so much damage!' He looked at Fern's concerned face and took her hand again. 'Look. We both need a day off and I know a great little secluded beach along the coast. Wes booked a table for lunch and we may as well take advantage of it.'

'Supposing he goes there with his wife?' asked Fern, giggling suddenly.

Jessie grinned and tucked her under his arm. 'She hates seafood,' he said, 'and sand.'

Fern laughed and snuggled into his arm as they both headed towards the back steps where his car was parked behind the shop.

Jessie held the door of his little black sports car open and she paused and raised an eyebrow at him. 'I know, I know. You expected a campervan with a board on top, or a truck of some sort.'

When Fern laughed he felt his breath hitch in his chest. Her laugh made him feel a bit lightheaded. 'I do own a van for transporting my custom boards, but when I lost out with the shop, I went and bought myself a sports car in pique.'

Fern gawped. 'You didn't?'

Jessie threw back his head and laughed at her clear discomfort. 'Of course not! I was so annoyed when Wes cancelled that I told him he had to let me have his precious car for the day. Monique can drive over to his place. He was so apologetic, he'd have agreed to anything. I'm already insured as we often travel together on weekends, or we have over the past year,' he paused for a moment. 'I guess that might all end now Monique is back on the scene.'

Fern made herself comfortable in the plush leather interior of the car. The roof was down and she looked damn sexy as a few loose tendrils of her hair caressed her face.

'I'm sure he'll still make time for you. He obviously trusts you if he's insured you on his beautiful car,' she laughed.

Jessie shrugged and got into the driver's seat. 'He has to keep me sweet. I know too much about him,' he joked, making her laugh again.

'I'm guessing that works both ways,' teased Fern.

He grinned and revved the engine theatrically, before sweeping into the traffic on the main road and heading for the little beach along the coast before the usual throng of holiday makers got there. Luckily the restaurant Wes had chosen had its own private stretch of sand, the posh bastard. Jessie was intent on using every minute of this time alone with Fern. His feelings for her were confusing, but growing every day. He now had the suspicion that, if she'd gone out with his devilishly handsome, kind and generous mate, he might have spent the day pacing his shop and growling at his customers.

'I hope you like secluded restaurants and private beaches.' He knew he'd said the wrong thing immediately, by the sudden flush on Fern's face and he winced. He put his hand on her leg and she didn't flinch.

'I'm not trying to hide you away. I'm not Brad. Wes chose this spot because it's gorgeous and he was trying to impress you. There will be lots of people there and I can't wait to introduce you to Dennis who runs the place. He's one of my customers and you can probably hear his voice from the next cove, even though his restaurant is supposed to be the epitome of zen,' he said lightly, hoping to make her smile.

Fern tried to hide her face and looked out of the window, but she rested her hand on top of his for a moment before he put it back on the wheel. Then she turned and smiled at him shyly and his guts wrenched. What was it about needing to make this woman happy? He'd only known her for a short while but it seemed a daily smile from Fern powered his day. He gripped the steering wheel a bit harder and cursed himself for being such a sap.

'You don't need to explain yourself,' she said quietly. 'I'm OK. I'm just used to my boyfriend hiding our relationship... I know you're not my boyfriend,' she joked feebly and flushed again. 'I spoke to Brad,'

It was Jessie's turn to be surprised. 'I thought you didn't want anything to do with him?' Suddenly the blood in his veins seemed to be boiling. What the hell was she thinking of?

She brushed her hair away from her face and sat straighter in the seat. 'I told him I'm not interested, that he treated me appallingly and to be honest I wished I'd never set eyes on him.' She took a deep breath as if to calm herself. 'He wasted three years of my life.' She grinned suddenly and all of the air whooshed out of his lungs, when he hadn't realised he'd been holding his breath. How would he have felt if she'd said Brad was back on the scene? Luckily it seemed that Brad was no longer an issue that Jessie had to worry about.

He felt a smile play around his lips as he swung the car into the car park in front of the restaurant and turned the engine off. They both jumped out and he enjoyed the look of awe of her face as she took in the all-white restaurant. It sat in a secluded cove and was built from whitewashed timber and sleek metal. Both materials contrasted but worked in tune with each other. The metal was lit by the late morning sun, and the timber seemed to breathe in the sea air and welcome them into a special paradise. The palm trees swayed in the gentle breeze and he could almost imagine them being somewhere tropical – except for the fact that they were in Essex and, although the scenery was beautiful, the sun hid from them for much of the year. For now it was warm, though, so Jessie wasn't complaining.

'I thought our corner of the coast was divine, but this is something else!'

She held her hand out to him and he took it as if that was

the most natural thing in the world, before leading her inside.

He watched her take in the beautiful deck, with tables set up for lunch. The glass balustrading gave a clear view over the beach and the rhythmic back and forth of the waves lapping at the sand. The inside of the restaurant had intimate round tables, set with crisp white linen and sparkling crystal glasses. A few people were already being served their appetisers, which looked delicious and made Jessie's stomach growl after his missed breakfast. The staff were smartly dressed in white with muted grey aprons tied at their waists and were milling around checking on their customers. The restaurant oozed serenity. Jessie knew he could do with that, after the previous evening arguing with Khloe.

Today he wanted to spend some downtime with his new friend Fern – who incidentally was still holding his hand. She let go as Dennis spotted them and came over to slap Jessie on the back and then give him a warm hug, loudly telling him off for not visiting sooner, which a made a few of his patrons turn their way and smile.

Dennis personally showed them to their table with a flourish and a bow and Jessie hoped Fern didn't notice the big theatrical wink and thumbs up that Dennis gave him as he left to get their drinks. That man had the subtlety of a rhinoceros, which was pretty mind blowing, considering he'd built such a zen-like business.

After enjoying a sumptuous lunch of locally caught fish delicately flavoured with butter and herbs, complemented by a crisp salad and new potatoes, Fern rubbed her full stomach and Jessie laughed. It was good to see her body relax and a natural smile unfurl, rather than the watchful eyes and tense demeanour that she usually presented him with. He now realised that it was her coping mechanism after all the stress she'd been under, but he was determined that she'd enjoy their day. It was as if she expected people to hurt her. Jessie wished he had the opportunity to give her ex and her grandmother a piece of his mind.

After they both attempted to pay the bill, Fern acquiesced and insisted that she would pay next time. Jessie puffed out his chest at his dastardly plan. Now she'd said they should go out again. He was more than happy to pay the bill for his dates, but he understood that the person with him might like that opportunity too. Fern was an independent woman and he wasn't about to push the issue. If she wanted another lunch date, who was he to complain?

He tucked his wallet into his back pocket and reached for her hand. They wandered out and found a shady spot on the beach, where Jessie laid out two huge beach towels and they stripped off their clothes to reveal swimwear underneath. Fern was looking at everyone but him, so while he had the opportunity he drank in the sight of her long limbs and graceful style. Her dark blue bikini was dotted with tiny white stars and tied at each side of her hips, making his heart almost stop. It would take one pull from his fingers to make it all fall apart. His fingers twitched and he made fists with his hands as she turned and bashfully caught his eye. He busied himself with settling on his towel and giving her space to find a level of comfort in his company when they were both half-naked. He laid down in the sun after applying a coat of sunscreen and put his arms behind his head, feigning sleep, but really letting her eyes roam his own body freely in the hope that it might spark a mutual flame of attraction.

When he opened one eye a few moments later, she was turned on her side to face him with her head propped on one arm, her eyes watching him. He opened his eyes fully and grinned at her blatant inspection. 'Are you enjoying your day off?' he asked, his voice weirdly deep and raspy all of a sudden.

Her eyes sparkled with mischief and he felt his heartbeat ramp up a notch. 'It could be better,' she laughed, running her eyes over his body and then gazing around the cove at the glorious beach. She winked at him whilst reaching for his hand and pulling him up. Then she ran into the sea, as he stood for a moment watching her. Then his muscles whipped into action and he threw his sunglasses onto his towel before chasing after her into the cool surf, picking her up and spinning her around until she had her arms hooked together behind his slick shoulders and she was hanging on for dear life. Her chest was pressed firmly into his and their eyes met in mirth. He slowed down and they burst out laughing. She hooked her leg behind his as he was about to put her down and she sent them both collapsing into the sea. As they surfaced and brushed the water out of their eyes, Jessie's whole being wanted to pull her into his arms and kiss her for the first time.

CHAPTER TWENTY

*F*ern stretched and then winced. Her back was slightly burnt from the previous day on the beach with Jessie. He'd spent ages rubbing suntan oil into her shoulders, but must have missed a patch of skin. She carefully moved to throw on a light T-shirt and shorts and closed her tired eyes. The butterflies were back in her stomach and she was a bit confused about where she stood with Jessie. They had laughed so much yesterday and she'd felt a spark ignite between them, but at the end of the evening he hadn't tried to kiss her. She wasn't sure if she was glad or annoyed. There had also been a moment on the beach when she'd thought he might, but then someone had appeared that he knew and they'd called him over to say hi.

Her phone rang and when she answered it was Milly, sounding wound up and a bit fraught. 'How are you?' she asked Fern. 'We've missed you. You must be exhausted, but I'm glad to hear the new cupcake café is ready to open.'

'You sound worn out, too,' said Fern, frowning. Milly was usually energetic and noisy on the phone and in person. Fern often had to rub her ears after a long conversation, but today the feeling was sombre. Milly was nosey, too, but Fern mostly let her get away with that, as they had a lot of catching up to do with each other's lives. 'You OK?' she asked.

'Your grandmother is driving me mad with her demands,' sighed Milly. 'She keeps coming into the shop and trying to take over, even though she's never run a café in her life. She knows you've left and seems to think her baking is just as good if not better,' Milly snorted and Fern grinned too. 'So… we are moving,' said Milly firmly. 'As soon as humanly possible!'

Fern gasped. She'd known this was coming, but had thought it might take a while to find new owners for her little café in Cornwall. It had only sold so quickly before because Milly and James had snapped it up for a very fair price.

'Sorry,' said Milly, real contrition in her voice. 'I'm annoyed with my mother that I didn't think about your feelings about the business that you built from nothing. We're so proud of all you've achieved and it's a wrench to leave your beautiful café and customers… well, all except one. It must have been a million times harder for you. When we left our café on your coast, it was failing and we were too tired to listen to new ideas. The hard part was leaving Genie,' she said honestly. They'd not really spoken about that in detail before and Fern winced.

'Um… It's OK,' said Fern, realising for the first time that the thought of her old home didn't hurt. 'Really,' she reassured Milly. 'I can see why you love the coast round here in Essex and you have the rest of your family here. I know Genie misses you and understands why you did what you had to do – and I get it too,' she said truthfully. The feeling of oppression had gone and she was able to see how much Milly and James had given up to help her. She was more able to stand back and see what they'd done from afar. She had enjoyed Milly's infectious energy and James' quiet strength and had got used to having them around and leaning on them.

'We will be pretty much selling everything with the café and coming back with a couple of suitcases,' said Milly tentatively. 'The new owner is a young woman and she's excited to run the café as it is. She's actually a regular customer.'

'Oh?'

'Yes. She used to come in and try out all of your new recipes and it inspired her to enrol on some cookery courses. Now she's ready to start her own business and couldn't believe her luck when the café came up for sale. She's going to run it with her best friend, who has already owned a food business. They came here yesterday and offered us a deal for everything. Do you need anything from this shop for the new café?'

Fern pictured her shiny chef's kitchen with its sparkling metal surfaces, then the much loved little shop she'd left behind. 'No,' she said finally, after mentally itemising what she'd kept and the equipment left behind so that the café could run without her. 'I brought my mixer and the baking utensils my parents bought me, when I moved. Anything else can go.' She grimaced when she realised she'd said her parents – but that was what they'd always be. She hadn't quite worked out where Milly and James fitted into her life just yet. 'Sorry,' she said with a sigh.

Milly's voice took on an over-bright tone. 'It's OK. They were your parents. They brought you up and we will always be eternally grateful for them and the love they gave you. You don't ever have to apologise to anyone for calling them what they were, your parents,' said Milly with finality in her tone. Fern let out the breath she didn't know she'd been holding and smiled. Milly was fierce.

'We want a fresh start, too. Even if it is back where we began,' joked Milly. 'James is determined to put me off the idea of opening another restaurant, but he's already talking about running a portable hot dog stand,' she laughed, as if this was the most absurd thing she'd ever heard. 'He hates walking half a mile, let alone along ten kilometres of beach.'

Fern enjoyed hearing Milly sounding so happy suddenly, as Genie had expressed concern about her parents' marriage and the stress they had been under before they hot-footed it to Cornwall.

Fern had grown to love them over the past year. Milly and James were a lively pair. Bill and Irene had been quieter, thoughtful in every choice they made around her, possibly because they were scared of losing her. She sniffed and her eyes stung with tears. She blinked them away. Lucinda had a lot to answer for, but Fern was very thankful for her adoptive parents, so at least her grandmother had chosen right. And her new family were still surprising her. She chewed her lip, while Milly chatted happily now about how James couldn't pack up fast enough to be near to his girls and his dad again.

Her new family could be slightly overwhelming at times. Fern screwed up her face as her sunburnt skin brushed against her T-shirt and she pulled it away and wriggled to make that section looser. Her sister Genie was a whirlwind and slightly intimidating in her success. Meanwhile Milly had kept hugging Fern and stroking her hair when they'd run the Cornwall café together. Milly said it reminded her of their first hugs as a baby before she'd had to let her go, which broke Fern's heart, but she still found it unsettling. James was more reserved, but he seemed to enjoy the effervescence of the women in his life and went along for the ride. Fern fidgeted in her seat and wondered if she'd ever match up.

Her granddad, Gus, seemed happy with Ada. They had

popped in to the flat and café a few times. Ada had insisted on grabbing an apron and helping to clean, while Gus had wandered around finding broken things to collect and fix later. Fern could picture Genie rolling her eyes at this as he already had a shed full of junk in the small garden behind the ice cream shop. She did love the insulated baskets he'd designed to keep Genie's coffee deliveries warm on their way to the beach and fleetingly thought again about a delivery service for cupcakes and cocktails, but shook her head to clear that image. The café was enough for now, though she would store the idea to chat to Gus about later. Currently, she just wanted to get the shop open and find some customers.

'How about coming for the grand opening of the café? Do you think you'll make it back in time for a visit?' she asked Milly, breaking into a stream of chat about a customer who had insisted on ordering a cup of milky tea in a bone china cup and saucer – for her dog. Fern loved dogs and allowed well-behaved pooches inside her cafés, but she had never had a request like that before.

Milly paused for a second and then squealed with delight. Fern winced and held the phone away from her ear. When she gingerly listened again, Milly was calling to James. 'I'm putting you on speaker phone,' she announced, 'so James can hear.' Fern waited patiently until James joined them and said his hellos. 'Now we're in the process of selling the shop,' continued Milly, leaving dramatic pauses every few minutes, 'we need to be here to sort everything out for a few months... but the new owners want a trial run and we agreed they can take over for four days while we visit you and Genie!'

Fern smiled and could picture Milly, eyes sparkling, and James standing with his arm around her.

'Can you tell Milly's excited to come home?' asked James,

laughing. Fern loved the sound of his calm voice. His obvious happiness at this news eased away the day's tension.

'I'm so glad you're coming!' she said, a wide smile stretching across her face. 'I've missed you both,' she said suddenly, shocking herself as much as them, as they all fell silent.

'We've missed you too,' said James. 'It's time we were back home and all together. We'll see you at the launch – and we're bringing a surprise.'

Fern flinched and almost dropped her phone. 'It's not Brad or Lucinda is it?'

Then they all burst out laughing and Fern felt the last of the worry about them selling the shop dissipate.

'I promise you, it's not that,' said James. 'Did Milly tell you we are thinking of opening a bed and breakfast in our old house?'

'The town grapevine told me,' teased Fern. 'Genie and I both think that's a marvellous idea. You certainly have the hospitality experience and can send your customers to at least two local eateries,' she laughed.

'Brad has been seen in town, having coffee with Lucinda,' said Milly quietly, as if hoping that throwing facts like that into a conversation made them easier to take. Fern rolled her eyes heavenward. Lucinda? What the hell!

'Why on earth would he do that?' she asked out loud.

'To make you notice him,' said James simply.

'Well, that tells me that he never really knew me, or listened to what I said. I told him I was devastated by Lucinda's deceit.'

'Let's not worry about the past now,' soothed Milly. 'We're building a future and we can't wait to see you at the grand opening of your new café. We can leave all of our troubles behind,' she said. 'My mother and your ex.'

Fern said her goodbyes, put down the phone and paced

the room. Why was Brad interfering in her life, and with Lucinda of all people? He'd been texting Fern and demanding to know where she was, then the messages became pleas for a meeting. She had almost given in a couple of times, but they had been her only weaknesses. It had been an incredibly lonely time for her recently and she was only human. She pictured his seductive glances and knowing smile, but she was far away now. Brad was not likely to travel to be with her. She could see clearly that she'd been a mere convenience to him... a local place to get fed and have sex. She cringed at her own stupidity. She picked up a small crumbly slice of gingerbread cake that she'd made the day before and stuffed the whole thing into her mouth, almost going cross eyed in bliss and at the hit of spice and sugar. Who needed men when you had cake?

CHAPTER TWENTY-ONE

*T*he day of the grand opening was filled with glorious sunshine. Rays of light bounced off the waves and the beach looked picture perfect. Fern had spent the last few days tossing and turning in her sleep and having nightmares about no one turning up. Now she was rushing around her kitchen, watching her two new staff members polish cutlery, set out menu cards and straighten tablecloths. She stopped for a minute to take in the scene before her, the scent of sugar and spice filled the air.

The café was full to bursting with delicate cakes and chocolates. She'd made hundreds of alcoholic cake pop samples for the cart outside and had two additional bar staff ready to serve drinks from the beautiful display of bottles that were organised inside and along the top two glistening glass shelves. Her branding stood out from the awning and on every menu card. Her graphic designer, Allison, had pulled out all the stops with tiny branded flags for the cupcakes and beautiful signage along each of the back counters. It was breathtaking. She'd woven ivy garlands with pale blue and gold ribbons and wrapped them around all the doorframes. It felt as if you were stepping into another world where your senses were heightened and your mouth started salivating immediately. There were leafy plants dotted everywhere and the sight was fresh and inspiring. Garlands were strung across doorframes and from the balustrade posts outside, and fairly lights were entwined around some of the ivy to bring an ambience when the sun dipped behind the horizon.

Genie was speaking quietly to Ada and her grandad, Gus, who were on door duty to welcome all of their guests. If the growing crowds outside were anything to go by, the evening would be a resounding success. Fern's heart was racing and she hoped she didn't look like a sweaty madwoman. She'd brushed her long blond hair to within an inch of its life and it hung like a glossy curtain. Genie had approved of the pale blue aprons they all wore, with 'Fern's' scrolled in gold lettering across the front with a little cupcake. All the waiting staff were dressed in short-sleeved black shirts and tailored trousers, with name badges on their lapels. The cakes were glistening like gems on crystal cake stands, and the staff knew to tempt customers with exciting new flavours to try.

Fern had been thinking of making the grand opening pretty low key, but once word had got out, it had taken on a life of its own. Her stomach was churning and her hands were sweating, so she quickly washed and dried them and then took a deep breath, smiling a bit manically to her sister and nodding that it was OK to open the doors. She had stood firm on speeches and ribbon cutting, as the horde of people in front of her were almost enough to scare her back into her old safe life. She felt a hand slip into hers and another cup her waist and pull her in close and she sighed at the contact from Jessie. She looked up into his eyes and grinned. 'How did you get in before them?' she tilted her head towards the line of guests that was 'oohing' and 'ahhing' at the décor and selection of coffees and cakes.

'I bribed your grandad Gus, by promising to be a bodyguard if there was any trouble,' he joked. She immediately bristled and he kissed her cheek. 'I told him you and Genie had enough spark to get rid of anyone you wanted to and he laughed, agreed, and let me in anyway,' he grinned, dropping a quick kiss on her lips before gently nudging her away from the kitchen door and forward to greet her future customers.

She didn't have time to think about that searing kiss, before she felt a genuine smile unfurl and that energy of a full café seeped through her bones. She shook hands with people and enjoyed every minute of their questions about the renovations and how glad everyone seemed to be that she was finally open for business. A group of friends of Jessie's, who had already set up instruments outside, began strumming guitars and singing and the bar cart seemed to be popular already. She was offering cake samples, tall glasses of frothy coffee and delicately fragrant teas for free, but alcoholic drinks would be charged in full to cover some of her outlay. She could already see customers waving phones and credit cards around and enquiring about the pretty boxes of cupcakes and clear bags of intricately iced biscuits that she had set up.

She worked her way outside to the bar where both Genie and Cal were also taking money and serving drinks, while Milly and James led guests on a tour of the public areas. James looked like his chest might explode with pride, it was so puffed out. Genie caught Fern's eye and smiled and winked, before turning back to yet another eager customer.

Milly and James had arrived the night before with their surprise. A very excitable Viv had exploded into the room in the brightest pair of lime green leggings that Fern had ever seen, with a bright pink baseball cap perched on her thick bouncy grey curls. They had hugged and cried and Milly had explained that they'd asked Viv if she'd like to join them for their short visit and see Fern's new business for herself. Needless to say Viv had packed a small suitcase in record time and they'd all jumped in the car and driven down. Viv was already settled in one corner and regaling Fern's new customers with stories of her many awards and glorious baking. Fern's eyes misted over at the sight of old and new coming together to create something special.

As the evening progressed, different people drifted into the shop or on to the beach with their purchases and Fern felt pride fill her at the sight of a roomful of smiling customers. She'd barely had time to speak to anyone properly, but she'd had several enquiries for birthday cake or cupcake orders already and there was even talk of hiring the bar cart out for events. It wasn't something she'd thought of and she didn't know if it was logistically possible, but a traveling cocktail and cupcake cart could be great for parties or fairs, if she ever decided to buy another one.

Jessie had brushed passed her a few times during the evening and the hairs on the back of her neck had stood up as he'd caught her hand and given it a squeeze of congratulations. He'd had to pop back to his own shop as customers were asking about his board designs too. She felt a frisson of excitement that her little corner of paradise might help other locals, especially Jessie.

Fern was finally taking the chance to talk to Harry about one of her cupcake recipes when there was a bit of a commotion outside. There had been a couple of journalists and a photographer there earlier in the day taking photos for local newspapers, which was exciting and terrifying at the same time, but suddenly there seemed to be something big happening, with flashbulbs going off. Surely her little café wasn't important enough for a bigger newspaper to be interested? How would they have heard about it anyway? She frowned and pushed her way to the door, only to see Brad chatting happily to some of her customers after stepping out of a sleek black car. She recoiled and her brain tried to compute what she was seeing. How would photographers have known he was coming? She turned and saw that Jessie had left his shop to see what was happening too. Their eyes met, hers confused, his angry. She lifted her palms to show him she'd had no idea about this and he quickly stepped around a few people and came to her side.

'How did he know where you were?'

'My only guess is that Lucinda worked it out. Milly told me he'd been meeting her. She'd have made him meet her in public to show him off. I bet he hated that.' She felt bile rise in her throat and it begin to close in panic. She needed her asthma inhaler but it was in a drawer in her flat. She took a few deep breaths and tried to calm down. 'Lucinda likes to have the upper hand.'

'A bit like Brad,' said Jessie under his breath, but she heard him.

'You think he alerted the press?' Her head whipped round to face him. Her jaw dropped in stunned comprehension and her hand slid into Jessie's.

'I'm certain,' he said with ice in his tone. 'He's backing you into a corner.'

'He's stealing my thunder,' she said angrily, dropping his hand and straightening her shoulders just as Brad spotted her and gave her a megawatt grin. Women for miles were probably swooning from the heat of it, but her eyes glinted coldly as she moved forward to greet him, having no other choice without causing a scene. It was either look ridiculous in front of her new customers, or grin and bear it by welcoming him into her café. He was not about to ruin one more moment of her life.

She plastered a warm smile onto her face, blinking as more flashbulbs exploded in her face, and then Brad swept her up, taking her into his arms in front of everyone, and kissed her on the lips. She was so stunned that she didn't react for a moment, as a big cheer went up in the crowd, and then she pushed against his chest and made him release her.

'What the hell are you playing at?' she hissed in his ear.

'I've missed you,' he said loudly enough for anyone standing nearby to hear. He signalled to his driver, who reached into the back of the car and brought out the most beautiful flower arrangement she'd ever seen, with pale blue flowers and golden twigs and trailing ivy, to match her branding. She stood speechless for a few seconds, while Brad handed them to her and more photos were taken. She took them mutely and then turned to see Genie, Jessie and the rest of her family had gathered to one side to see what was happening.

Genie clearly understood Fern's anguished silent appeal for help and nudged Cal and Milly, who both rushed forward to draw them all inside as they profusely thanked guests and dodged questions about why a famous film star was suddenly in their midst and declaring his feelings for one of their own.

James put his large frame between Brad and Fern with enquiring eyes, and ushered them inside the café and into the back staffroom.

'You OK?' Genie asked Fern, as she eyed Brad with a tight smile and then signalled for everyone else to leave the room.

Fern rubbed her tired eyes and took a fortifying breath. This was supposed to be the best day of her life, and she'd be damned if Brad was going to ruin it, whatever his motive, as she was pretty sure he'd have one. She threw her keys at Genie, who caught them in one hand.

'Can you take Brad up to my flat and leave him there for a while?'

Brad started to speak but she put out a hand to stop him. 'I've got a shop full of customers and now I'm going to have to answer a thousand questions about you, Brad. Thank you for that.'

'I thought me turning up today would help your business,' he said smoothly, clearly not ruffled by the reception she was giving him.

'Her business is doing just fine without you, Brad,' said Genie helpfully, in a monotone voice. Fern knew from experience that fire would be bubbling just below the surface. Fern's lashes swept over her eyes and she had to smother a laugh. No one messed with Genie or her family and came out unscathed. She'd had to fight for her heritage and build it up from the ground, so a man like Brad would mean nothing to her, other than an irritation. Genie didn't suffer fools gladly and Fern felt that some of that girl power had rubbed off on her lately.

'Go and wait in my flat, Brad. You being here today of all days is less than helpful and now you'll have to wait until everyone's gone home until we can talk.'

Brad grinned easily and put his arm along the back of the sofa he was lounging on. 'I've already sent my car home, so I'm all yours for the night.' Fern felt her blood warming up to boiling point and she gripped her hands into fists.

Genie gently placed a calming hand on her arm and their eyes met. 'I'll show Brad up to the flat and he can make himself comfortable until you're ready. It might be a long wait,' she said, turning to Brad and jangling the keys in her other hand. 'Come on. I'll show you out the back way.'

Brad got up and tried to touch Fern's waist as he passed, but she moved just out of reach. When the door closed behind him and she finally had the room to herself she let out the breath she'd been holding. She brushed a crumb off her apron, rushed into the kitchen to grab a fresh tray of strawberry and raspberry liqueur cupcakes, then pushed open the door to go back and face her guests.

Suddenly everyone wanted to speak to her and, although the grand opening had been a wonderful success, it had been a lot more relaxed before Brad arrived. Now it seemed that everyone knew he was around and loads more people had arrived. Milly and James were trying to serve customers and Ada and Gus were talking animatedly to Jessie. All three looked up as she arrived. Ada moved forward and handed the tray of cakes to a member of staff and she pulled Fern into a hug.

'Are you OK, Fern?'

Fern looked around the throng of expectant faces and decided that she was. She sank into the hug and then grinned at them all.

'I don't want him here,' she said quietly, 'but I can't get rid of him with these crowds around. We might as well make use of the situation and sell everything we've got!'

Ada's eyes sparkled. 'That's our girl!' she said happily as Gus looked on, the concern on his face easing.

'I don't need to hit him with my walking stick then?' he enquired conversationally.

Fern laughed, as Gus was a sprightly eighty-four and had never been in need of one.

'No, but thank you for the offer,' she said solemnly. She glanced at Jessie but couldn't quite meet his eye for a moment. When she did finally look up, he stared straight at her and she flushed. She could see the questions about Brad in his gaze. She was mortified at Brad's arrival, but she didn't feel secure enough in her fledgling friendship with Jessie to ask for his support. Though she guessed the fact he was still there said something.

Jessie reached a hand around her waist and pulled their hips into contact for a fleeting moment, then let go. His tanned face was pinched with frown lines and his eyes were darting around. 'You OK?' he asked quietly. When she nodded, he continued. 'Why did he show up today?'

Fern scoffed. 'He said it was to help with my launch.' They both looked around the now heaving throng of people. 'I guess he brought more custom.'

'You already had enough custom,' said Jessie. 'Now it's more of a free for all! Where is he?'

'He's in my flat, waiting for me.'

Jessie's eyes narrowed like lasers. 'Do you want me to tell him to leave?'

She put a hand on his arm. 'No. Thank you, but I can handle it. He wants to talk and I can't chuck him out. Those photographers are still here and after his big show of affection with the flowers, who the hell knows what will be splashed all over the front covers tomorrow. It certainly won't be about my shop. Brad's spent years manipulating the press to his advantage. That's the reason he's here.'

'He's here for you!' said Jessie incredulously. 'Why wouldn't he be? Maybe someone saw us on the beach and it got back to him.'

He ran his hands through his hair distractedly, as he always did, and it only made him look more gorgeous. How she had ever thought Brad was God's gift to women, she could never now work out.

'We're just friends, though,' Fern said carefully, feeling her skin start to warn up and her palms sweat.

'Are we?' asked Jessie, making her freeze in shock. A customer nudged into their conversation and asked about her cocktail cake pops, so with an apologetic smile to Jessie, she let herself be led away. She could see the tills ringing while the second batch of cakes had almost sold out, so she pushed any doubts aside and concentrated on this important night for her career. Genie had scraped her long dark hair into a high ponytail and was wiping her brow, while her eyes darted along the cake shelves, no doubt to check stock levels. Fern watched as Cal swiftly kissed her sister's neck before turning to answer a question from a customer. A warm fuzzy feeling spread into Fern's heart, despite the annoying Lothario making himself at home, upstairs in her flat. This was her family now and she was exactly where she belonged.

CHAPTER TWENTY-TWO

*F*ern paused for a moment to try and find some extra energy, but every part of her body ached. She just wanted to crawl beneath her crisp sheets and sleep for about a week. The evening had been a huge success and she'd managed to kind of explain Brad away as an old friend who'd turned up to surprise her. She'd fielded questions about him all night and she knew he'd be getting restless in her flat, but that was his own fault for turning up in the first place.

She glanced over at Jessie's window, sorely tempted to ask if she could sleep on his couch, but then she remembered his question about them being just friends and decided her life was quite complicated enough right now without throwing that into the mix.

She was surprised to see Brad was still awake, as it must be well past midnight. But he'd made himself at home with a glass of wine and the leftover pasta she'd put in the fridge in case she didn't get time to eat that night, which she hadn't. Her stomach growled at the thought of food, but then a flare of heat hit her as she stared at her ex. She hated the way her body betrayed her, but there was no getting away from Brad's magnetism. She took a steadying breath and summoned a kind smile, the type she always found for her customers, however tired she was. He jumped up when he saw her and he swept her into his arms and was kissing her before she had a chance to splutter a protest.

She responded for a split second, then pushed against his chest, making him release her. 'Brad! What the hell were you thinking? You can't just waltz in here after such a long time and expect everything to be the same.' She walked over to the kitchen counter and poured herself a huge glass of red wine, taking a sip gratefully.

'Why didn't you answer my calls or text messages?' he asked.

'Because we were over,' she said, exhaustion showing in her voice, so he led her to the couch to sit down. He ignored her last statement.

'I wanted to support you on your big night.'

'Why did you do that?' she really wanted to know. 'We haven't spoken in months. We aren't dating.'

He took hold of her hand and she was too tired to draw it back onto her lap. His knees were too close to hers and she could smell the familiar fruity scent of his aftershave. She gulped and tried to move further back into her seat.

'I've missed you,' he said simply.

'Why?'

'Because we spent three years together,' he said as if speaking to a small child, tension underlying his words as he drank the last of his wine and set the glass down. 'You mean a lot to me.'

'No I don't,' she scoffed, standing up and putting space between them. 'You wouldn't ever be seen with me in public in that three years. I was just a booty call.'

He got up and tried to reach out to her, but her icy gaze

made him halt. He wasn't used to a Fern that didn't simper in his presence and he frowned at her hostility. 'It was more than that. You know I cared for you. I just had to listen to my agent and my management company. I was told to be seen out with someone famous for my own profile. I always came home to you.' He shrugged and gave her one of his most seductive smiles.

Annoyingly, her body still felt the pull of attraction and she pushed it back down. Now was not the time to crave intimacy. Not that her sex life with Brad had ever been that intimate. It was always hot and rushed. She realised now that she'd enjoyed this as much as he had, but his hollow promises of a future had kept her coming back for more. The stress of keeping their relationship hidden and the underlying feeling that she was never good enough for him had chipped away at her self-esteem and left her pining after a shadow of a relationship, instead of looking for something fulfilling and healthy. She pictured Jessie's smiling face as he laughed at one of her lame jokes and his hand gently touching her leg when they'd lain side by side on the beach. She'd been on her own for a while now and finally the amazing people around her had shown her her worth. A man like Brad would never deserve her loyalty.

'Suddenly you turn up on my doorstep again, very publicly. Why? And don't give me that nonsense about helping me out. It was an absolute nightmare after you arrived. We had to call out all of Genie's staff, half of whom were in bed for the night, and ask them to help manage the crowd.'

She rubbed her aching back and sat down, stretching her legs out in front of her and wriggling her toes as she kicked off her shoes with a sigh. 'I couldn't talk to customers about my cakes because of the screaming 'Brad' fans. It must have pained you to stay inside with that adoration so close by.'

Fern stared up at him, then got to her feet with her last reserves of energy. She was raging now and didn't care who heard it. Jessie might be trying to get to sleep next door, but Brad needed to hear this. 'Why are you here?' she repeated, her shoulders sagging suddenly and her bones feeling like lead. She walked over to the kitchen and ran a glass under the cold water tap. She pressed the icy glass to her forehead for a moment before quenching her parched throat. She leant on the small breakfast bar and waited.

Brad moved to the other side of the bar and for once he didn't seem so sure of himself. The smile had drooped and she could almost see his brain whirring about what to say next to win her over. 'I really did miss you,' he said simply, holding out open palms to her and then placing them on the kitchen top when she didn't move. 'I kept going to the coffee shop, but there was no sign of you.' He ran his fingers through his thick dark hair and rubbed his perfectly shaved jaw, succeeding in making himself look even more mussed up and sexy. Fern gulped, her mouth suddenly dry again. She'd dreamt of this moment for so long, now she was confused. 'In the end I had to reach out to Lucinda. I didn't know what else to do.'

Fern scoffed. 'I bet she loved that!'

Brad just rolled his eyes and smiled, their eyes meeting. For the first time, she didn't turn away.

'I'm sorry for the way I treated you. It's true when they say you don't know what you have until it's gone,' he said, coming round and taking her in his arms. Her body sighed at the contact for a moment, then she gently pushed him away.

'I'm glad to hear that,' said Fern gently, 'but it's too little, too late. A year ago, I'd have fallen into your arms, but not now.'

He stood back and she could see admiration shining in

his eyes. She rolled hers now. Typical! He was enjoying the challenge. 'I mean it, Brad. It's over.'

He paused for a moment, as if gauging her mood, then sighed and went to stare out at the inky night sky. A few stars were dotted around with the lights from the shops along the seafront. She could hear the gentle lapping of the waves on the shore. 'You've found a beautiful place. I can see why you love it here.'

'It's my home. My dad was born here and although I'll always love the Cornish coastline, this place is in my heart too.'

He turned to face her. 'I'm not, though?'

'You had that opportunity, more than once.'

'I'm sorry. Can you give me a chance to prove myself to you?' His eyes searched hers as he waited for an answer.

'It's too late. I've moved on.'

'Can we at least be friends?' he appealed solemnly.

Fern smiled, and switched the kettle on to make them both a mug of hot chocolate, a ritual they had often followed after a night together. 'We can.'

'Can I stay the night?' he asked, suddenly solicitous again. Fern knew that question would be coming, for where the hell else was he going to go at this time in the morning? She glanced at the timer on her oven and stifled a yawn. It had been one of the biggest days in her life, for more than one reason, and sleeping in the same bed as Brad without snuggling up next to his warm body would be a huge challenge. She wasn't dead!

Fern grabbed some spare bedding from the cupboard by the front door and threw him a duvet and some pillows. One of the pillows nearly hit his head and he ducked.

'You can sleep on the couch. It's a sofa bed,' she said.

He grinned at her as he picked the bedding up from the floor and stood facing her with it in his arms. 'Don't try that look on me. It won't work,' she grinned back. She quickly finished making their hot drinks, placed one on the coffee table for him, gave him a quick kiss on the cheek and said goodnight as he began to undress. Closing her bedroom door behind her, she leaned back against it and took a fortifying breath. What a day!

CHAPTER TWENTY-THREE

When Fern woke up the next morning, she rubbed her eyes and rolled over, her body creaking in protest. She looked at the clock beside her bed and groaned. She needed to get up, shower and be in the shop in less than two hours. She could see the sun coming through her curtains and, although she'd prepped for her first full day of trade, last night's commotion had meant a horde of extra customers – they had pretty much sold out of stock. They'd had to start charging for cakes in the end, but no one had seemed to care! So now she needed to get all her ovens running, and soon.

Hearing someone singing beautifully from her kitchen, she remembered that Brad was still there. Swinging her legs out of bed she quickly rubbed her feet, sore from all the rushing around the night before. But she actually enjoyed the feeling of a hard day's work done successfully. Brad was just a hiccup. She'd endured worse.

She rushed into her tiny en-suite and showered, then walked into the kitchen as fresh as she could be on such a tight time schedule. She'd brushed her hair until it hung in glossy waves down her back and donned her work uniform of fitted back trousers and a short-sleeved shirt. She felt like a sexy Ninja about to kick arse, she grinned to herself. Brad smiled and handed her a fresh cup of coffee as she walked into the kitchen. The sliding doors to the deck were open and Brad was standing there in a pair of black boxer shorts and nothing else, his tanned chest taunting her. She gulped in some air and gave him a breezy smile. 'I've got to get to work. Are you OK letting yourself out?'

Brad smiled genially. 'I thought I might as well take a look at the coastline for a few days now I'm here. I don't often get time off.'

'You want to spend it here?' she asked him incredulously.

'I want to spend it near you,' he said simply.

Fern took a fortifying breath and glanced outside. The sun was getting higher and she needed to get baking. Those cupcakes wouldn't ice themselves.

'We can be friends, but that's all,' she warned. 'I told you last night. You can't stay here.'

Brad came and gave her a kiss on the cheek. He smelt divine, spicy and warm. 'I know what you said. I understand I behaved like a moron and I need to prove myself to you.'

'You really don't,' said Fern, frowning. 'I'm happy that we're friends again, but that's all we'll ever be.'

'Look,' said Brad, taking her hand, just as Jessie came to sit on the deck with his usual cup of morning coffee. He glanced their way, noting their linked hands and then turned away to sit and look out to sea. Brad dropped his voice. 'I'm going to stay in a hotel up the road for a few days. I'd love it if we could have dinner together one night and I'd love to meet the rest of your family while I'm here. I know we're just friends now, but I want to be proper friends, who are part of each other's lives. I'll be around if you ever need me. I care about you more than you'll ever know. We're part of each other's history.'

Fern stood still in shock for a moment, feeling her anger towards him wane a little, then gave him a quick hug and said goodbye. 'Look, I've got to get to the café. If you want to stay around that's up to you. Let yourself out when you're ready and we can talk later. You have my number,' she said and he laughed, throwing his head back and then taking a sip of his coffee, watching her over the rim of the mug.

'Have a great day,' he called after her, as she said a quick hello to Jessie and rushed to the café. 'I'll speak to you tonight,' said Brad, in a clear voice, staring directly at Jessie, his smile dropping as he turned away to shower and change.

~

*J*essie tried to calm his racing heartbeat at the sight of a half-naked man and Fern holding hands. He flushed as he remembered her fingers interlaced with his own hand on their beach date and he gritted his teeth and sighed. Fern wasn't his property and she could spend the night with whoever she liked. How could he compete with someone like Brad, with his movie star good looks and smooth talk? Fern had told him it was over, but it didn't look that way to Jessie. Plus they'd clearly agreed to speak again that evening and Brad was still in her home.

Jessie didn't like the sinking feeling in his stomach and decided he might as well go for a surf before work to try and ease out some tension. He felt like kicking something, so he knew he'd better go before he told Brad a few home truths about how to treat women... although Fern didn't seem upset that morning, so maybe he should just stay out of it. She was strong enough to make her own decisions, however hopeful Jessie had been about their fledgling feelings, if he was completely honest with himself.

He had a huge crush on Fern and he just wished she stared at him the way she had at Brad when he'd rocked up last night with the flowers. She'd said she was upset to see him, but he'd clearly stayed the night. And, by the smug look on his face, it hadn't been on the couch. Jessie's stomach turned over and he stood up and pushed back his chair. Brad came and shook his hand before he left that morning and introduced himself as a 'friend' of Fern's. He was clearly marking his territory and Jessie wasn't about to get mixed up with another woman who wasn't available.

Jessie sighed and refrained from kicking a plant pot. He knew how much Fern liked them and they all now over-flowed with fragrant blooms. She'd spent ages tending to the half-dead plants and bringing them back to life. He stomped into his lounge and grabbed his keys, before turning and locking the door behind him. He wished he had another rich client to go and visit, before his heart was well and truly lost to his new neighbour. The problem was, he had a sneaking feeling that it was already too late.

CHAPTER TWENTY-FOUR

*A*fter a hectic first week, Fern wandered along the beach and then sank down onto the warm sand, gazing out to sea. The rhythmic coming and going of the waves soothed her mind and she let the tension of the last few days drift away on the gentle early evening breeze.

Brad had hung around long enough for her name to be mentioned alongside his in the newspapers and for her phone to have rung off the hook all week. In the end she'd had to turn it to silent, which was a nightmare for her first week of trading.

He'd arranged a surprise dinner with her family after they'd called a truce. Although Genie and Cal had been wary of his motives, they'd all been intrigued enough to attend. Brad had been charming and on his best behaviour, but for her, the evening had been an attack on her nerves and her hand had been shaking when she'd tried to sip her sparkling wine. She'd just wanted him to go home. Jessie hadn't really spoken to her since the opening night and this added to her confusion. What his problem was, she didn't know. She wasn't back with Brad and had made this clear in any statements she'd given to the press. Not that they'd listened as Brad was happy to gush about their special bond. Now he'd gone home, she finally felt she could breathe. Maybe this was what he'd always known she wasn't ready for. Someone used to the limelight might bask in it. For her, it was a living nightmare.

Now she let a handful of sand trail through her fingers. It had actually been a great week financially and her cupcake café was now officially on the map, much faster than she could ever have dreamed. She wasn't fool enough to think the full coffee shop was just down to her cakes, however delicious they were. She was new to the area and had been ready to build her reputation through great products and service. Now the story about her relationship with Brad had brought a wealth of extra business to her door. As a result she'd had to step up much faster and keep the level of customer care on par, if not better. People kept looking at her and whispering about the news stories, probably wondering how such an exhausted-looking woman could bag a film star. No one seemed to care that they weren't dating any more. The fact that Brad had made such a big show, by personally bringing her flowers for her launch, told them all that he wasn't over her, apparently. That was the most frequent story she overheard.

Everyone seemed to be looking at her with fresh interest, as if wondering how she'd pulled off being the focus of a lovesick, and incredibly gorgeous, famous hunk's affection. She sometimes wondered if Jessie had to listen to the same things. Everyone seemed to know her name now. She was determined not to succumb to the urge to turn her shop sign to closed and to run and hide. It was overwhelming.

She'd hired a new member of staff already and the café was full to bursting most days. She assumed this would tail off eventually, but for now, her kitchen was maxing out at full steam.

She let the cool evening breeze blow the anxiety away and tried to enjoy the buzzy feeling of running such a successful shop. Lots of local business owners had popped by to offer their congratulations, while she'd apologised for all the extra people hanging around due to the press. But the traders were excited and they thanked her for bringing new people to the area – so finally she'd had to accept it and let herself enjoy the ride.

If Jessie had been around more it would have been even better, but she squashed any fledgling feelings she'd had for him. She'd seen his ex-girlfriend hanging around a lot lately and the last thing she needed was another messy entanglement. She did miss their evening glasses of wine, or chats over dinner on the deck, though. Jessie didn't seem to have much time for her since Brad's reappearance. Maybe he was glad to get rid of his annoying neighbour? She'd been avoiding the deck herself for that very reason.

Even though Brad had gone home with just a quick hug and a kiss on the cheek she still had a feeling that he had an underlying agenda. He'd had chance after chance to meet her family before, but had never bothered. Now he suddenly had time for fancy dinners and hotel stays? She didn't think so. Something was definitely up. Her family had been gracious and kind, but they hadn't really any idea of why he'd invited them all out, either! Still, he was gone now, so perhaps she could return to her quiet life and concentrate on her blossoming new business. She looked at her phone as a text dropped in. It was a message from Brad saying he'd got back safely and that he hoped he'd be able to visit again soon, as his filming schedule was bringing him nearby for a month. She sighed and turned her phone over, too tired to answer.

She looked up as a shadow fell over her face and her

eyes travelled up Jessie's firm legs to his waist and further up, to his eyes. He was wearing a pair of loose surf shorts and a shirt that was open and moving in the breeze to expose even more of his taut stomach. Fern gulped and shielded her eyes as he sat down next to her, their legs touching.

He had a small cool bag hooked over his shoulder and he opened it without saying a word. He passed her two glasses, then opened the wine he'd stored in the bag and poured them both a generous glass. Fern took a sip of the crisp wine and tasted blackberries and a hint of lavender. 'It's delicious. Thank you,' she said, forcing herself to look him in the eye and not to blush. She didn't want him to see the hurt she felt at not spending time with him lately.

'I've missed you,' was all he said as he gazed out to sea, his bare feet resting on the sand.

Her bottom lip wobbled and she quickly took another sip of wine. 'I've missed you too. Where have you been?'

He took a moment to turn and their eyes met. 'I didn't want to cause a problem between you and Brad now you're back together.'

'We aren't together! We parted amicably,' said Fern, striving to keep her voice steady. It wasn't easy being so near to Jessie and not touching him.

'Khloe told me she saw you having a cosy family dinner with him in a posh hotel. I was pretty sure that wouldn't happen if you were just friends?'

Fern brushed her hair out of her eyes and frowned. 'Would it matter?'

Jessie sighed and stared out to sea again. 'More than you know,' he said, before facing her again.

Fern's heart melted and she put her hand on his leg, enjoying the feel of firm muscle. She'd never met a man who was so upfront with his emotions before but she knew it must still be hard for him to say that, when he wasn't sure where her loyalties lay.

She'd spent years with Brad ducking questions and giving evasive answers. Jessie's openness was refreshing. She leaned forward and touched her lips to his gently before pulling back, her insides fizzing with excitement. She licked her lips and her eyes never left his.

'I haven't been with Brad for over a year and I'm certainly not with him now. We've decided to remain friends, but he threw me a very fancy dinner with my family before he went home. It was some kind of weird truce, I think.'

She tilted her head forward again and before she could say anything else, Jessie had dropped his glass in the sand and his fingers were gently entwining in her hair as he pulled her mouth to meet his. Her hands slid around his back and met warm skin, which made her gasp and catch her breath. Her body ignited with lust and she pulled him closer to deepen the kiss. It was like nothing she'd ever experienced before and she was hungry for more. They both drew apart moments later, their eyes dilated and their breathing fast.

Jessie looked back at their flats and she nodded, blushing slightly. It had been a while since she'd been alone with such a gorgeous man. Her pulse rate picked up even further and she couldn't look at him. He gently lifted her face so that their eyes met. His had a question in them. She smiled, kissed him briefly and then got up, reaching for his hand. He quickly placed the glasses and wine back into the bag and took her hand, tucking her into his side with his arm as they strolled home together. She turned and grinned at him suddenly and he laughed as they both picked up their pace and raced to get indoors. Sliding the door closed behind them at Jessie's place, he swept her up into his arms and carried her to his bedroom.

CHAPTER TWENTY-FIVE

*F*ern hadn't stopped smiling for the past two weeks. Her café was looking incredible with sparkling glassware and spotless tables. Customers were happily chatting over coffee at the little round tables and the fresh flowers in the centre of each one left a lingering scent in the air that mixed with the cupcake frosting and coffee beans. She had two full time staff members and two part-time, but felt she could really do with more.

Her days were spent in a cloud of icing sugar, keeping up with such a busy shop. Luckily she wrote lists for everything and she had her recipes and flavours planned months in advance. They offered big slices of cakes like coffee and walnut and lemon and raspberry, then people could buy boxes of cupcakes in the same flavour to take home, or eat in store. Fern offered alcoholic cupcakes from her cocktail cart and, as the weather was getting warmer with summer now in full swing, she had bought a frozen cocktail machine. She loved seeing the long line of customers coming from the beach at the weekend. Word was obviously getting out, as weekdays were filling up too.

She leant in to speak to her newest staff member, Pam, who had been recommended to her by Genie. Genie had a full staff and although Pam already worked in Genie's ice cream shop part time, she needed a full-time job. Fern had been happy to offer Pam more hours and Genie had been relieved, as she hated to lose good staff. Pam had so much experience that she was a breeze to work with.

'I've decided we are going to start adding the mocktails we tried at the weekend to the main menu. Lots of people drive to the beach and we don't want them to miss out.'

Pam nodded her agreement and immediately began writing a list of ingredients they would need, and the costings for a separate ice machine. Fern grinned and left her to it. She wanted to pull her latest bakes out of the oven and give them time to cool before frosting them. The windows to the beach were all open and a cooling, salty breeze, was gently wafting in from the sea. She stopped for a moment to enjoy seeing so many happy customers and waved to two of her regulars as they came in looking for a table. Regulars! Even though Brad had shown up, it was her cakes and customer service that kept people coming back.

Thinking of Brad made her wince as he was still texting her, even though she'd told him she wasn't interested. They were supposed to be friends now as she was a cosmopolitan woman who could stay friends with an ex, even one as annoying as Brad. The texts were leaning towards being quite flirty again and she wasn't sure if she should mention Jessie. Their fledgling relationship was too new and exciting to put a label on and it wasn't something they'd discussed anyway. They'd kind of fallen into a routine of hidden kisses, so no one else knew what they were doing, and then meeting for an early dinner on the deck, before they shoved the plates in the sink, forlorn and forgotten, while they ran their hands over each other's bodies and ended up with tangled limbs, in bed. It didn't seem to matter which flat they 'slept' in, but the consensus was that they spent practically every night together.

Fern's skin prickled at the memory of Jessie's confident touch and hot suggestions about what he'd like to be doing to her, as they passed each other in the mornings. Then he'd grab her hand and pull her into the shower with him, so now they had to get up increasingly early to get to work on time, when they both lived above their shops. The man was insatiable! Not that Fern was complaining. She was just the same. She couldn't seem to get enough of him and she worried that she'd started to fall for him. He hadn't given her any inclination that this was anything serious, but for now, she was having too much fun to care.

Milly and James had gone back to Cornwall after the café opening to finish up handing over the other café and would be returning tomorrow, full time. They were leaving their new manager to do the hand over, as she would be staying on to help the women who had bought the business. As they had bought the stock and fittings too, there wasn't much for Milly and James to stick around for. Fern suspected they'd all need to help them get their house ready for bed and breakfast customers, so she'd been preparing herself for walking into what could have been her childhood home. She knew it was rented out at the moment, so Milly and James' personal items weren't there, but they would be when they moved back. Most of their belongings had gone into storage when they'd moved into the flat above the café in Cornwall, as it was quite small.

Fern had loved growing up with her own parents, but she had always missed a sibling, just as she knew Genie had. What would it have been like to grow up beside such a feisty sister? Would they have argued and fallen out? She didn't think so. The family bond seemed so strong between them all, so she was pretty sure they would have worked it out. The same way they had now. She wondered what she'd be doing with her life now if she'd grown up within that boisterous family, then shook her head. Genie owned a restaurant, so there was her answer. She'd probably have ended up with the same shop she had now! Her eyes crinkled at the corners and she smiled to herself.

By the early evening most of her customers had gone. 'You can go home now, Pam,' she called over her shoulder as she wiped the last of the tables down. Pam grinned and grabbed her handbag from behind the counter, waving her goodbyes as she walked out and shielding her eyes from the evening sunshine. Fern saw her check that all of the tables outside were empty, the gate to the terrace was shut and the closed sign hanging jauntily. It was great to not have to worry about those things because she knew her staff double-checked before leaving. She presented the bill to her final customers for the day and they spoke for a few moments about a possible birthday cake order. Fern handed them a leaflet and encouraged them to take a look at her photo gallery online.

She had just flopped down and swung her aching feet up onto a chair opposite when the bell above the door to the shopping street chimed. Fern slid her feet back to the floor and plastered on a smile. People often knocked on the door if they saw her in there, to enquire about traybakes or celebration cakes. They didn't seem to notice the opening hours, but she didn't mind. She loved that people were interested in her cake business. She gasped in surprise to see Milly, looking stunning in a little green sundress with daisies dotted all over it. Her hair was like a silky wave of sunshine and her eyes were sparkling. She was looking around the shop in awe. Following her in was James, who seemed to tower in the space, and behind him was Mr Aldous. 'What are you all doing here?' she exclaimed, rushing over to greet them. 'I thought you were back tomorrow,' she said to Milly and James.

Milly laughed and hugged her so tightly she thought she might pop a rib. James came over and prised her out of Milly's arms, so that he could envelop her in his own for a moment. He rested his chin on her head and sighed, as if he needed this as much as she did.

'We've missed you and couldn't wait a moment longer to see you,' said Milly, glancing around. 'We bumped into Harry as we were walking up and he was on his way to see how you are getting on with the shop. It looks incredible!' She picked up the new menu cards and ran her hands along one of the tables. 'It's even better than on opening day. You've simpli-fied the menu and moved a few tables around. It really works,' she said admiringly.

'We're very proud of our girls,' said James, flushing slightly.

Harry patted him on the back and his eyes watered as he looked around at the beautifully designed table settings and the leafy green plants in golden pots that sat along every wall. 'It's like a hidden paradise,' he said. 'I could never have imagined it looking this good, even when we first opened. There were so many people here on your opening day that I couldn't get a proper look. Congratulations, Fern!'

Fern felt her eyes begin to fill up and she blinked the tears away. She hadn't realised how important it was for Harry to like what she'd done. She didn't want to wash away his legacy, which was why she'd retained as many original features as she could. The kiosk had just been given a spruce-up and the kitchen area was still the same layout, she'd only updated the appliances. She'd even framed a few photos of the old shop along the back wall. 'Thanks, Harry. Would you like a tour of the kitchens while I make Milly and James a coffee?' She glanced at them with a smile and they seemed happy to sit and admire the view of the sea for a while.

Fern felt her legs wobble a bit at showing Harry her kitchen as this was her sacred space, but she knew that she'd have to get another baker in soon if the business was to keep thriving. Harry ran his hands along surfaces and opened and closed the huge fridges and freezers she'd had installed, all the while telling her how much he loved the changes. 'I knew you'd be the right fit for this kitchen,' he said, turning to her. He reached inside his jacket pocket and pulled out some well-used sheets of paper, before laying them out on one of the kitchen surfaces. They were covered in food stains and spidery handwriting. Fern squinted and moved closer to see what he had brought.

'These are my own recipes,' he said, running his fingers over the paper affectionately. 'I know you are an incredible chef, but I thought you might like to try one or two of these. They were created here and served me very well.' Fern gasped and turned to hug Harry. She knew how much these recipes must mean to him and for him to share them was humbling.

'Are you sure?' Her eyes were bright with wonder and she quickly ran her eyes along the lines of text, deciphering the ingredients he'd used. She carefully put each sheet aside and took note of the next. They were full of fresh fruit and spices and flavours her mouth watered to taste. 'If Milly and James weren't here I'd try them right now,' then she slapped her hand over her mouth in horror as Harry threw his head back and laughed. 'I don't mean I'm not pleased to see them, of course!'

Harry kept on laughing for a moment and then patted her hand. 'I know what you mean. The pull of a new recipe is such temptation for a baker. You can keep them and try them out any time. I brought them for you.'

'Thank you! What a treat,' said Fern, taking the papers and putting them in a clear folder next to the notebook she kept for ideas. 'I promise to take good care of them. I'll add some to the menu.'

Harry's eyes crinkled at the corners and he carried on his inspection of the room while she made them all a coffee. Just as she placed the cups on the table, the little bell above the door jangled again. She glanced up to see her sister and Cal walk in, hand in hand and smiling. Fern let out the breath she'd been holding and relief filled her veins. She'd been quietly worrying about how little Genie and Cal actually managed to see each other, so their entwined hands lifted her spirits even more. Genie was a master at dodging personal questions, for such an inquisitive person herself, but Fern hoped this meant everything was OK. They all shuffled up along one of the bigger tables that looked out over the ocean and Fern grabbed two more drinks.

When she returned, Harry was in his element, regaling them all with stories about his new life as a fancy-free bachelor. 'I'm so happy to see such good energy in this place again. I wanted it to go to someone who would love it as much as I do. You've made an old man very proud,' he said, looking at both Genie and Fern. 'You make a great team. World domination!' he joked, and they all laughed. James took Milly's hand and Fern could feel how much this meant to them too.

She wasn't used to big family gatherings. She hesitated as Jessie walked by, but Cal knocked on the window which made him jump. 'Join us,' called Cal, gesturing to a spare seat next to Fern. Her heart skipped a beat, as he looked so gorgeous in cut-off jean shorts and a simple white T-shirt, showing off impressive arm muscles from all the physical work he did. Fern's brain switched to the memory of touching those muscles and her face flushed, so she looked down for a moment and let her hair cover her cheeks before anyone saw her. Genie was looking at her with interest and a glint came into her eye as Fern tried to regulate her breathing and looked up again. Genie gave her a cheeky wink and Fern rolled her eyes.

Jessie came in and greeted them all with a hug. He slid in beside Fern when they sat down again and their legs touched, making her skin heat up. She couldn't seem to be near this man without combusting into flames. He put his hand on her leg under the table while he spoke to Cal about his day and she froze like a cat caught in car headlights. Then he removed his hand as he laughed at something Genie said and Fern avoided looking into her sister's knowing eyes.

The hours rolled by and it didn't seem like anyone was inclined to go home, so Fern got up, trying not to lean into the warmth of Jessie's body. He got on so well with everyone, but was still treating her like just a friend, so she needed to put a little bit of space between them. 'Shall I rustle us all up something for dinner?' Everyone rushed to agree and while Genie, Milly and Jessie stayed at the table, Cal, James and Harry jumped up to help.

'You don't need to do anything,' she laughed, as they all followed her into the kitchen and started opening cupboards as if they owned the place. That's what you get for having several chefs in the family, she supposed, smiling to herself and enjoying the intrusion in her kitchen. She darted a glance around to see what everyone would do. Her café wasn't set up for big meals, but she had ingredients for a simple dinner. Having both a famous chef like Cal and a legend like Harry around was a bit intimidating, and she was thankful for James' steady presence. She'd often watched him work in the kitchen of her old shop and although his food was simple it was tasty and he always left the customers happy. Cal, on the other hand, was already making a huge Greek salad from what she could see, and Harry was rustling up the ingredients for a cinnamon loaf for dessert.

'Sorry Fern!' said Cal, when he finally noticed that she and James were standing and watching them. 'I do tend to take over in a kitchen. It's my natural instinct.'

Fern laughed and went to grab some cutlery and plates. 'It's actually a joy to watch. I'm pretty mesmerised by your skill. I haven't stopped because I'm upset. I absolutely love having you all here. This is a family kitchen,' she said resolutely, making sure Harry knew he was honorary family too. Tears glistened in his eyes before he went back to his baking. James took the plates from her and went to lay the table as she cut some cubes of lamb and pepper and placed them on skewers, before rolling them in a spice rub Cal had just handed to her with a smile. She had tubs of potato salad already made in the fridge, so she pulled one of those out and gave that and a green salad to James. The kitchen filled with scents of thyme, tarragon and bay leaf, mixed with a heady undertone of cinnamon.

When they finally put all the dishes on the table, it was almost bursting with succulent food. It was a veritable feast. Milly stood up and handed people plates of delicious food.

'This is incredible,' said Jessie. 'There was me thinking I'd have to make myself a sandwich for dinner.' They all laughed and he caught Fern's eye, as they'd spent most of the last week feasting on each other and ignoring food. She felt her skin grow warm and she flushed, making his eyes dilate before he turned to speak to Genie.

After their stomachs were full and they'd spent a raucous evening sharing jokes and catching up on each other's news, Jessie offered to make them all a coffee and Fern jumped up to help him. Fern didn't miss the shared look between Genie and Milly, but she was too fired up to care. It had been a lovely evening, but she needed a moment alone with Jessie.

As soon as they closed the kitchen door behind them, he backed her up against the door and kissed her with such passion that he almost took her breath away. Her knees buckled and she wrapped her arms around his neck and pulled him even closer. When they finally drew apart they were both panting, and then they doubled over and burst out laughing.

'We're behaving like teenagers,' Fern said, as she moved away and switched on the coffee machine. Jessie kept coming up behind her and kissing her neck while they made the coffees and then he put a healthy dash of rum in each one from her cocktail supplies. Kissing one more time, they loaded up the trays and went back into the café. Everyone stopped talking and looked at them, and then they all started again suddenly. Fern ignored them and handed out the coffees, enjoying their double-take when the rum hit home.

'Yum!' said Genie. 'Whatever magic you conjured up in the kitchen should be on the menu,' she teased Jessie, bumping shoulders with Cal who put his arm round her and grinned. They all got up and started helping to tidy away and Fern watched them sharing the tasks with a smile. This was her family now. She watched Jessie's broad shoulders as he passed the clean cutlery to James to put away and wondered where he fitted in with them all. Was she a casual fling, or something more? Her feelings for him were growing and the fear of being hurt was beginning to seep in.

The almost daily texts she now got from Brad were a reminder of her past, but she couldn't go back. He seemed to think he was still in with a chance, however blunt she was. He'd mentioned being in the area again soon, but there was no real reason for him to come by any more. His attentiveness still didn't add up. She knew he'd said he was a changed man, but she wasn't that stupid. Brad would always put himself first and whatever he was after was for his own gain. Yes, he might miss having her hanging on his every word, but he could find any number of women to do that.

She filched the last half-slice of Harry's cinnamon cake and sighed in bliss as the burst of flavour hit her tongue. His baking was sublime. An idea popped into her head and she wandered over to stand next to him. He was straightening up the pile of tea towels and stopped when she joined him. 'Why did you really give up this shop when you love it so much?' she asked quietly.

Harry smiled and took her hand in his. 'I'm too old to run it on my own and was too tired to rejuvenate it. In my heyday this was a bustling venue, but lately I'd lost my passion. Seeing it reborn has made me fall in love with it all over again. That's down to you, Fern.' He gently kissed her cheek and she gave him a warm hug. 'I'm happy to leave it to you youngsters while I return as a customer. I must admit that I'm already a bit bored and I need a new place to live in, though. The flat I was hoping to buy fell through. Considering I was very decisive about moving, I'm now dithering about going away,' he confessed.

'Rent out our annexe!' said Milly, butting in on their conversation after clearly eavesdropping.

'Great idea!' said Genie and Fern in unison.

Harry's mouth dropped open in shock. 'I couldn't, surely?'

'Why not?' asked James. 'You've always been considered as part of the family. You're one of my dad's best friends. You've been there loads of times when Dad was living there. Would it suit you?'

Harry started blustering and looking around the room at them all. 'I do know the annexe well. Gus and I have spent many a night talking over a glass of whiskey there.' He looked at Jessie, who was smiling too. He nodded his head.

'Take a chance,' said Genie. 'I know we are a lot…' she winked at Jessie, who grinned widely, 'but we're a great family to be part of. You won't ever feel alone.'

'You won't get a moment's peace,' joked Cal, earning a poke in the ribs from Genie. He kissed her on the lips and snuggled her into his side. 'Other than my own, of course, it's the best family on earth.'

Harry blinked back tears. 'I don't have a family of my own and I have come to regret that over the past few years. I was a bit of a playboy in my day and old habits die hard,' he admitted to wolf whistles from Cal and Genie. They all laughed and it seemed the deal was done.

'I was wondering…' mentioned Fern. 'Would you pop back for a couple of afternoons each week to help me with the café?' For once they were all speechless, until all hell broke loose and Genie headed back into the kitchen to break open some sparkling wine.

She handed them all a glass and Cal filled them with the golden liquid. They all toasted to new memories being made. 'What an inspired idea!' said Genie. 'I wish I'd thought of it first.'

'Aren't I too old for a hip place like this?' asked Harry. 'My hips are a bit creaky these days.' Fern almost choked on her wine and Jessie rubbed her back.

'Ada and Gus help Genie with her place and although they don't cook, half of the customers only come in to see them,' she winked at Genie who stuck out her tongue but then acknowledged how integral they both were to her success.

'I honestly don't know what I'd have done without Ada's support,' said Genie then winced as she saw Milly flinch. 'Sorry, Mum,' she soothed.

'It's OK,' said Milly, brightly. 'It's the truth. Ada might be a retired movie star, but she sure knows how to run a successful business. James and I are very grateful to her and also to you, Harry. Because of you, we now have both of our girls home.'

CHAPTER TWENTY-SIX

Fern stretched out her arms and turned to lie on her side, looking out at the horizon. She'd enjoyed the raucous dinner the night before, but it had been a bit of a revelation too. She'd never experienced such a rowdy family dinner before. The evening out with Brad had been much more refined and everyone had clearly been on their best behaviour.

She'd always had quiet and relaxed meals with her adoptive parents in their formal dining room in Cornwall. Her mum had shooed her away from helping, saying she cooked all week, which was true. So she and her dad spent time catching up on news while her mum was in the kitchen. Her dad set the table and cleared up, insisting once again that she found time to relax and that her mum should let him tidy away as she cooked. It was a team effort, but nothing like the handing around plates of food to be shared and sticking their heads over each other's shoulders to see what they were cooking. It made her insides churn that she might be being disloyal, to have enjoyed the evening so much. She'd loved her evenings with her parents and a tear slipped out of her eye and ran down her cheek. She sniffed and brushed it away, sitting up and hugging her knees as she watched the tide come in and a few people walk along the beach, hand in hand with their partners or children.

She missed her parents so much at that moment that it physically hurt. They'd been such gentle and kind people. She hoped they'd be happy for her in her new life. In fact she knew they'd be proud of anything she achieved. Although she'd loved the previous evening's shenanigans, at some points she'd also felt like she was watching everything from the outside. It had been a lot of fun and she hadn't wanted them to leave, but she'd run away from Cornwall when her new family had become all-encompassing and now she was in the same situation here.

She'd wanted time to get to know her sister, but it seemed that Milly and James would not accept life away from her after so many years apart. Warmth spread into her heart and she decided that maybe it was time to step out of her comfort zone and open up a bit to having a big, noisy and talented family. You could never have too many people to love, she decided, straightening her shoulders and going to wash away her doubts with a refreshing shower. Genie had bought her some zingy orange and lime body wash and it was like being splashed in the face with a bucket of cold water, making her skin tingle in shock. Genie used it to drag herself awake when she had a busy day planned. Fern was sure there were better ways to start the day, but she was willing to give it another try.

Once washed and dressed in her work uniform of black trousers and short-sleeved shirt, she slid on her flip flops, grabbed her keys and decided she'd go for a stroll along the beach before the café was due to open. She stopped when she saw a group of girls chatting happily to a couple of young men who had surf boards propped in the sand by their feet, with wet hair from the sea. Had Fern ever been that carefree? She didn't think so. Brad had swept into her life and she'd been enamoured by his vibrancy after her elderly parents had kept her sheltered. He'd been exciting and dynamic and downright bossy, but she'd adored him. She hadn't even minded keeping their relationship secret. She'd stupidly been understanding about how difficult it must have been for him, someone who was in the public eye, dating an ordinary girl like her. She'd always flinched when she saw pictures of him in the papers and magazines with other women, but he'd explained that this was just for show. In the end it had all been lies, though. She was pretty sure that he'd been seeing someone else all along. A glamorous 'starlet' who hung on his every word and looked incredible in the designer clothes he bought her. She'd appeared in photos one too many times for it to be a coincidence. He'd never admitted it, but being away from him had given Fern clarity.

Occasionally, he'd bought them both the same outfit, but whilst the starlet wore hers to the premieres, the dresses hung unworn in Fern's wardrobe. He'd probably got a two for one deal, she smirked to herself, glad she'd not ever worn those clothes. They were beautiful, but Fern's vibe was more boho than supermodel. She knew she looked good in most clothes, but she loved her curves and tight, blingy dresses weren't her style. She preferred dresses that skimmed her hips and hugged her waist, and simply designed tops that made her feel confident and occasionally a bit flirty. She certainly wasn't someone who needed all eyes in the room on her. Her flirt game could definitely do with some practice, though. Then she thought of the sexy man who was usually in her bed and grinned to herself. Maybe she was better at it than she thought! Jessie seemed to find her irresistible.

Not that she was complaining. She was enjoying every moment of seemingly driving a man like Jessie insane with lust. He grabbed her for kisses any chance he got and often popped into the shop for a coffee and a chat and then managed to communicate his need for her in wanton looks or by brushing his hand on hers. Her pulse rate was usually bouncing around for most of the day in expectation of a possible tryst, and they saw each other most evenings.

She sighed heavily and rubbed her eyes. She was still unsure what to do about Brad's texts. He would be coming to visit again soon. She couldn't help but glance over her shoulder at Jessie's shop. It was such a cool place to hang out, with lots of natural wood and colourful clothes and boards strategically placed throughout. If you walked past, you couldn't help but stop and want to go inside. She often ran her hand along the handmade wooden service area and then crept into his workshop at the back to do the same to his shoulders or legs. She couldn't seem to keep away from him for very long and it was beginning to worry her. Supposing he didn't feel the same, and this was just a casual fling? Maybe he was like this with everyone he dated.

Could she survive another heartbreak? She really didn't know. There was no way she was ever leaving her beautiful new café, so they had to stay friendly whatever happened. Her stomach turned over at the thought of another woman touching Jessie, but that feeling wasn't there any more for Brad. She'd have to make it clear again when they met that they were never getting back together. Jessie deserved that, if nothing else.

She looked up and realised that she'd already strolled halfway up the beach. She turned back and started walking towards the café, keys jangling loosely in her hand. The sight of her little café with its soft blue awnings and her name in gold lettering never failed to brighten her day. She walked up the small sandy incline in front of her shop, crossed over the path and opened the back door. After stepping over the threshold and switching on the lights, she took a deep breath in. The air was full of the scent of sugar. She grinned as she decided to experiment with some of Harry's recipes. She grabbed her baking apron and set to work, handsome neighbours and annoying movie stars forgotten.

CHAPTER TWENTY-SEVEN

Fern smiled. Harry had started whistling while he whipped up a cake batter. They'd got into an easy routine and she loved having him around. He reminded her a little bit of her adoptive dad, when he'd stepped in to help when she had a big order come in. Harry was a hugger and she'd also got used to him coming in for his shift and embracing her. At first she'd been a bit shy, but now she was getting used to her new extended family and friendship circle, who all seemed to enjoy hugs!

She'd made a few tentative friendships with regular customers and the other shop owners along the street and the two evening cocktail and cake sessions she'd held had been a roaring success. She hadn't seen much of Genie in the past few days as they were both so busy in their respective shops, but James and Milly were now settled back into their house and renovations to make it into the most fabulous bed and breakfast for miles around were underway.

'How are you finding living with James and Milly?' asked Fern, as Harry slid the first two trays of cakes into one of her industrial ovens and brushed his hands on his apron, dusting it with flour.

'I was worried I'd be imposing at first, but your granddad had already sectioned off a little bit of garden and it's pretty separate from the house. I love it!' he grinned happily, checking to see the oven temperature was right and then pulling out a few tubs of ingredients from the fridge.

It was surprising how well they danced around each other in the kitchen without invading each other's space. She had paced around her lounge a few times wondering if Harry would come in and commandeer her beautiful new kitchen, but he'd been graceful and asked simply what needed to be done.

Now she pulled out a rack of cakes she'd been hiding and her eyes sparkled. She placed them on the gleaming surface in front of him, just as one of her staff popped in to grab more coffee beans and then left again with a quick nod in their direction. Fern loved the way everyone here was efficient and just got on with their roles. She'd done staff training, but they all had service experience, which was so lucky for her!

Harry eyed the jewel-like cupcakes in front of him. Each of the smooth chocolate cupcakes was covered with whipped strawberry icing and topped with a single fresh strawberry dipped in chocolate, and they gave off the heady scent of temptation.

Harry gasped and reverently picked one up. 'You followed one of my recipes?' He turned to her with delight on his face. Fern grinned and bit into the soft sponge, sighing in bliss. Harry hurried to do the same and they both rolled their eyes as the flavours burst in their mouths.

'This is so delicious,' said Fern. 'I've tried out several of the recipes you left here, but this is my favourite. Do you mind if we add it to the menu?'

'I'd be delighted,' said Harry. 'I didn't bother with most of my recipes once the shop got quieter. It will make me so happy to see them displayed once again.' He placed his hand on Fern's arm and looked around him. 'You've really given an old man a new lease of life.'

Fern let out the breath she'd been holding. She'd loved making the cupcakes but didn't want Harry to feel she was overstepping the mark by selling them.

'It's blending the old with the new,' she said.

They both walked over to the kiosk window and she handed the tray to Harry so that he could add them to the display. She'd already hand-written a sign to say 'Harry's Strawberry and Chocolate Delights', and he smiled from ear to ear when he saw it and gave her another warm hug.

'I had a bit of a panic about ending up alone in the shop and covered in cobwebs, undiscovered for years,' said Harry sheepishly, arranging the last cupcake. 'It's made me feel years younger seeing it like this.'

'Maybe you should start dating again?' teased Fern, making Harry throw back his head and laugh. The customers closest to them jumped, but then grinned too.

'I don't think the town is ready for that yet,' said Harry, but then a light twinkled in eyes. 'Never say never, though! If Ada and Gus weren't such a perfect couple, I'd give him a run for his money,' he joked, winking. Fern laughed until her sides hurt and she felt the real, flirty Harry emerge. She bet he had been a real hit with the women before he'd hidden himself away.

She stood back and waved to a couple of her regulars as they walked by and then checked over the shop floor to see if anyone needed anything. Luckily it was running like clock-work and all she could see was a room full of satisfied customers. She loved watching Harry chat to them. She had felt that maybe he was a bit lonely, but he seemed much happier now.

Fern had already spoken to Genie about her takeaway service and how she could do something similar on this stretch of beach. Now a queue was once again forming for their cocktail and mocktail slushies. She grabbed some supplies to top up the biodegradable cups they used and headed out to the bar cart to help with the line of customers.

Jessie had popped in for a coffee a few times and they'd spoken about how busy they both were – and made out in the kitchen when no one else was there. Jessie said he could understand Harry's reasoning about why she had got the premises, and not him. Both shops were now inundated with customers.

Fern wasn't so sure Jessie was completely over it, but she was very grateful it had happened that way. She wondered if Harry wished he hadn't been so impulsive now he could see the butterfly of a shop that had emerged from the dusty chrysalis, but he seemed very happy and Genie said she hadn't seen him smile so much in years.

~

*F*ern sighed with relief after she closed the door and turned the sign to closed. It had been a long day but at least having Harry there had meant she didn't have to spend the next few hours baking for tomorrow.

She picked at one of her nails and then flinched when it hurt. She'd been keeping a secret for days and it was about time she decided what to do about it. She went into her little office, one of the few places she hadn't renovated too much, and looked at the small neat desk and table and the natural wood walls and floor. There was a window out to the back and a door that led to the small patio area that linked up with

Jessie's shop. Beyond that was the café's seating area by the sea and the big double sliding doors to the interior of the café.

She went over to the uneven patch of flooring she'd discovered and bent down once again to lift out the small carved box she'd found hidden there. At first she'd been excited to discover its contents, but now she wished she'd covered the floorboards with cheap vinyl and hadn't been so picky about straight lines. That way she might not have tutted and tried to push the floorboard straight. Doing so had made the other end pop up. She lifted the box out and put it on her desk. Then she sat down, picked up her phone and called Genie.

CHAPTER TWENTY-EIGHT

enie and Fern sat crossed-legged on the floor in Fern's office. There was barely room to move as the desk took up one whole wall. The lights were dim and curtains drawn, as if they were in some sort of spy movie. They spoke in hushed tones and the offending box sat between them, looking innocent and harmless.

Genie had dropped everything and rushed straight round. Luckily it had been closing time and she had just been locking up. The sisters both stared at the box as if it would open itself and speak.

Then Fern gingerly opened the lid and lifted out the small stack of letters hidden inside. She'd only read a few lines of the top one and then had stuffed them back inside and under the floor once again while she thought about what to do. She knew she'd have to tell Genie, but what about everyone else? This could destroy the whole community, just when she'd begun to fit in. She knew the phrase 'don't shoot the messenger' but she could picture angry faces turning to her for bringing this information to light. She was totally the wrong person to have discovered it, because her whole childhood had been a lie and it had irrevocably changed her. She didn't want that to happen to someone else.

'What do you think?' she asked Genie. 'Should we read them?'

Genie was unusually quiet and her eyes were like saucers. 'How long have you had them?'

'Only a few days. I didn't want to cause anyone any pain. I thought maybe you could help me decide what to do.'

'Shove them back in the floor?'

'Is that what you want?' asked Fern.

'No,' sighed Genie. 'It's too late now you've seen them. There's no way I'd have been able to keep quiet either. If they are what you think they might be, then all hell is going to break loose.' They reverently placed the letters on the floor between them.

'Which one shall we read first? It feels weird to read love letters to someone else.'

'Some of them have been marked 'return to sender', which makes it even more heart-breaking. I've just glanced at the top one, but I already feel sick about the trouble this might cause.'

Genie picked a letter up carefully. 'Well I for one want answers and it's not like we'd get a straight one from Gran. She's never told the truth to any of us.'

They bent their heads over the letters and spent the next few hours reading every word on the crinkled pages. At one point Fern got up and made them both a sandwich and a strong coffee laced with rum, like the ones Jessie made. They sat in silence together, concentrating hard. Their phones dinged with texts, probably asking where they were, but they ignored them. For the first time in ages, Fern felt a tell-tale tightness in her chest and picked up her asthma inhaler from her desk drawer. She inhaled deeply, feeling her breathing regulate and her lungs ease up.

'Your gran's parents originally owned this building,' said Fern eventually, placing the inhaler in her trouser pocket.

'She's your gran too,' said Genie, tiredness clearly making her irritable. It was unusual for her to be anything but feisty or sunny, so Fern wasn't sure how to react. Perhaps she should start calling Milly, James and Lucinda 'Mum', 'Dad' and 'Gran' – but it still felt a bit alien to her.

'Sorry,' said Genie. 'I just want us to be one family.'

Fern gave her a wobbly smile and took a sip of her coffee. It was now cold, so she winced at the bitter taste of the rum. 'Did you know that our grandparents were wealthy land-lords?' she asked Genie. 'They used to own this shop! How weird is that? What the hell?'

'Do you think that's why Harry offered you the shop – because it used to be in our family?' asked Genie. They both sat back on their heels in shock.

'Possibly,' said Fern. 'Wow, this is complicated. My brain hurts.'

Genie placed all the letters back in the little box. 'He was pleading with Gran to come back and run the shop with him and telling her he'd make something of himself to support her.'

'How do we tell Milly that Harry was one of her mum's boyfriends?'

'Was Harry Lucinda's first love, do you think? Was she his?' asked Genie.

'It seems it, from what he's written. There's so much passion on those pages, it almost felt wrong to read them. I always thought Harry was a ladies' man,' said Fern quietly, as if the walls had ears.

'Maybe that was his way of getting over her?'

'Why did they separate, do you think?' mused Fern. 'Maybe Harry rebelled after Lucinda left, but no one could match her – and he's still single. How sad!'

She tried to work out the timings but it must have been before Milly was born. She could see Genie frowning too and decided that they needed to sleep on it and then decide what to do.

'Do you think Milly knows about this?' Fern inclined her head towards the letters.

'Mum,' corrected Genie distractedly. 'No. But I think she'd be a bit shocked to find out that Lucinda and Harry were lovers.'

CHAPTER TWENTY-NINE

*T*he next few days were hectic, so Fern and Genie agreed not to rush into a decision. Milly and James seemed to be enjoying the challenges of running their new business and Harry had settled into his new role. Would Milly feel like Harry had cheated her, by still trying to be part of her mother's life, and had Harry brought Fern here by selling her the shop, with the ulterior motive of luring Lucinda back? It was all too confusing.

Fern tried to distance herself from it all and concentrate on her new venture, but even the success of her café couldn't stop the gnawing worry that something was terribly wrong. They needed to tell Milly, and as soon as possible, but neither child wanted to cause her pain, or explain that Lucinda might end up back on these shores if Harry had his way. Argh!

The bell above the door rang and Jessie stepped inside. It was bright sunshine outside so the branded parasols were up over the outside tables and most people were wearing sunglasses. Jessie looked tanned and sexy and a few of her customers stopped what they were doing to admire him for a moment. She didn't blame them. She'd been too busy to meet up for a few nights and she'd missed him. They avoided the subject of Brad and now she tried not to mention Harry or her family either. It was easier to just sit at home on her own at the moment. If Jessie found out about the shop he might think she'd conned him, or something. She didn't actually know what was going on herself, but she was determined to find out. Her heart fluttered when he walked up to the counter and ordered a takeaway coffee, his eyes searching hers.

'Want to go for a stroll on the beach after work?' he asked quietly. Her heart missed a beat.

'Um...'

'I feel like I haven't seen much of you lately,' he said, making sure there weren't any customers in earshot. Fern tried to bite down her frustration at him still keeping their relationship, if that's what it was, a secret.

She smiled, but it didn't reach her eyes. The past few days had taken a toll on her and she felt she could happily sleep for a week right now. Her phone rang in the kitchen and she apologised and went to answer it, after saying that she already had plans that night. She was fed up with pandering to men who weren't proud to be seen out with her. She was thankful for the reprieve from her emotions – until she heard Genie on the other end of the line. 'We have to make a decision about what to tell Mum,' she said.

Fern glanced around to make sure no one was around. All her staff were busily getting on with their jobs and luckily Harry wasn't working that day.

'I know,' she replied. 'This whole mess is making my stomach churn.'

Fern wasn't sure how she felt about Harry now. Although they had fallen into an easy pattern of working in harmony alongside each other, she often found herself staring at him while he worked and wondering if selling the shop to her was a ploy to get Lucinda to come back to the beautiful Essex coast.

From what Genie had told her, Lucinda rarely visited now, demanding that they all travelled to Cornwall instead. But the fact that Harry was eternally single made Fern wonder if Lucinda gave him just enough hope to string him along. She'd lied easily to Fern's adoptive mum and dad for so long and done the same to Genie and her parents… their parents. She still winced when she thought of Milly and James that way and hated the thought of being disloyal to the mum and dad that had raised her. It was hard to navigate, because Milly had tried to find her for years and had herself been tricked into giving her child away by her own mother, who let her think she'd been abandoned by James and would be shaming the family. Lucinda had been so 'shamed' that she'd let her own grandchild think she was her godmother, and had been part of her life since she was born! Fern found she was grinding her teeth again and hated the new habit that had crept in while she was agonising about what to do.

In a way it was a welcome distraction from her unpredictable feelings about Brad and Jessie. Perhaps she should move on from both of them and enjoy being single for a while? Her business took up most of her time, but brushing past Jessie on the stairs to the flats and seeing him walk past every day was its own kind of torture. Having Harry working alongside her was the same. How the hell had she got into this mess!

'Let's try and tell Milly tonight. We ought to have Dad there too. Just in case she starts throwing things and blaming us,' said Genie.

Fern smiled at this. Milly was quite highly strung and James was usually a calming presence, but when he was riled up about his family, James could yell with the best of them.

Plus he already hated Lucinda for what she'd done. He'd missed his oldest child growing up and that wasn't easily forgiven when it could have been avoided. 'I agree. We can't keep anyone in the dark this time. Then they can decide what to say to Harry.'

'You haven't spoken to him about it, then?' asked Genie.

'I wouldn't know what to say,' said Fern. "By the way, Harry, we know you were in love with our grandmother and we think that's why you sold me your shop," she said flatly.

Genie giggled and Fern smiled at the sound. 'It is pretty weird,' Genie agreed. 'What if he sold you the shop to get her to follow you?'

'Exactly!' said Fern. 'I'm not giving up my shop for anyone now. It's mine and I've worked hard for it. But if she moves here, I might have to consider it.'

'Don't worry,' said Genie, soothingly. 'You were the obvious choice for the shop and it's given Harry a new lease of life. No one can dispute that.'

'How are we going to broach the subject of my newest staff member possibly having an ulterior motive for getting closer to our family? He's living in Milly and James' annexe, for goodness sake!'

'Mum and Dad,' corrected Genie. 'He cooks the evening meals for their guests too now! His feet are firmly under the family table.'

'Do you want to tell them on your own? You know how they'll react better than me.'

'No way! You're the one who found the letters. Maybe it should just be you,' said Genie, clearly very tactically.

'OK, OK,' said Fern, with a big sigh. 'I'm free tonight if you want me to come over.'

'I'm busy tonight, the restaurant is full and I'm on shift, but tomorrow will be easier. I think their second set of guests are checking out too, so they won't have an excuse to say no. Not that Mum would turn down a night with both her girls,' joked Genie. 'She was moaning the other day that we are too busy to spend time with our 'old' mum,' she laughed and Fern couldn't help but smile too.

Milly was about as glamorous a woman as it got. She worked so hard, but was immaculate in every way these days, from her straight blond hair to her soft pink lipstick. Fern often wondered how she did it, as those genes certainly hadn't transposed to her or Genie, who were both a bit more of a mess, sometimes looking like they'd been spat out of the sea like a piece of seaweed. Fern fleetingly remembered Jessie saying she had looked like a Siren with her green shorts and top combo, but she didn't have time to dwell on that now.

Genie spoke to someone in the distance and then told Fern she had to go as a customer was enquiring about something. 'Before I forget,' she added, 'I tried one of Harry's cake recipes, making it into an ice cream, and it's out of this world. It's the strawberry and chocolate one, but with chunks of bitter chocolate to balance the sugar. I made two tubs last night and I've already sold out. You might want to serve it with those cupcakes you make when you next bake them.'

'Great idea!' Fern's tastebuds were already tingling while she wondered which of his other recipes would work well as ice cream flavours.

'I also need to order an extra box of your savoury cheese and courgette muffins, as they've sold out.'

Fern grinned and mentally added that to her list. She would be baking for the rest of the day, but she loved surrounding herself with flour, butter and eggs. The scent of fresh pastries and cupcakes filled her with joy and made her customers keep coming back for more. She pressed a button to end the call and almost skipped into her kitchen to start making batches of cake batter.

CHAPTER THIRTY

*F*ern's feet were aching when she finally closed up for the day, but she felt satisfied that she was doing a great job. Her customers were happy and she'd been invited out by a couple of the other shop owners, for a proper grown-up drink in a few days time. She was partial to the odd glass of wine. There was a beautiful Tudor pub down the road by the water and she loved strolling past and chatting to Charley, the owner. She hadn't ventured in for a drink yet, as she didn't feel quite settled enough to walk in on her own, but she was looking forward to going there with a small group of locals. The pub had hanging baskets outside with ivy trailing towards the floor and deep pink flowers, which were in full bloom.

As she turned the key in her door and headed for the stairs leading to the two flats, she almost jumped out of her skin. She'd been looking down, putting one foot in front of the other – and there was Jessie, lounging against the bottom wooden railing. He was clearly waiting for someone.

She gave him a half smile and prepared to step around him, but he gently took her arm, making her catch her breath and stop. He let her go and brushed his hair out of his face, as his piercing blue eyes searched hers. 'Have I done something to upset you? I get the feeling you're avoiding me,' he said, sitting on the third step and facing her, so that she couldn't move around him without climbing onto his lap. He took her hands and made her look at him.

'I just had plans for tonight,' she said prissily, whilst enjoying the feel of her hands encased in his. He raised an eyebrow at her and tilted his head to one side, a half smile on his face. 'OK,' she sighed. 'I'm avoiding you.' He frowned and pulled her closer so that her legs were touching his.

'Why?' he asked, brushing a stray hair out of her eyes. Then his hand caressed her cheek and made her mind fuddled for a moment. She tried to think of a plausible lie, then her shoulders sagged and she leaned her body into his and kissed him softly on the lips, not really caring who saw them. He responded instantly and deepened the kiss, until her heart felt like it was beating out of her chest and she pulled back.

'I'm fed up with having secret relationships,' she said defiantly, fire sparking in her eyes.

Jessie looked confused and gazed around. 'We're out in the open now. I thought you didn't want your family to know about me, after the Brad situation. You don't touch me in front of them. I was following your lead.'

It was Fern's turn to frown as she whizzed back through her memory, and realised what he was saying was true. She didn't feel comfortable enough in front of her new family to be openly affectionate with someone they probably knew better than they knew her. His arms had looped behind her now and he pulled her to sit on his lap, so she snuggled into his chest. It felt good to be held and unafraid of who happened to walk by.

'I didn't realise,' said Fern. 'I'm sorry. I thought you wanted to keep us a secret.'

'Like Brad did?' he asked, dropping a kiss onto her nose.

'Umm… I guess. I'm just used to hiding any affection I have for a man, so I didn't know I was doing it. Plus I wasn't sure how you felt. Are we kind of dating, or casually seeing each other? I don't really know, so it's easier to keep you at a distance.'

Jessie's arms tightened around her and he kissed her again, making her heart flutter. 'I'd say it's more than a fling and although we haven't been out on many dates, we have spent practically every night together recently. I assumed that meant we were dating,' he said seriously, frowning again.

'Maybe we should have spoken about it. I don't want to keep mentioning Brad, but he left me feeling insecure and anxious for three years.'

'I'm not Brad,' he said firmly, placing his arm around her shoulder and gazing out to sea. There were a few people strolling along the sandy shores and the sea was gently lapping at the beach as the sun dropped to the horizon. Fern shivered and Jessie picked her up and stood up, placing her feet back on the ground, his arms still around her. 'So, you're my girlfriend?' he questioned, with a cheeky smile, his face offering a promise of untold pleasure.

She grinned and wrapped her arms around him, happily. 'That sounds good to me. I quite like the idea of having a sexy boyfriend next door, especially when he brings me wine,' she teased, a lightness filling her chest. No one had officially called her their girlfriend before. Brad had only done that in private, which meant it didn't count. They both turned as they heard someone approach.

Brad stopped suddenly at the sight of them in each other's arms. His eyes narrowed and his cheeks flushed. Fern dropped her arms from Jessie, but he kept his arm around her shoulder and turned to face Brad.

'Brad,' said Fern, enjoying the solid feel of Jessie's body next to hers. 'I didn't know you were in the area.'

Brad ran his hand through his hair and his gaze travelled over her face, as if searing it onto his memory. He looked pointedly at Jessie's arm over her shoulder, but Jessie didn't move an inch.

'I told you I was coming via my texts,' he said, through gritted teeth. He looked like he'd just stepped out of a magazine photoshoot, with inky blue jeans and a perfectly pressed shirt rolled up at the sleeves. He had a lightweight jacket slung over his shoulder and he didn't seem too happy to see them together. Fern broke away from Jessie and kissed Brad lightly on the cheek.

'No press entourage today?' asked Jessie dryly. Fern tried to hide a smile but turned to Brad brightly instead.

'Um. I was just about to go and make some dinner for Jessie and me,' she gave Jessie an apologetic look. 'Would you like to join us?'

Brad wrinkled his nose like he'd just smelt something bad but didn't have much choice but to comply. 'Sure. I was hoping I could talk to you alone,' he glanced at his fancy designer watch and then noticed a few people looking their way. Fern saw it too and quickly ushered both men up the stairs to her flat.

She was sure she'd look back and find this comical – having two stunning men in her home – but for now it was an inconvenience. Just when she'd had a breakthrough with Jessie, Brad had arrived to muck it all up. She hoped Jessie didn't change his mind about her being his girlfriend now Brad was here. Then she faltered for a minute and almost missed the last step.

She'd been very clear with Brad about them both being

single now, but he'd been equally clear he wanted more, so what if he still thought of her as his girlfriend? Oh man! She smiled to a couple who were walking by with their dog and watching them all with interest and practically shoved both men into her flat.

She looked imploringly at Jessie and took a deep breath. 'Would you mind if I had a moment alone with Brad while I make us all some dinner?'

Jessie rolled his eyes, but just leaned in and gave her a quick kiss on the lips.

'How about I cook dinner while you two sort out... whatever it is you need to. Come by in about forty minutes.'

She grabbed his hand as he began to leave and squeezed it, pulling him back in for one more swift kiss, which made him smile finally. 'I'll see you later, Brad,' he said as he left to go into his own flat.

'Bye,' said Brad sarcastically, then turned to face her. 'You move on pretty quickly.'

Fern threw up her arms and then went to fetch them both a glass of red wine. She handed one to him and asked him to sit down in her little living room. There was only one small couch, so she chose to sit on one of the two chairs she and Jessie often used out on the deck. She took a fortifying sip of wine. 'You and I haven't been together for a while now and even when we were, I hardly saw you.' She couldn't help the resentment that crept into her voice. 'You can't expect me to wait around while you decide between me and your career.'

'I choose you,' he said, his hands reaching out to take hers. She put her glass down and moved her other hand out of his reach.

'It's too late. If you'd told me that last year, I'd have been ecstatic, but not now. You're right. I've moved on.'

'With the bloke next door? You've got to be kidding me!'

Brad stood up and started pacing the room. 'What does he even do for a living?'

'Why does that matter?'

'He won't be able to take care of you like I do.'

Fern's mouth dropped open and her skin started fizzing with heat. She stood up and faced him.

'You have never taken care of me! I have had to rely on myself for years. I'm financially independent because I work hard. I don't need a man for that. Jessie has offered me more emotional support in the past few weeks than you ever did. I was just one of your girlfriends.'

'You were my only girlfriend,' said Bad with passion.

'Only girlfriend?' scoffed Fern. 'That's comical. You dated half of the starlets on your last film and the one before that. I'm not stupid. I was just in love and gullible. I believed your lies.'

'I never cheated,' said Brad, not quite meeting her eye.

'It doesn't matter now. I don't care enough to want to know. I understood you needed the publicity they gave you and we were never official.'

'You *were* my girlfriend,' said Brad vehemently. 'I know I didn't appreciate you enough or show you off to the world, but I didn't think that was your scene.'

Fern scoffed scornfully, motioning around at her small flat. 'But you do now? Did you ever ask me?'

'I need you,' he said, walking over to stare out of the window at the sea.

'Why?' she paused, as she did want to know what this was really about.

'You always know when I need support,' said Brad, turning to face her. 'It's hard when a new film is out and the last one didn't get such great reviews. We have to use every contact to back us up and you do that for me. You're always in my corner.'

'You managed just fine before,' said Fern, closing her eyes, enlightenment dawning. She shook her head sadly. 'Doesn't your latest co-star have the contacts to keep negative press at bay? Is the film that bad?'

Brad went and sat down, sipping his wine, clearly trying to think of what to say. 'It's not a bad film, but after the last one bombed at the box office, it has to get positive press.' He looked at her for a second, then wouldn't meet her eyes.

Fern suddenly put two and two together. She took a huge gulp of wine to calm the fires of hell that had just ignited within her and them slammed it back down on the table, making him jump.

'So little old Fern has finally become useful?' she asked.

'You've always been my main support,' he said warily.

'Just one that wasn't good enough to tell anyone about until now?'

'I don't want us to hide away any more,' said Brad.

'You made it very clear at my launch you wanted us to go public,' snarled Fern. 'But that was just after you learnt that my sister's boyfriend is massively famous and his grandmother is Hollywood royalty. I'm sure Ada and Cal loved the dinner you threw us so that you could all meet. Unfortunately, they were as confused as I was about your intentions, seeing as we clearly haven't been dating, or even been close friends, for a very long time.'

Brad flushed and got up to try and hug her, but she stepped back. 'Do not come near me. You need Ada, don't you? Do not lie to me.' Her gaze pierced his and he tried to stand straight, but his shoulders hunched over.

'I really have missed you. I didn't realise what I had until it was gone. Now the studio are pressuring me to get in front of the public and show off a positive image. I thought that having my gorgeous girlfriend and her big family by my side couldn't hurt. It would be a double win.' He held a hand out to her, but she stared at it in disgust.

'Get out.'

'Fern. I love you. You know I do,' he pleaded.

She turned her back on him and waited until he grabbed his coat and left the same way he'd arrived. She stood stock-still for a moment, trying to calm her body and stop herself from screaming out in pain. She might not want Brad any more, but she'd hoped they could be friends. She picked up her wine and drained the glass.

Jessie came back in and when he saw she was shaking, he wrapped her in his arms as a torrent of tears finally broke loose and she let herself grieve for the loss of her past life, as her final connection to it floated away.

'Did he hurt you?' asked Jessie, when she finally calmed down. 'If he did…'

Fern snuggled into his chest, then raised her head and gave him a watery smile. 'Not physically, but he's gone and done it again emotionally.'

'He wants you back?' Fear had crept into his voice, and it gave her strength.

'He wants the backing of my famous family for his new film,' she gulped and then burst out laughing at the shock on his face.

'You have got to be kidding me?'

'Oh, he wants me back too,' she said, enjoying his suddenly ferocious look. 'He thinks me being by his side will up his street cred now.'

They both burst out laughing and then she swatted his backside for laughing quite so hard. 'I'm very cool, don't you know. All of the hottest celebs want to be my friend.'

Jessie swooped down and kissed her and she linked her arms behind his head and deepened the kiss. When they both came up for air, he picked her up into his arms and strode to his flat, food clearly long forgotten.

'What about dinner?' giggled Fern into his neck.

'I ordered a takeaway,' laughed Jessie. 'It's warming in the oven and we definitely need to work up an appetite first!'

CHAPTER THIRTY-ONE

*F*ern's legs wobbled as she strolled down the beach to Genie's ice cream shop. There had been so many changes in her life recently. It felt amazing waking up in the arms of her boyfriend and kissing him over a shared breakfast. She wasn't sure if it was good that they spent too much time together, in case she started relying on him. She was supposed to be a strong independent woman. Then she shook herself out of her funk. She had sold her business, met her birth parents, moved away from the only home she'd ever known and begun a new life. She was strong enough – and she would make a success of it. Her adoptive parents had taught her well about business and she'd also learnt a lot from observing how Milly and James operated. Although they hadn't been good at change either, she'd since learned, they had uprooted their whole life for her and survived.

As she approached the lights of Genie's ice cream shop, she stopped and enjoyed watching the bustling café for a moment. She knew Genie had a night off, but she was still walking in between tables and checking on her customers. She smiled and waved when she spotted Fern and after calling out to her staff that she was leaving, they linked arms and walked up to the wine bar where they were meeting James and Milly. Genie had said it had a terrace that was quiet at this time of night, so they could hopefully speak without the local grapevine going into overdrive.

They were guided to their table by the owner, after they'd stopped for a quick chat about how all their respective businesses were doing. Milly jumped up excitedly when she saw them and started waving, which was funny as they were only a few tables away by then. James smiled at them as they got closer and then got up from his seat at the tall bar table that was situated at the edge of the deck by the sea. He hugged them both and asked what they'd like to drink, before disappearing for his own quick chat with the owner.

Milly watched him go. 'He wants to find out more about the wine they suggested we try. It really is delicious,' Milly took a sip, as if to make sure. 'He wants to pair it with one of Harry's recipes. He made a really rich boeuf bourguignon the other night. He only cooks for two evenings and your dad does the rest, but he really is a life saver. It means we can have the odd night off.'

At the mention of Harry's name, both girls blanched and Milly frowned. 'Is everything OK?'

'Let's wait for Dad to get back,' said Genie.

'You're worrying me now,' said Milly.

'What's happened?' asked James as he returned with extra drinks, looking from his daughters to his wife.

'They won't tell me,' said Milly.

'It's about Harry,' said Genie.

'Harry?' Milly looked confused and James quietly sipped his drink, whilst resting one hand on top of Milly's.

Fern took some calming breaths before taking a quick mouthful of the Mojito she'd just ordered for extra courage. She procrastinated for a moment by savouring the hint of mint and then a punch of rum. 'Um... you know when they renovated my little office at the café?'

'Yes,' said Milly. 'What about it?'

'Well, I found a box of letters.'

'Letters?' asked James, frowning. 'Who from?'

'From Harry to our grandmother,' said Genie, suddenly, as if she couldn't bear to keep the secret in a moment longer.

'What?' asked James and Milly in unison.

'What do you mean, letters from Harry to Mum? What kind of letters?'

Fern cleared her suddenly parched throat. 'Love letters.'

James almost spat out his drink and Milly gasped.

'Harry, *Harry*? The one who now lives in our annexe and who sold you the shop?' clarified James.

'Yes,' said Fern, pulling a face like she'd just sucked a lemon. 'That Harry.'

'But what does that mean?' asked Milly. 'She's never even mentioned him. Maybe it was just a fling a long time ago. I know my grandparents visited here often as they were land-lords with properties all over this area. James and I thought it was hilarious at first that we ended up meeting and falling for each other, when he's from here. I've seen a few old photos of the coastline. There were one or two hung in the old ice cream shop. Do you remember?' she asked Genie.

'Ah... yes. I do,' said Genie, wincing.

'Mum said she hated the area and that's why she rarely comes to visit. She makes us come to her. She said she spent loads of her childhood here,' recalled Milly. 'I assumed that was when she was very young.'

'I felt awful reading the letters, but once I started, I couldn't stop,' admitted Fern.

Genie hung her head. 'Me too.'

'How long have you known about this?' Milly demanded to know.

'A few weeks,' said Fern. 'We weren't quite sure how to broach the subject, as by then Harry was working with me and living with you.'

'How old was she when this was all happening?' asked Milly.

'From late teens right up until about twenty years ago. Many of the letters have been returned to sender, but he kept trying.'

'Maybe he's stalking the family now, as he can't have the woman he loves,' said Milly, dramatically.

'Or maybe he's lonely and saw selling the shop as a way to bring you here, Fern. But why?' said James thoughtfully. 'He's not a stalker, that's for sure,' he gently chided his wife.

'Perhaps he misguidedly thought that as Lucinda clearly wants to be in my life, she might follow me here?' said Fern gently and they all sat quietly for a few minutes while they digested this and pulled faces of disgust at the thought of Lucinda living nearby again.

'In love with your mother,' said James, puffing out his cheeks and leaning back in his chair. 'Is he mad?'

Genie and Fern tried not to laugh and Milly took a huge gulp of wine.

'Maybe she visited the area more than we thought?' asked Genie.

'No,' said Milly. 'She was married and pregnant by the time she was twenty, so we only came here about once a year with my grandparents. She always said how much she hated coming back and that it was under duress as her parents made her join them. I need to call her. No, that will give her time to work out more lies. It's time she came here for a visit.' James put his head in his hands and groaned and Genie and Fern patted his back in a show of solidarity. Milly gave them all a pained look and signalled to the waiter for another bottle of wine.

CHAPTER THIRTY-TWO

$\mathcal{I}$t had taken a week to persuade Lucinda to visit, but in the end she had given in and agreed to travel down by train. Milly's dad, Edward, was on a golfing holiday, so she'd been rattling around their bungalow on her own anyway.

Luckily Milly and James had a full house of bed and breakfast guests, so there was no room for her mum to stay with them. They booked her into a pretty little hotel further along the beach. Milly sighed with relief when that was done. Now all she had to do was face her mother and demand answers for even more lies. Lucinda had never mentioned that she knew Harry when Milly had spoken about him, even though he was now their lodger. Milly had kept communication with her mother to an absolute minimum since their awful argument about Fern being kept a secret, but the time had come to find out the truth.

Milly didn't want the girls or James to be there for this first confrontation, even though she'd have loved their support. She planned to meet up with everyone that evening to tell them Lucinda's explanation for why her old lover had sold his shop to Lucinda's granddaughter over Jessie's head, especially as they now knew Harry loved Jessie dearly. Something didn't add up.

Milly sighed and stood in front of the mirror in her bedroom. It wouldn't do to be anything but immaculate when faced with her mother. She combed a stray hair into place with her fingers and checked her shell pink nail polish wasn't chipped. Pausing, and then deciding she couldn't put it off any longer, she made her way to the hotel.

It was a beautiful sunny day, so the walk was energising, but as soon as the hotel sign came into view and she had to turn away from her beloved beach, her stomach sank to her toes. She was sure other people's parents didn't cause reactions like this. She'd loved James' mum with all her heart. Milly missed her warm smiles and comforting embrace. She racked her brain to remember the last time her own mother had held her, but other than once when she was ten and had fallen over and badly cut her knee, she couldn't picture it. Even then Lucinda had brushed her down and told her in a matter-of-fact tone that she was a big girl and not to cry. No wonder Milly lavished so much love on her own children. She never wanted them to feel the way she had. She was so grateful to Fern's adoptive parents for every single cuddle they'd given her daughter when she couldn't.

She stopped in front of the hotel and took a fortifying breath. Her mother had caused enough chaos. Perhaps there was a simple reason why Harry was now firmly ensconced in all of their lives.

Her mother was waiting for her in the hotel lounge, looking fresh and beautiful in fitted white trousers and a soft beige top. Her hair was swept up into a chignon and she was chatting happily to the waitress who had just set tea for two on the table in front of her. Lucinda smiled when she saw Milly, but didn't get up.

Milly dutifully kissed her mother's cheek and sat in the armchair opposite her. They were the only people in the lounge. Her mother had chosen a table by the window that overlooked the sea. To anyone looking in, this was a relaxing mother and daughter get together. Milly gritted her teeth and commanded her body to stay ramrod straight and not sink into the comfy sofa the way she wanted to, and cry. Lucinda always brought her close to tears, but it didn't usually happen the first moment they met! Milly rallied and gave her mother a tight smile.

'Hello Mother.'

Lucinda straightened the teacups before pouring them both some tea and taking a sip, looking expectantly at her daughter. 'What was so urgent that I had to come down here? You know I don't like travelling without Daddy.'

Milly tried to stop the eye roll she always did when her mum called her father 'Daddy'. Milly hadn't called him that since she was five. They didn't have the strong father-daughter bond some of her peers had with their fathers. She'd never been a 'daddy's girl'. Her father had always been too busy working or playing golf to spend time with her.

'I do appreciate you coming all this way, Mum. I know it can't have been easy for you. I want to talk to you about Harry.' Her eyes never left her mother's face.

Lucinda paused with her cup midway to her lips, then slowly took a sip, not looking at Milly. 'Harry who?' she said.

Milly gave her a hard stare and didn't speak. Her mother sniffed and put her teacup down, staring out to sea. 'What about him?' she said finally. She folded her hands in her lap and waited for Milly to answer.

Milly could feel her heartbeat ramp up. She had a compulsion to pick her fingernails, which she hadn't done since she was a small child, waiting to find out from her mother what she'd done wrong now. In the end her mum had painted this awful-tasting nail gel on her fingers to get her to stop. It was disgusting, but it had worked. Milly glanced at her perfectly manicured nails and winced.

'You know Harry lives with us.' It was a statement of fact.

Lucinda's cheeks flushed but she looked defiant. 'What has that got to do with me?'

'Exactly. What *has* that got to do with you?' asked Milly. 'Fern found a box of love letters between you, under the floorboards of the shop Harry made damn sure she bought.'

Lucinda's skin flushed bright red this time and she gasped in shock. 'Those were private! I thought he'd destroyed them.'

'Well, he didn't.' said Milly drily. 'I guess they were too important to destroy.'

Lucinda drew in a sharp breath and then her whole body seemed to crumple. She put out a hand and placed it on the arm of the chair.

Milly got up and crouched down in front of her while she caught her breath. 'Tell me what happened,' she said gently.

She really did want to know. She liked Harry, but now she felt he'd been underhand somehow. She couldn't quite work out the connections. But however awful Lucinda was, Milly's loyalty stayed with her mother. She'd always held onto a tenuous thread of hope that her mother might one day turn into a better version of herself. *Maybe today was that day*, she thought wistfully.

Lucinda straightened her shoulders and sat back in her chair, watching her daughter. *Would she tell her the truth?* Milly wondered.

'My parents made me come here every year. I spent my childhood holidays on this coast.' She sighed and finally met Milly's eye. 'My family owned property here, including shops. You already know this,' she said impatiently. 'They were landlords. It's how they made their fortune, but my father was always working, my mother too.' She picked up the now cold tea and winced at the bitter taste before replacing the cup in the saucer, spilling a few drops on the side but not noticing. 'I was bored.'

'So they left you alone a lot?' asked Milly.

'I acted out. I wanted their attention. Then I met Harry.' Milly felt that she didn't dare breathe for a moment, in case her mother stopped speaking. 'He seemed wild and exciting. He had a motorbike,' she said, as if that explained everything.

'You fell in love?'

Her mother stared into the distance for a moment before answering. 'Yes. I suppose we did. We spent all our time together and he was my first proper boyfriend. But when my parents found out, they were so angry,' she turned to Milly as if that would explain everything.

'They didn't want you and Harry to date?'

Lucinda sniffed and brushed an invisible crumb from her knee. 'They felt that he wasn't good enough for me. He didn't have a proper job.'

Milly was aghast. 'What is a proper job?'

'One that could support us both.' Lucinda threw up her hands and sat back in her seat. 'He was a trainee baker at the time. They said he didn't have prospects befitting our status.'

Lucinda's eyes filled with tears for a moment and Milly was almost rooted to the spot in shock. She'd never seen her mother cry. Lucinda got a handkerchief out of her handbag and dabbed at her eyes. 'I was devastated, but I'd never gone against my parents, so I complied. Times were very different then.'

Milly sat forward in her seat and her fists bunched, then she jumped up and stood by the window.

'But that's the same way you treated James!' she shouted at Lucinda. 'How could you do that to me, when you'd gone through it yourself? Plus I was pregnant!'

Lucinda went bright red and wouldn't meet her eye.

'Oh my God! You were pregnant too! Is that why you married Dad so quickly?'

Millie sat down in shock, but didn't give her mother another chance to lie. 'How old were you?' she demanded to know.

'Of course I wasn't pregnant!' shrilled Lucinda, jumping up too, pacing around the room and then stopping to look at her daughter's angry face.

'Don't lie to me,' said Milly with steel in her voice. 'How old were you?'

Lucinda sighed theatrically, suddenly dry-eyed, clearly buying time. She walked over to the couch and sat facing her daughter, her cheeks flushed.

'Eighteen, when we met.' She wrung her hands in her lap and then straightened the hem of her dress. 'Harry and I spent the two whole summers together. Yes, we did fall in love,' she looked imploringly at Milly to understand but was met with a steely glare.

'I was twenty when Harry asked for my hand in marriage, but my parents refused. I was heartbroken, but I understood. He didn't have much money. How could he support me?'

Milly's mouth dropped open in shock, though why the hell she was surprised by anything her mother said was beyond her.

'So you dumped him?'

Her mother harrumped and then moved to make herself more comfortable. 'I didn't dump him. I realised that what my parents said was true, and I tried to forget about him.'

'But?'

'But what?'

'Do not lie to me.'

Lucinda flushed again and kept her eyes on the floor. 'I

met your father, but then I found out I was pregnant. My parents would have disowned me.'

'Harry would have married you, though.' Milly said through gritted teeth.

'Yes, but how would we have managed? He was just running a cake shop by then, for goodness sake!'

Milly felt like her heart was breaking for Harry's suffering – and for the non- existent relationship she'd always had with her dad. Now that made sense too. And why he favoured her sister so much. Milly had always striven to make him proud, but it had never quite happened. Now she knew why. He hadn't been cruel or unkind, he'd just with-held a part of himself. That had been cruel enough when she was a small child. 'So, Dad isn't my father?'

Milly's heart was splintering into a thousand pieces. She sobbed and turned her back so no one else in the hotel would see her suffering.

'Of course he is!' said her mother in horror. 'He's brought you up and been an incredible father.' Lucinda went to try and touch her arm, but Milly flinched and moved, frantically wiping tears away with the back of her hand.

'But he's not my biological dad?' Milly sat down heavily on the chair facing her mother, her face red and puffy. When her mother didn't speak Milly smacked her hands on the table to get her attention. 'Is he?'

'You father knew I was pregnant by another man and wanted to marry me anyway. He had his own business and could look after us in Cornwall, near my parents. Not that I saw as much of them after that. I didn't have a choice. I would have disgraced my family!'

'Did you love him?'

Her mum faltered. 'I grew to love him. I could see that what Harry and I had was frivolous and not realistic. I had made a mistake.'

'Did Harry see it that way? Did he know about me?'

'Of course not! I didn't tell anyone except Edward.'

'But Harry knew anyway?'

Her mother got up and started fussing with her hair. 'He may have guessed. I was worried that he'd ask me in some of those letters, which is why I stopped responding. We used to come here for holidays after you were born, with my parents, and Harry saw you once or twice.'

'For God's sake, Mother! That must have been torture!' Milly's hands were shaking but when a worried looking staff member glanced over, she tried to smile at them. 'Why?'

'I needed to see him from time to time,' Lucinda said quietly.

'So, you still loved him?'

'No… no… of course not. But we'd shared a bond and my family still owned property here, and a holiday home. I eventually persuaded my parents to sell Harry the shop and I think as they always suspected, they wanted to keep him quiet.'

'It must have almost killed you when a boy from this town got your own daughter pregnant,' spat Milly. 'You made me suffer even more than you did yourself. You let my child believe I was dead, but stayed in her life yourself. How could you?'

Then Milly brushed the tears from her eyes and laughed almost manically. 'I shouldn't have expected anything less from the woman who married for money and gave her own granddaughter away.'

Milly then got up and left the room without a backward glance, knowing she'd happily never set eyes on her mother again.

She didn't know how she felt about Harry, but it must have been hard on him to wonder what the truth was and have to lie to everyone. Her heart broke a little further for him too. Those bloody letters! She didn't know whether to feel grateful or horrified that they had been uncovered.

She'd have to speak to her dad, Edward, about it and there would be tears there too. It was a complete mess. She could only guess that he didn't know that Harry was her father, or he'd never have brought his little family here on holiday. It must have killed him to take on another man's child, but to his credit, he had been a good dad, even if he hadn't quite managed to let her in completely. She'd read stories about men knowingly and happily bringing up other men's children, but it clearly hadn't worked out that well for her own father. He hadn't been able to treat both of his daughters the same. Now that Milly knew why, her broken heart split apart even more. So much so that she feared that she'd never recover.

CHAPTER THIRTY-THREE

*F*ern put down the phone after speaking to Milly, puffed out her cheeks and then stuffed a piece of cupcake into her mouth. She chewed it and for once ignored the heavenly flavours of blueberry and white chocolate and thought instead about the family meeting that was scheduled for that evening. Milly had sounded awful, but she hadn't given much away during their conversation. She'd said that they all needed to talk, face to face. A feeling of foreboding was swirling around Fern's stomach, but she tried to squash it down.

Things were going swimmingly between her and Jessie and even Genie had mentioned that she and Cal were managing to spend time together, which was good news. Genie was smiling more and that was one less worry for Fern. Genie and Cal were perfect together and as they were both feisty, each gave as good as they got. She wondered if Cal would be there that evening and wished she could invite Jessie, but she hadn't told them about him yet. They were not hiding anything any more, but there hadn't really been an opportunity for anyone to see them as a couple either. They tended to spend the evenings eating together or in bed and during the day their respective jobs kept them busy. She adored it when he popped in for coffee, but there was always a counter between them. Tonight probably wasn't the right time to announce she had a new boyfriend to her family, so once again, it would have to wait.

She also didn't quite know what to mention to him about Harry, as Jessie, without knowing it, was slap bang in the middle of the drama. Supposing he hated her when he found out Harry had sold her the shop because he'd been in love with Lucinda for years! There was no way she was going to give up her dream business now. Even for Jessie.

She glanced up when she heard Harry come back into the kitchen and she hated that the hairs on the back of her neck prickled whenever he was near now. She had this massive secret, but Harry had no clue that it was about him. She'd spoken to Genie about the possibility that he'd purposely left the letters for her to find, but he didn't seem jumpy or worried if she had. Perhaps an old girlfriend didn't mean so much now, and he'd forgotten about her. His impassioned pleas for Lucinda to return to him were heart-wrenching, but they'd been written a long time ago.

She watched Harry slide three trays of cupcakes into the oven and then stood beside him and helped him clean the surfaces he'd been working on.

'Is it weird being here with me owning the shop?' she asked him carefully.

Harry turned to her and gave her a warm smile, passing a bowl for her to put away in the cupboard by her head. She did it without looking and kept her eyes focussed on him. 'Not at all. I was ready to let go and move on.'

Fern's heart stilled for a moment. 'Let go? Of what?'

Harry paused and he tilted his head as he looked at her, then ran his hands over his apron to dry them. 'The past,' he said. 'I was holding on to the memory of the shop and how it used to be. I guess I was hoping that something might change for me, and it did. Just not how I expected.'

Fern frowned and leaned on the counter. 'What do you mean?'

'I was missing something in my life and the shop filled that gap for a while,' he said honestly, grabbing some tea towels and folding them into a neat pile, before tucking them in a drawer for the next day's service. He was a neat freak like Fern. 'Then I decided I needed to move on and sell the shop. Stop using it as a crutch when I wasn't really doing it a service by keeping it fresh. I was tired and a bit angry at myself for wasting time. That's why I decided to sell quickly. Before I changed my mind.'

'Was it the right decision?'

'Of course.' He said, his eyes sparkling. 'I don't think I've ever been happier. I'm working with you and your parents and I don't feel so alone any more.'

Fern sighed and smiled too. She held such affection for the man standing next to her that she didn't know if she really cared how she had got the shop, as long as it made both her and Harry happy.

'You kind of feel like a surrogate family,' said Harry, then put his hand over his mouth in shock. 'Sorry. I know you've been through so much with everyone.'

'It's OK,' laughed Fern. 'You are part of the family now whether you like it or not. We are all so mixed up. I still can't call Milly and James 'Mum' and 'Dad' yet,' then she slammed her hand over her own mouth and cringed. 'Sorry. Over-sharing.'

Harry grinned and he took her hand. 'You have two very special sets of parents and I'm sure any of them would be honoured to be called your mum and dad. Take your time and do what feels right for you.'

'Thanks Harry,' said Fern, snuggling into his arms for a warm hug. 'I'm seeing Milly and James tonight, so I am trying to get used to being part of such a big family. Lucinda is here too.'

Harry's body froze for a moment and Fern looked up to see if he was OK. He smiled brightly at her and then bustled away, saying he needed to check on their stock levels of icing sugar before heading back into the restaurant. Fern pulled a face and then shrugged. If Harry still held a torch for Lucinda, then that was for them to sort out. For now she had a busy café to run and three batches of cupcakes to take out of the oven to cool down.

CHAPTER THIRTY-FOUR

$\mathcal{F}$ern wondered if this was what it was like to be a part of a bigger family? Someone summoned you and everyone dropped whatever they were doing and met up.

She'd just finished decorating a birthday cake for one of her new customers and she hadn't had time to run to her flat and change, so she was covered in the sweet scent of icing sugar and was still wearing her work uniform of three-quarter length black trousers and a short-sleeved blouse with 'Fern's' written on the pocket in pale blue scrolled lettering.

She brushed her hands through her hair to try and tidy it a bit and had slapped on some lipstick, so it looked like she'd made a bit of an effort. The sun had been shining for weeks now, so she had a smattering of freckles on her nose and, although she spent a lot of time indoors, she had started wandering along the beach just as the sun began to set and her skin was softly tanned. She hoped it made her appear less exhausted. Running her new shop was a revelation. She'd never had so many customers and she barely had a moment to sit down or regroup her energy. Seeing Jessie most nights wore her out even more! Who needed sleep when you had a delicious man in your bed? She grinned suddenly, smiling at how much her life had turned around in the past year.

As she walked up to Genie's ice cream parlour, she breathed in the salty scent of the sea air and let the slight breeze blow away the stress of the day. She adored what she was doing, but she hadn't banked on the demand for her coffee and cake combinations or how well her little bar cart would do. It seemed that the picturesque cove that her little café was snuggled into had been ripe for a new place to eat and drink. 'Fern's' was fast becoming a destination of its own and, after discussing it with Genie, she knew she was going to have to hire more staff. It was exciting and scary at the same time. She already had a small group of part-time staff, but she'd wear herself out and lose all creativity if she didn't find more help soon. Perhaps Harry might like more hours? But she knew he'd sold the shop to retire, not be back where he started yet no longer the boss.

Fern saw that Genie's ice cream shop was quiet and the lighting low. It was early closing that day, but inevitably there usually ended up being a few customers still milling around. Being more of a restaurant that a café, 'Genie's' had longer opening hours than 'Fern's', for which Fern was quite grateful.

She smiled when she saw Milly, James and Genie sitting at a secluded table near the till, but the grin slid from her face when she saw Milly's tearful face.

'What's happened?' she asked as she rushed over and hugged Milly before pulling out a chair and sitting down. She turned to Genie, but her sister just shrugged and seemed as worried as she was. 'Did Lucinda say something to upset you?'

Genie didn't bother to correct her to 'grandmother', so something must be terribly wrong.

Genie took one of her mum's hands and Fern reached for the other. Milly gave them both a watery smile, but James' usually amiable face was pinched with anger.

'We wanted to speak to you both together, as this affects us all,' said James gravely. Fern's stomach flipped over and her throat was suddenly parched. She sipped from one of the tumblers of ice-cold water that Genie had provided for them all, alongside huge glasses of rich ruby-red wine.

James sighed and put his arm around Milly's shoulders. 'Your mum spoke to her mother about Harry and, in usual Lucinda fashion, it took her a while to get to the truth.'

'Which is?' asked Genie, taking a big slug of her wine. James' glance darted to Milly, who nodded her assent.

'You already know that your grandmother used to come here on holiday with her parents and that they owned property here, including your shop, Fern.' Both girls sat back in their seats and frowned. This was old news. Fern reached for her wine and pulled it closer on the table beside her. 'Harry and Lucinda had a relationship for a while, but her parents didn't approve, so they split up. But by then she was pregnant.'

Genie and Fern gasped and Fern held her hand over her mouth and her eyes almost bugged out of their sockets. What the hell?

'What about Granddad?' asked Genie with a cry of anguish. 'Did Harry and Grandmother lose the child, or put it up for adoption? I don't understand.'

'Have you got another sibling?' asked Fern, reaching for the wine and taking a hefty slug of it.

'No,' said Milly carefully, her eyes darting between her two daughters' faces. '*I* am that child.' She winced and watched the reaction of both girls, before wiping away the tears that escaped from her eyes.

'But…' said Genie.

'Your grandmother and her parents agreed that Harry couldn't support her and a child, but your granddad could. Edward knew about the baby and wanted to marry Lucinda anyway,' said James in a sombre voice, clearly containing his anger by the way he was gripping his glass. Fern worried he might snap the stem clean off.

'So... Granddad's not my biological grandfather?' said Genie, tears springing to her own eyes as a sob escaped her lips.

'I'm sorry,' said Milly, brushing yet more tears away.

Genie jumped up, pushing her chair away with such force that it clattered to the ground. She hugged her mum fiercely and then buried her face in her dad's chest and cried. Fern jumped up too and just stood there, not knowing what the hell to do. James stroked Genie's hair and then opened his spare arm for Fern to snuggle into. Feeling his arm wrap around her filled her with warmth and eased some of the fog in her brain.

Genie straightened up and pulled her mum into her arms. 'It's not your fault, Mum! I'm so confused.' They all sat down again and Genie rested her head in her hands for a moment, before looking up and meeting Fern's eye, and then turning to her mum. 'So Harry's your dad... my granddad... Fern's granddad. Does he know?'

'I think so,' said Milly gently, reaching out to take both of their hands again. 'Lucinda came back for family holidays and he got to see me sometimes. She never confirmed I was his, but he suspected, apparently.'

'Poor Harry!' said Fern, sniffing away her own tears. 'Is that why he gave me the shop?'

'Probably,' said Genie. 'Let's face it, that's the only reasonable conclusion to why he really stepped over Jessie to get to you... to all of us,' she sighed and rubbed her eyes. 'By doing this he's now part of our family by default, without ever having to tell us. Even without the job and home, we would have been indebted to him in some way for the cheap sale price of Fern's shop.'

'I don't think it was that calculated,' said Fern. 'I know him quite well now and he was probably thinking of asking you to buy it Genie, but you mentioned me. That way he got all of us back. He must have known Milly and James would want to come back to you. And with me here too, there would be no reason to stay in Cornwall. It was probably an educated guess to help us all stay together.'

'I feel like I can't even look at Harry in case I burst into tears,' said Milly. 'My dad... Edward, has always held back love and affection from me and I could never understand why. It causes jealousy between my sister and I, and in the end it made me want to move away.' She fiddled with the stem of her wine glass and then took a deep breath before continuing. 'I called him,' she squeezed her eyes shut for a moment as if reliving an awful memory, before continuing. 'He was devastated, but said he'd always dreaded this day. He'd tried to keep himself apart from me to ease the pain when I found out, but didn't realise the hurt he'd caused me. He thought he'd hidden it well as he loves me so much. He's spent so many years worrying that I'd find out. We both cried rivers of tears and I actually think we can now start to build something new. This wasn't his fault, or of his making, but he does have a part in the way it's been handled.'

'Oh Mum,' said Genie, squeezing her hand and then letting go. 'This is so hard for you. Listen, we need to do this on full stomachs. There's some leftover meat pie from today's service, let's have that.'

James got up to help her and Fern stayed holding Milly's hand.

'I'm so sorry for what you're going through,' said Fern in a wobbly voice. Milly gave her a half smile and leaned over the table to kiss her cheek.

'You've helped me get through it.'

'Me? How?' Fern was incredulous, as she was the one who had started this whole mess off by finding the letters.

'You've been through so much and you've handled it with such grace, Fern. I'm very proud of you. Your dad is too.' Then she blushed at calling James her dad. 'Sorry.'

'You don't need to apologise,' said Fern earnestly. 'He is my dad and I'm thankful for all of my parents. You can never have too many,' she joked, finally making Milly splutter and laugh.

Genie and James came back with bowls of salad drizzled with a herb dressing, and a deliciously baked and heavenly scented pie. As James served them all their portions, they gazed at each other and grinned.

'What a mess!' said Milly with a smile. 'Thank you all for being here for me. I know you'll have to process your own feelings. You now have an extra granddad.'

Genie chewed on her lip and Fern nudged her out of her reverie. 'It will be OK,' said Fern.

She spooned a mouthful of the pie into her mouth and sighed with bliss. Genie's tummy rumbled and they all smiled as they tucked in.

'We will have to tell Harry, though. Lucinda's lied to us all for most of our lives and that's not going to be easy for someone who probably still loves her. Harry might like to dream that we're his family, but he doesn't know for sure,' Fern said sadly. 'Lucinda misled him while parading his own child along the shoreline he lives on. How can he ever get over that? Plus he's missed so many years of all of our lives, the same way you missed mine,' she said to them all, her lip wobbling. 'We are all so lucky that we found other people to love and to love us, but what about the man who was left behind?'

Tears formed in Milly's eyes again, but it was James who spoke up. 'That woman will not be destroying any more lives, and Harry will be told and welcomed as part of the family, if that's what he wants. Now he knows us he might run for the hills!' he teased, making them all smile.

'Jokes aside,' James continued. 'Harry made his own decision to bring us all back together and for that I'm eternally grateful. I've got my beautiful wife and two daughters beside me and I for one have never been happier. Let's tell Harry what we've found out and see what he thinks.'

When Milly sniffed and looked at the ground, he gently lifted her chin up. Her eyes were sparkling with unshed tears, so he kissed her nose and handed her a napkin. 'He will be the happiest man alive to have you as his daughter, Milly. Honestly, you have nothing to worry about.'

Grabbing his wine glass and looking around the table, James proposed a toast. 'To the strong, creative and talented women of this family. Long may our adventures together continue.'

They all laughed and raised their glasses together, but Fern couldn't help but wonder about the news they had uncovered and what the dawning of a new day might bring. They still had to deal with Lucinda, and poor Harry, who was none the wiser about the absolutely catastrophic chain of events he'd begun by leaving that innocent-looking box of love letters to be discovered.

CHAPTER THIRTY-FIVE

*F*ern knew she should go inside as it was starting to get cold, but the rhythmic lapping of the sea was soothing her brain after such an emotional evening. Harry was her granddad? She'd only met Edward a few times and was still getting used to both him and Lucinda… Yet now there was Harry, too. She'd felt a connection with him from the moment they'd met, but she wasn't sure how she felt about what he'd done. He must have thought she was his granddaughter, to go to so much trouble to make sure the shop stayed in the family line.

She'd also decided in the past ten minutes that she'd have to tell Jessie. She was putting off going into her flat in case he came and asked her how her evening had gone. He knew something was up, but she'd felt it was unfair to discuss it with him without speaking to her family first. Plus she hadn't had a clue, at that point, that Harry was part of that family too.

She shivered and watched a few stars twinkling in the moonlit sky, then she jumped as she felt a warm blanket slide over her shoulders. She heard the deep sound of Jessie's laugh and she turned as he came and sit next to her. 'Sorry. I didn't want to make you jump, but the temperature was dropping and you looked cold. I haven't seen much of you lately.'

She sighed and wrapped the blanket around her arms, realising she'd missed him too. She was used to spending practically every evening with him, but the last few days had been an emotional whirlwind and she'd craved solitude. 'It's OK. I was just thinking about you anyway.'

She smiled and looked into his beautiful blue eyes. He was smiling back, but she could see from the way he was hugging his knees and not touching her that he was confused.

'What were you thinking about?' he asked. 'Is this relationship all a bit much for you? I know we've been quite full on, and we still haven't really told anyone about us.'

Fern rearranged the blanket to wrap it around them both, so he had to move closer. She placed her hands on his face and they rested their foreheads together, before breaking apart so that they could touch lips. It was the sweetest of kisses and the roaring sound in her ears wasn't from the surf, but from her own heart. What this man did to her with one simple kiss was as scary as hell, but also more exciting than anything she'd ever experienced. She felt a pang of unease about how he would take what she knew she had to tell him. His arm went around her, as if he sensed she needed his support.

'I found a box of letters under the floorboards at the shop.'

Jessie frowned. 'OK. What did the letters say?'

Fern closed her eyes for a moment and then gazed out to sea while she tried to think of a way to tell him everything without hurting him. She also had to trust that her words would stay between them and not become local gossip. It was a risk she needed to take, to show how much he meant to her. 'They were love letters, between Harry and my grandmother,' she said softly.

'What? I didn't know they even knew each other,' he said, rubbing his jaw.

'Neither did we,' said Fern. 'I think Harry wanted us to find out, though.'

'Why does it matter that he dated your grandmother? Surely that was a long time ago?' He gently stroked her face with his hand and she kissed his palm, then laced his fingers with her own.

'I've just got back from dinner with Genie, Milly and James. Lucinda's in town and Milly demanded answers from her. It seems that Milly is Harry's child. He's... my grandfather,' she winced and waited for him to get angry, but he just looked confused – and then enlightened. His jaw dropped in shock and she tried to quell the fear burning in her body.

'Harry is your granddad? Milly's dad? Bloody hell.' Jessie stared at the shoreline and then his eyes turned back to her. 'You had no idea?'

'None. When we found the letters, we just thought they were young and in love. We wondered if that was why he sold me the shop. No one could have expected that he would be Milly's biological dad. Her own dad had been scared that she would find out for years, and it had put distance between them. He married Lucinda knowing she was carrying another man's baby. Whatever you say about Lucinda, she sure knows how to win a man's loyalty.'

'This is crazy!' said Jessie, standing up and letting the blanket fall on the ground. He reached out for her and pulled her up too. Grabbing the blanket, she followed him towards their flats. 'I think we need wine for this.'

Fern pictured the huge glass of red she'd gulped down with her family, but she readily agreed with him. It had been a long and tiring day… and she still didn't know if he'd hate her when he finally realised why she'd got the shop.

Jessie went inside and came out with an ice-cold beer for him and a big glass of red wine for her. She sniffed the black-berry scent appreciatively, buying time. They sat facing each other and Jessie placed the blanket over her legs. 'So… Harry sold you the shop because he knew you were family?' he asked directly.

'I don't think he knows for sure,' said Fern, sipping her wine and sighing appreciatively. 'We think he suspected and as Lucinda would never confirm it, he had no way to find out without destroying her family. He doesn't know that my other granddad, Edward, knew the whole time. They came here for holidays, which must have been so hard on both men. I think Edward made excuses not to join them most of the time. Now Milly knows why. She's devastated. She doesn't know what to do and is kind of hiding from Harry, which is ridiculous as they live in the same house.'

'Poor Milly,' said Jessie, without judgement.

'I know. How do you feel about it all?'

'Me?'

'Yes,' said Fern. 'About the shop, and me buying it.'

'Oh that.' Jessie ran his finger through his hair and shrugged. The beautiful planes of his face were sun-kissed and his sandy-coloured hair had even blonder highlights from the sun. 'You're family. It makes much more sense now. I know he said it was to do with Khloe, but that never quite sat well with me. I can see it might have affected his decision, but this would have driven it. I'd want my shop to stay in my family line too.'

His eyes crinkled as he waggled his eyebrows at her – and she burst out laughing. She held her stomach and her shoul-ders drooped in relief.

'I thought you might be upset.'

He pulled her onto his lap and kissed her deeply before rubbing his stubbly jaw again. 'I got over that ages ago. If Harry hadn't sold the shop to you, we might not have ever met. I've got enough on my plate juggling my ever-growing clientele and having a sexy girlfriend next door who is bringing in new custom at a rate of knots. They come to buy your heavenly cupcakes and then wander next door. I've never had my hands so full,' he joked and grabbed her bottom in his palms.

She squealed and kissed him passionately with all of the pent-up longing she'd held inside her for the last few days. Jessie's eye's dilated with lust and he picked her up and carried her indoors. Her legs wound around his waist and all thoughts of troublesome families slipped through her mind and out into the evening breeze.

CHAPTER THIRTY-SIX

Genie was lying on her stomach on her old bed when Fern walked in. She had been to Genie's childhood home a few times now and she couldn't help but stare at every little thing. She knew it had changed a lot since Genie grew up there and that it had been rented out, but the fact that this was the room her sister had gone through her teenage years in, possibly staring out to sea and wishing for a sibling, while Fern had done the same from her own coastline, made the hairs on the back of Fern's neck stand up. She plonked herself down next to her sister and stroked her back. 'You OK?' she asked.

Genie rolled over and then sat up next to Fern. 'I'm not sure how to feel. Gran and Grandad have never been cuddly and welcoming, like Dad's parents, so I'm confused about how to feel. Apparently, Granddad came back early from his golf weekend and that's unheard of. Lucinda's going home tomorrow. I'd like to be a fly on the wall for that conversation... not,' she joked feebly.

Fern hugged Genie and something unfurled inside her. Was this what it felt like to be an older sister who looked out for her younger siblings? It was good to be there for Genie. Genie had grown up in this family, whereas for Fern every single feeling was new. She didn't have to balance how she felt about grandparents old and new. But then she breathed in sharply – that was exactly what she'd been dealing with, from the moment her adoptive parents had died. How could she call Milly and James 'Mum' and 'Dad' when she already had parents, even if they weren't alive now? She was gradually realising that what she had with Milly and James was very important to her too, and that maybe her adoptive parents would be glad she wasn't alone, and was now back with her original family. They were such giving people that she knew they'd have loved Milly and James. She squeezed Genie a little too hard and she protested.

'Give yourself time to take all of this in,' said Fern. 'You can't be expected to be OK with it straight away, but you will be in time.'

Genie looked at her with big brown inquisitive eyes. 'Like you, you mean?'

Fern looked out of the window. It was a blustery day outside and it fitted her mood perfectly. It was still warm but she could see the breeze propelling people along the sand, they were holding their hair out of their eyes and laughing. 'Yes. I suppose. It's taken me a while to feel comfortable in this new family dynamic, but I'm grateful to you all. I don't know what I would have done without you.'

Genie kissed her cheek and linked her arms around Fern's waist to rest her head on her shoulder. 'You'd have been just fine. You have moved halfway across the country, sold one business, started another from scratch and met a sex god in the mix,' she joked and poked Fern in the ribs. Fern gasped. 'Don't even try to deny it. We're all waiting with bated breath for you to fess up. How the hell anyone in this family hasn't cornered you for answers yet is beyond me,' she joked.

Fern blushed and her hair fell over her face to cover her eyes. Then she looked at her sister and grinned. 'Sex god?' she laughed. 'Maybe that's one good thing that runs in the family,' she said.

Genie fell about laughing and then Milly opened the door and peered in to see what all the commotion was about. She smiled when she saw her daughters messing about together and then sighed. 'Harry's downstairs. It's time we told him.' Fern and Genie stopped laughing and the room fell silent.

'OK,' said Genie. 'Let's do this.'

~

It was a bit surreal, Fern thought, walking down the stairs of her family home to meet her granddad properly. It felt different to when she had first met Milly and James, because she'd already met Harry and he had a special place in her heart. He'd been looking out for her, whether she was his blood or not.

Harry looked up from the newspaper he'd been reading while James and Milly made them all a cup of tea. His smile faded into confusion when he saw Fern and Genie's faces. Fern tried to smile, but she knew her expression was pained. Genie took her hand and they went to sit opposite him in the light and airy lounge. Genie had told her that it hadn't always looked this way, as her parents had often been too exhausted after long days at the ice cream shop to take care of their home. It had been clean, but a bit unloved, apparently. You wouldn't know that now. The walls were freshly painted in the palest blue and there were vases of fresh flowers everywhere. The scent of peonies filled the air and the delicate white jasmine flowers in the pots on the windowsill made her smile. That had been one of her mother's favourites. Her eyes watered and she smiled a bit manically at Harry to reassure him as James walked in with a tray of drinks, Milly not far behind him. Milly was dressed all in black, which was so unlike her usual stylish flair that Genie and Fern exchanged glances. Had somebody died?

Genie shrugged and the sisters shared a secret smile. Milly expressed herself with her clothes, so she must be feeling like this occasion warranted the sombre style. Her hair was still beautifully brushed and her make-up impeccable.

Fern felt butterflies unfurl their wings in her stomach. She hated to see Milly upset and, although she might have found her exuberance hard to deal with at first, Milly was one of the kindest people she knew and she was proud to be her daughter.

Fern darted a glance at the jasmine plants and then out at the beautiful shoreline vista you could see from the three big windows facing the sea. The tide was going out and a few children were running around on the sand with their parents or siblings. Harry must have sensed her sadness, as he gently put his hand on her arm to bring her back to the room. He gave her a reassuring smile and the barrier she'd built up around her heart began to crack a little. Maybe she could have one big family, rather than seeing the new additions as a threat to her past?

She gave Harry a watery smile as Milly handed her a steaming mug of tea. They all sat facing each other. No one said anything for a moment.

Milly rolled her neck and then gave them all an over-bright smile. 'Sorry to drag you away from your morning newspaper, Harry, but we all have something to tell you. I'm just not really sure how to say it.'

Harry put his mug down and moved forward in his seat.

His smart linen shirt had short sleeves and he linked his hands, almost as if in prayer. 'Have I done something to upset you?' His gaze flitted around to each of them, frown lines appearing on his forehead.

'Of course not!' said Genie, taking one of his hands. 'The thing is... Fern found a box of letters under the floorboards of the shop.'

Oh great! Thought Fern. *Now I'm the baddie.* She winced as Harry turned to her. Genie was also pulling a pained face and mouthed, 'Sorry!' to her.

'I just read part of the top letter,' she said carefully, 'then I told Genie.'

She grinned and Genie stuck her tongue out at her and laughed, breaking the tension.

Genie went on. 'We thought maybe you and Lucinda had had a holiday romance or something, but when we told Milly, she asked her mum to come here and talk to us about it.'

Harry sat back, his jaw dropping. 'Lucinda is still here? I assumed she'd popped by in passing, when you mentioned it at the shop.'

'She's at a hotel down the road,' said Milly, staring at Harry. 'She told me... well, there's no easy way to say this... You're my dad...'

Harry gasped and the colour drained from his face. They all jumped up and Fern rushed to get him a glass of water. Milly ran to his side and crouched down. 'Are you OK?'

He had tears in his eyes and he brushed them away angrily. 'I never dared to hope... I wondered, of course, but Lucinda would never confirm it. Then she got married to Edward and I had no choice but to watch you grow up with another man as your father. He *was* your father, as far as I knew. I had to watch and my heart bled thinking that maybe it should have been me holding your hand, or taking you onto the beach.'

Milly was crying openly now. She laughed but it was hollow. 'My dad never took me to the beach or held my hand. He was trying to protect his own heart.'

'He knew?' said Harry with fire in his voice. 'How could he do that to another man? He stole my child – my memories.'

He stood up and began pacing, before seeing how upset Milly was and scooping her into his arms while they both sobbed.

Genie grabbed Fern's hand and led her into the kitchen to get them all a stronger drink. Their own eyes were filled with tears. Fern's heart had shattered into a million pieces, as she finally realised the hell that Milly and James had been through in missing her childhood. Genie tucked Fern under her arm, as if reading her mind and they hugged for all the sadness before.

Then Genie stood Fern in front of her and wiped away her tears. 'This is a fresh start for all of us. No more misunderstandings – and hopefully no more hidden family!' she joked, making then both double over with giggles, holding their sides at the pain of it all.

James came in and hugged them both. 'I'm so proud of you two. Your mum and Harry have had a moment to chat and they want to talk to us all.'

When they were all sat down once again, each with a dash of Amaretto in their glasses, the emotions in the room hit Fern. She sipped the deep amber liquid and enjoyed the strong hit of almond and apricot that dulled her other senses for a moment and she took a steadying breath.

'Although I'd never had it confirmed, I hoped Milly was mine,' said Harry, looking at his daughter with wonder. 'The timings seemed so odd. I didn't really recover, or have other children. I loved Lucinda with all my heart and never got over her.'

He paused to take in all of their faces, as if he was imprinting this moment onto his memory forever. He reached for Milly and she moved over and sat next to him, as if they never wanted to be apart again.

'When I found out what Lucinda had done to Milly and Fern, I was so angry!' he looked at Milly and she nodded for him to continue.

No one there was that happy with Lucinda, so he wasn't going to offend anyone, thought Fern with a grimace.

'Even if you weren't my child, Milly, I have always watched over you and to hear that you were in so much pain was almost my undoing. I thought that if Lucinda could lie about Fern, what other untruths had she told? So I planned to get the shop back into the hands of her granddaughters to try and compensate for what you'd been through. To find out you are actually my own granddaughters, too, is beyond my wildest hopes,' he got a handkerchief out of his pocket and dabbed his eyes.

There was a stunned silence in the room and they sat back and sipped their drinks.

'Do you want your shop back?' asked Fern, a tremor in her voice.

'Not at all! It's meant for you and I'm sure your maternal grandparents would be happy that it's back in the family too.'

'You've always been family,' said Milly quietly. 'But what on earth shall we do about my mum?'

At that moment the door flew open, and Lucinda came and stood in the middle of the room, gawping at them all. She had not a hair out of place, and her make-up was immaculate as always. She stood defiantly and looked at Milly, saying, 'So. You told him then?'

Fern gasped in horror and Harry stood up, his arm around Milly.

'My only child told me that I'm her father. Yes,' he said with fresh tears filling his eyes as he stared at the woman he'd loved for so long. 'Those words should have come from you, Lucinda.'

Harry spoke with such authority that Lucinda crumpled suddenly, but no one went to her aid. They all watched her theatrics, as she sobbed that she'd had no choice.

'You could have chosen me,' said Harry. 'I built a good business and ran it for decades. I would have supported you both.'

'How?' screeched Lucinda. 'My parents were against it and the shop was theirs. They said they'd throw you out. Finding employment was hard in those days.'

'It's hard now,' said Milly, with steel in her voice as she regarded her mother with clear scorn. 'I understand it was a difficult choice – but you did have a choice, unlike some.'

'I chose to give you stability,' said Lucinda, not giving an inch, her eyes suddenly dry.

'You chose to marry a man who wasn't my father and who knew I wasn't his child. He never loved me fully or let me into his life and I grew up resenting him. It caused problems with me and my sister, as she was his child and I could never work out why he favoured her so much.'

Real tears welled up in Lucinda's eyes this time and she brushed them away angrily. She looked around the room for support but there was none.

'I couldn't live around here with everyone knowing. They would have crucified me. We weren't married when I got pregnant,' she said.

'Not everyone's as judgemental as you,' said Milly through gritted teeth.

'We lived in different times. If I'd have told Harry, he'd have fought to keep you and I wanted you with me.'

'I would have fought for you both,' said Harry, disgust on his face.

'We were too young and you had so many dreams. You wanted to travel the world and experience different cultures and food,' Lucinda pleaded for understanding.

'But instead, I stayed here, hoping for a glimpse of you and our child every year, to see how much she'd grown. I knew in my heart she was mine, but could never tell a soul.'

Lucinda began openly crying now and James eased Genie and Fern from the room.

'I think we should leave them to talk this through now,' he said as they entered the kitchen. 'Let's go for a walk along the beach and get some ice creams from a really great place I know along the road. Then we can have cupcakes and cock-tails at another beautiful café further up the beach.'

He hugged them both to him and they stopped and listened out for cries of anger for a moment, before accepting that Milly, Lucinda and Harry should be left to talk.

James left the back door open to let in some of the fresh sea breeze and offered an arm to each daughter. Then he led them to find a quiet place to sit and watch the sun sink down below the horizon.

CHAPTER THIRTY-SEVEN

A few weeks had passed and the dust had settled on the revelations of the hidden love letters. Harry bustled in from the kitchen with a tray full of his signature strawberry and chocolate cupcakes with a fresh chocolate-dipped strawberry on top of each one. He slid them into the chilled window display and turned to chat to a customer. He seemed happier than ever. He had a spring in his step and Fern often heard him whistling while he baked. Her heart swelled at all the new memories they were making, working side by side in the cupcake shop. Milly and James popped in often and Milly, too, was always smiling these days.

The café was bustling with customers and Fern had loads of regulars now. The story of Harry being related to the family had spread like wildfire, but for once, they weren't trying to hide anything, and Fern enjoyed proudly introducing customers to her granddad. Harry's eyes welled up every time, so Genie and Fern had jokingly bought him a new box of handkerchiefs with the word Granddad embroidered on them. He'd kissed them both on the cheek and declared he'd tuck one in his breast pocket with pride.

Fern had put a reserved sign on the big table by the window, as Genie and Cal had rare days off and Fern had invited them all to join her for lunch in the cupcake shop. She'd found an incredible woman to join her staff and she ran the front of house effortlessly, so Fern finally felt that she could slow down a little and enjoy the balmy days and early evening sun.

Genie and Cal came in on a cloud of energy and stopped to chat to a few friendly faces from the town. Fern stayed where she was and enjoyed seeing them both radiating happiness and holding hands. Whatever hiccups they'd had along the way had clearly passed. She caught Genie's eye and waved towards the unoccupied table. Genie blew her a kiss and headed that way.

Milly and James walked in from the beach, where they must have been having a stroll, judging by the sand they brought in with them. Fern grinned and went round to give them a hug. She had already arranged for their food and drinks to be brought out and Harry had been instructed to join them. Fern watched him hesitate as he drew near, but she put her arm around him and nestled him in between Milly and herself after leaning in and hugging everyone else.

Lucinda had gone back to her comfortable life. She did finally apologise to Milly and Harry, but couldn't face the girls again, so she'd left soon after the night of the big argument. Fern and Genie had discussed it, but in the end they were both relieved. Neither of them were keen to rehash things with their grandmother and Fern felt that space was what they all needed from her right now. Milly was happy and that was all that mattered.

Milly had her hand on Harry's arm and his cheeks were rosy with pride as Milly chatted to him about their latest bed and breakfast guests. Plates of fresh ham and salad sandwiches and homemade crisps were placed in front of them all and they were about to tuck in when the bell above the door went and Fern automatically tensed. If a customer needed her, then they came first. Her gaze met the bluest eyes she'd ever seen and her heart turned over. Jessie grinned and then faltered when he saw who she was sitting with.

'Jessie,' she called, ignoring the few amused glances from her customers and family alike. 'Come and join us for lunch.' He looked a bit scared momentarily when faced with her whole family, but then took it on the chin and walked over to join them all.

'Hello everyone,' he said. 'I don't want to impose on your family time. I was just looking for Fern.'

'You are family,' said Milly, winking at Fern and making her blush. 'Move over and make room for your boyfriend, Fern,' she added. Genie snorted a laugh and Cal slapped him on the back as he walked past. Fern rolled her eyes and wished she'd kept her big mouth shut and not told everyone she was dating. Then Jessie's warm thigh touched hers and his arm slid around her shoulder in solidarity. She leant in for a quick kiss and decided that she didn't care who saw her. Jessie's eyes were sparkling and he grinned at everyone around the table.

'I didn't know if Fern had told anyone.'

'We knew from the very first kiss,' laughed Genie uproariously until Cal poked her in the ribs and she spluttered and leaned into him. 'You two are so obvious!'

Jessie and Fern's mouths hung open and they looked around the café to see everyone watching them happily, before going back to their own conversations.

'Right,' said James. 'Let's enjoy this beautiful lunch.' Fern handed Jessie half of her sandwich and then everyone started breaking off part of their food for him until he had a mountainous plate and they all laughed.

'What are we celebrating?' asked Jessie, his free hand on Fern's leg, making butterflies fizz in her stomach.

'We're welcoming you and Harry to the family and hoping you know what you've let yourselves in for,' said James, as he filched a sandwich from his wife while she was grinning at them all like a proud peacock.

'Oi,' she said, biting into the other half before he stole that too. Fern signalled for more sandwiches and the afternoon rolled into the evening. Fern jumped up now and then to check on the kitchen and bar cart, but her staff were managing beautifully.

There was a beach party vibe as the band she'd booked set up and started playing and they all decided to stand around by the bar and help out with the sudden surge in custom from people strolling along the beach and coming to see what was happening in the cove.

People flowed into café and bar and Jessie and Cal were serving drinks and chatting to some of Jessie's surfing customers who had just left the beach for the day. The twinkling fairy lights that Fern had strung around the outside lit up the sky and the delicate cupcakes filled the air with sugar and spice. Each outdoor table had flickering candlelight from open Mason jars, and the scene was magical.

Worrying for a second that her staff needed help, Fern noticed Genie was serving at the counter with Milly while James had disappeared with Harry into the kitchen to restock. *My family are the best!* thought Fern, then she caught her breath and tried to slow her beating heart.

Jessie came up behind her and slid his muscular arms around her waist, kissing her neck and making her body sigh at the contact. She leaned into him and threaded her hands through his. People were taking snaps on their phones and posting the photos to social media, and several would probably have images of her and Jessie together. He hadn't pushed her away or been embarrassed like Brad. He just pulled her in closer and said he was proud for the world to see his girl-friend and her amazing business.

As the evening wound down and everyone left, they cleared up and then Jessie locked the shop and led her down to the beach with a rug thrown over his shoulder. He laid the rug down on the still-warm sand and invited her to join him. Every part of Fern was exhausted, but being with Jessie made her body sing with joy. They snuggled together and gazed up at the moonlit sky, just as a shooting star flew across and disappeared into the inky ether.

CHAPTER THIRTY-EIGHT

*J*essie stood by the car, waiting for Fern, and she paused for a minute to admire both him and the vehicle! He'd borrowed his friend Wes' car again and his face lit up when he turned and saw her. She'd chosen to wear a light sundress with a pretty flowery pattern and had a lightweight jumper over her arm, as it was the end of the summer and the days could be a bit cooler now. Jessie was wearing jeans shorts that clung to his legs and a casual linen short-sleeved white shirt. Her mouth watered. Would she ever tire of the sight of him? She didn't think so.

He swept her up and spun her around when she reached him and then he kissed her thoroughly until she was breathless in his arms. She fanned her face with her hand and tried to cool her sizzling skin. 'We'll never get anywhere if you keep doing that every time we meet,' she joked, running her hand over his backside briefly and enjoying his sharp intake of breath.

He caught her hand and kissed it, before opening the door for her to get in. 'Not that I'm complaining,' she laughed, sliding her sunglasses onto her face and enjoying the admiring glances that came Jessie's way as he put her lightweight beach bag in the boot and then kissed her again before pulling the car out into a break in the traffic.

'Where are we going?' she asked, a wide smile on her face. She put her hand on his leg and enjoyed the feel of taut muscle under her palm.

He smiled back as he watched the road, fleetingly putting one hand on hers. 'It's a surprise.'

She sat back in her seat and gazed out of the window, enjoying the sight of endless sandy shores and boats bobbing up and down on the waves. When they pulled into the car park of the beautiful restaurant where they had had their first 'date' she felt excitement build in her chest and he turned off the engine and sat looking into her eyes for a moment. 'This is the place where we started our own story, so I wanted to bring you back. Hopefully we'll come here many times for all sorts of occasions and maybe bring the rest of your family here.'

Fern spluttered at that. 'Are you sure about that?'

Jessie threw back his head and laughed. 'Well, maybe not all of them.'

'Let's keep this just for us,' said Fern, opening the door and feeling the warmth of the sun touch her skin. Jessie's hand slipped into hers and they walked amiably to say hello to the restaurant owner and to find their table. Jessie had booked exactly the same one, overlooking the beach.

'What works for Wes...' joked Jessie, making Fern grin. They'd met with Wes and his wife for a drink one evening and the couple were firmly back together and now expecting their next child.

Jessie and Fern held hands under the table while they placed their order for white fish lightly dusted in flour and baked on an open fire, and a succulent tomato salad. When they'd finished their meal, Jessie led her down to the beach where there was a blanket laid out with a cool box next to it.

'Is this for us?' enquired Fern, as they sat down, and Jessie opened the box to pull out a chilled bottle of wine and two glasses. They clinked glasses, and then Jessie reached into the cooler for something else. Suddenly he was handing Fern a hand-carved box, tied with a white ribbon.

'This is for you,' he said, his eyes never leaving hers.

Fern gasped. 'It's just like the one of Harry's that I found under the floorboards,' she said as she untied the box and opened it. Inside was a stack of plain letters and envelopes and one of her own pale blue branded pens with 'Fern's' written in scrolled lettering on the side. She frowned and lifted it out reverently.

'I want us to begin our own adventure, but one that's out in the open and not hidden from sight. You're my girlfriend and a huge part of my life now.'

He flushed slightly and she put the box down and took his hand. 'I don't care where we live or what we do, just as long as we're together.' She threw her arms around him and before long they were entwined in the sand, the wine forgotten.

Fern kissed him in the afternoon haze of the sun and then giggled as they were in full sight of the restaurant. 'Well, this is certainly letting everyone know we're in love,' she said and then held her breath as the enormity of what she'd just said sunk in. Her face flushed bright red, but Jessie brushed a tendril of hair out of her face and kissed her.

'I love you too,' he said simply and she blushed again and didn't know what to say next.

'Did I tell you that Harry's not only working with me two afternoons a week and offering occasional evening meals for Mum and Dad's bed and breakfast guests, but he's also offered to deliver some of Genie's ice cream orders? He says he enjoys getting out and about,' she babbled, but Jessie tucked his arm round her as they gazed out to sea.

'Mum and Dad?'

Fern smiled and snuggled under his arm. 'I realise that it's OK to love more than one set of parents. I have room enough in my heart for all of them. I know it means a lot to Milly for me to call her Mum and after all she's been through, I guess my other mum would agree. They would have been friends, I think.'

'I think so too.' He kissed her softly on the lips and pulled her up, so they stood side by side. They strolled along beside the sea and watched the seagulls dip in and out of the surf. It was time for a new beginning and a world of possibilities stretched before them.

Fern had placed the box of unwritten letters into her bag and she could feel the weight of it next to her heart. She was determined to fill each page with a different step of her journey and maybe one day, somehow, someone else would find those letters hidden away and it would spark another magical journey.

THE END

Ready for a brand new series by Lizzie Chantree?
Check out book 1, in the Cherry Blossom Lane series, My Perfect Ex, now!

MY PERFECT EX. BLURB.

The brilliant new romance from the author of, The little ice cream shop by the sea.

Poppy Marlowe, a mental health advocate, moves into Cherry Blossom Lane to escape her past and build a future with her gorgeous, but troublesome, boyfriend, Dylan.

Dylan lives in the house across the street. But his reputation as a heartbreaker is legendary and Poppy reluctantly decides that she must walk away to protect her heart.

Poppy's friends think she is perfect for go-getter **Jared**, who's ready to step into Dylan's shoes and whisk her into his glamorous world.

Taking a chance on happiness is harder than Poppy imagined. Can she let go of her past and allow herself to fall in love with the same man again, or should she step into the limelight and walk towards a dazzling life with someone new?

A deliciously romantic story of friendship and second chances at love. It takes one click to lose yourself in the Cherry Blossom Lane series, today.

ABOUT THE AUTHOR

International bestselling author and award-winning inventor, Lizzie Chantree, started her own business at the age of 18 and became one of Fair Play London and The Patent Office's British Female Inventors of the Year in 2000. She discovered her love of writing fiction when her children were little and now works as a business mentor and runs a popular networking hour on social media, where creatives can support to each other. She writes books full of friendship and laughter, that are about women with unusual and adventurous businesses, who are far stronger than they realise. She lives with her family on the coast in Essex. Visit her website at www.lizziechantree.com or follow her on Twitter @Lizzie_Chantree

Subscribe to Lizzie's newsletter to find out about her latest writing news, new release alerts, competitions and exclusive giveaways:
www.lizziechantree.com

If you liked reading my novel, please consider leaving a review. Many readers look to the reviews first when deciding which book to choose, and seeing your review might help them discover this one. I appreciate your help and support. Make an author smile today. Leave a review! Thank you so much. From Lizzie :)

facebook.com/LizzieChantree

twitter.com/Lizzie_Chantree

instagram.com/lizzie_chantree

PRAISE FOR LIZZIE CHANTREE

'Books like this are the reason I love reading.'

'Rarely has a book held my heart in its hands the way, If You Love Me I'm Yours has. An incredibly uplifting romantic story that has had me laughing and crying over and over again.'

'Chantree has a way of creating an intriguing and seemingly innocent plot that slowly draws you in and all of your emotions are set afire – The Ice Cream Shop does all of this and more and I never saw where it was going until the end and, like in all of her books, I shed more than one tear.'

'If this was a TV play I would have been shouting at the telly and weeping 'discreetly' – I loved it – SUBLIME .'

'I really enjoyed reading this and devoured it in a day!'

'Well, what can I say about this book? It's gorgeous, clever, surprising and enthralling.'

'If you haven't had the pleasure of reading one of Lizzie's books yet - treat yourself!'

'My recommendation: Get a copy!'

'This diverse fusion of drama elevates the author to another level of romantic fiction and it's truly refreshing to indulge in a story with so many fascinating and page-turning layers. I loved it!'

'I stepped outside my normal genre comfort zone of crime thrillers to read this book; it had been recommended to me and I had my eyes and heart opened. I laughed, I cried and had a precious insight into the life of people who on the surface appear, okay. I have bought another book from this author and started reading it immediately – such exceptional writing. I do not hesitate to recommend this book.'

'Wow what a fantastic book, I didn't want it to end!'

'Fabulous book filled with fantastic characters and in a gorgeous setting. Lots of interesting things going on to keep me absolutely engaged.'

'It was a happy and funny book. Just a totally enjoyable read.'

A big and heartfelt thank you to everyone who takes the time to leave a lovely review for my books! They mean a lot to me. From Lizzie. X

MY PERFECT EX

The brand new uplifting, feel-good, romantic read to escape with.

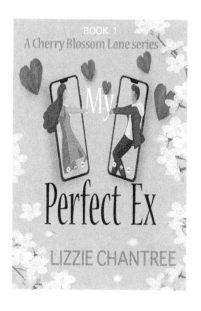

CHAPTER 1

Poppy threw her car keys into the little hand-painted bowl on the hall table. The rattle set her teeth on edge. Her hands were still shaking from the drive home, and the visit to her old school friends. She should have told them her secret. She'd wanted to, but her head had been full of worry about her mum, so it had just been impossible.

If Poppy's mum found out who she was dating, it might send her health spiralling. She'd been doing so well and Poppy wouldn't risk her mother's fragile mental well-being for anyone. The town grapevine would bring her the news in seconds, so Poppy had no choice but to keep her newfound happiness to herself. Their daughter dating Dylan wouldn't ever be a mother's first choice - he'd never settle down! Poppy saw a future for them, but for now it felt easier to keep her relationship status to herself. She was an independent woman and having a gorgeous boyfriend should be gratifying, but currently, it was a bit of a headache.

She wandered over to the couch and flopped down in between her two favourite men, Dylan, her boyfriend, and Billy, her personal assistant and best friend. Dylan immediately wrapped his arms around her and the pain in her head eased. This was her real home, not the place where she'd just been, the tiny flat she'd grown up in. She often felt torn in pieces, coming back here, to the palatial house she now owned. Even the design studio on Cherry Blossom Lane she'd just bought seemed a world away from the tower block she'd come from. She'd bought her studio because it sat on the edge of a pretty little rural village and it gave her mind room to breathe. The fields of wild flowers at the back of the property and the short stroll to the local pub, made it the perfect home for her growing business. Clients could feel relaxed there and Poppy never wanted to feel hemmed in by a town again. The new location set her soul free.

'Did you tell them about us?' Dylan asked her.

'I couldn't,' she admitted, rubbing her eyes with the back of her hand to try and wake herself up at bit. Dylan pulled her feet onto his lap and began to massage them, making her sigh in bliss. The sensation finally broke the tension of her horrible day. Then she giggled and shook him off. 'Ok. What are you up to?'

Both men looked at her innocently and she narrowed her eyes. She took in Dylan's strong arms, in a fitted white T-shirt that still had sawdust on the shoulder, and his blue eyes, framed by thick dark lashes. Her mouth watered at the sight of him. Then she turned to Billy. His blond hair was as immaculate as always, swept to one side in a quiff that he'd told her was bang on trend. He even had a little bit of designer stubble this week. She used to tease Billy that he matched his outfits to what his boyfriend, Ed, wore, but since Ed had left, he was a taboo subject. 'I would wonder how I got so lucky... except for the fact that you are obviously up to something. Spill.'

Billy caved first. 'We thought we'd cook you dinner to

cheer you up…' He started wriggling with excitement, he was such a fidget.

Poppy almost grimaced, but hid it in time. 'Uh… how lovely!' she said over-brightly and pushed herself up, using Dylan's thigh as leverage and enjoying the feel of taut leg muscle against her palm.

This was supposed to be her treat after a difficult day? It was all she needed. Both men were awful cooks. Dylan's mum had never let him inside her kitchen, as she ran a cake business from home and the place had to stay spotless. He hadn't even managed the basics. Billy was just a lazy arse who'd never bothered to learn. His attempts were based on photos in glamorous magazines. He didn't like to follow a recipe in case it 'dampened his creative energy'. The results were inedible. It was becoming increasingly difficult to keep making excuses to leave the table so she could spit it all out. Unfortunately, Billy had decided his new passion, other than their work, of course, was culinary art. The pounding pain in her head was back at the very thought. She took a deep breath and the scent of trimmed roses from her rose garden filled her senses. They were propped in a glass vase on the counter top, and a few soft petals had dropped onto the surface, mirroring her mood.

Then Dylan winked. 'But… I've just decided we're getting a takeaway instead.' The relief on her face must have shown. Billy frowned for a second, but then his eternal optimism kicked in, assuming Dylan was too tired to cook after a busy day at work. Poppy reached over and brushed the sawdust off Dylan's shoulder. 'Do you have to bring your work home with you?' she joked, running her fingers along his shoulder blade.

Dylan grinned and Poppy wandered over to the huge open plan kitchen-diner to fetch a bottle of wine. The floor-to-ceiling windows to the garden were open and the scent of freshly cut grass filled the air. She knew that job must have been done by Dylan, as Billy preferred sunning himself on the lawn, or posing for photos to fill his social media streams.

'How bad was it today?' Dylan asked Poppy.

'Pretty bad.'

He walked over and pulled her in for a cuddle and her body sighed at the contact. She loved the feel of his arms around her and couldn't believe he was hers. With his broad shoulders and tall frame, he caught glances from other women wherever he went. Poppy was used to it now, and she revelled in the fact that it was her that he wanted. She knew she could be annoyingly obsessive-compulsive about her work, downright stubborn and opinionated. She'd had to be, to survive. But he loved her. She could never quite work out how it had happened.

'So what did you say to them?' he asked.

She gently shrugged him off, biting back her irritation. 'It was the same as usual. I wanted to tell them, but the words wouldn't come out.' Her eyes clouded over and her shoulders drooped.

His voice rose slightly. 'You said you'd let them into your new life. How much longer can you go on like this?' He was an easy-going man, but she knew even he had his limits. He took the wine she offered him and sipped the rich red liquid, watching her. Then he reached past her and picked up a small remote control. As he pressed the top button, the television built into the wall began playing soft music and scenes of places Poppy wanted to visit around the world. The views never failed to soothe her.

Inspiring images were a big part of the Poppy Marlowe homes and mood panels she designed. There was a lot of talk in the press at the moment about mental health, but it was something Poppy had always been passionate about. She'd trained night and day to get where she was, and finally her dreams were being realised. She was designing the interiors of homes and helping people. She'd created a certain lifestyle for herself, too, but making others happy and advocating mental health issues, was at the forefront of her work. She just wished she could open up to her three oldest friends... and her mum, about who she was dating.

They still met for lunch in the same place they had for years. Sasha, Demi and Anne, wouldn't even try a new sandwich bar, not that she didn't love the one they gathered in. They were all fiercely supportive of Chris, who ran the café right next to the tower block. Her closest friends would tell her off for risking her heart for Dylan, even though it was going well. Poppy had obsessed about him at school, as he'd attended one nearby with his brothers and they'd earnt the reputations of 'the heartbreak kids'. All of the girls swooned over them. It somehow felt easier to keep her dating status vague, in case everything burnt to ashes around her and Dylan realised she wasn't for him. They'd look at her with pity in their eyes and say they told her so. It was a repetitive theme when they'd been at school. The Taylor brothers were trouble. Her body had quaked with fear every single time she lied to her best friends, but a laser-like determination to prove them wrong, spurred her on. It had started off with her telling a few fibs about what she was doing and who she was spending time with, but the untruths had snowballed. Now she was stuck in her own web of lies. She watched the screen, hoping for inspiration or answers.

Dylan looked into her troubled eyes and then put down his glass. He reached for her shoulders and gently eased the stress away for real this time. His gorgeous face always made her heart pick up speed and he often kissed his way up her neck when they were alone. The combination was intoxicating. Whenever she was in the same room as him, her eyes followed him around of their own volition.

Poppy sighed and turned to face him, noticing Billy eavesdropping from the lounge. 'I couldn't tell them about you.'

'Why?' asked Dylan.

'They'll hate me. I should have just told them at the start, but I wobbled and fibbed.'

'They won't hate you,' he leaned down and brushed his lips with hers. The taste of wine was delicious, but she resisted pouting, or leaning in for more kisses.

'They won't understand. I've left it too long to explain it all now. They think I'm having a casual fling with someone mysterious,' she waggled her eyebrows at him, reaching for humour and failing miserably.

He gave her a measured look and she tried to control the frisson of heat it always ignited inside her. 'Why won't you tell them about me?' he asked.

She couldn't meet his eyes, and pressed her face into his shoulder. 'I told them I'm seeing someone, but I didn't say your name.'

'Do they think you're dating one of your clients? You spend so much time in your studio at Cherry Blossom Lane. Most of your clients are over sixty and have gone grey!'

His own shoulders drooped now and she realised how much it meant to him. She had to tell her school friends about her relationship. She sipped her wine, then chewed on her lip, making it sore. Even the stunning photos on the screen of the trees in bloom, that lined the street to her studio, weren't raising her spirits tonight. She pressed the button to turn them off.

Billy, who had given up eavesdropping and clearly wanted to be part of the conversation, waltzed over and poured himself a glass of wine, sniffing it appreciatively.

'They think you're sleeping with a client?' He roared with laughter at the idea. Poppy knew she was too uptight to mix business and pleasure – but Billy didn't need to laugh quite so loudly about it.

'They know I've been on some dates,' she chided Billy and looked at Dylan, hoping that might cheer him up, but Dylan's mouth was set and his beautiful blue eyes bored into hers. 'But I didn't say it was you, Dylan. They added me to some dating app ages ago and although I never look at it, I pretended that I've met a few people from there. I'm sorry,' she hung her head in shame. 'They know you. You know them. It's a bit messy.'

'Surely that's a good thing?' he walked to stare out into the garden. It was just beginning to get dark. 'And I thought they liked me.'

She rushed over and hugged him, linking her arms around his waist and resting her face on his chest, but he was immoveable. 'Of course they like you. They love you!' she said, carefully omitting that her friends called him and his brothers, Casanovas.

'Then what's the problem?' Dylan said. 'I thought you liked smoulderingly sexy men who are good with their hands?' he joked, smiling – but it didn't quite reach his eyes.

'Sexy?' asked Billy, pretending to look scornfully at Dylan's thick dark locks and impressive arms. Dylan looked miffed for a second, then he and Billy both laughed. Poppy relaxed. She loved it when her two men lightened her mood. When she was feeling down, she sometimes wondered if she was too much like her mum. Then she shook that thought away. They were poles apart.

Her mum, June, had suffered from clinical depression when Poppy was a child. As Poppy grew up, the illness progressed. Poppy had learnt her triggers and had taken on the role of carer at home sometimes. The world had felt like it was closing in on her and she didn't have anyone to turn to. Eventually her mum had needed to have residential treatment and Poppy had coped with that alone too. No one knew how bad it had been for her, or her amazing mum, and she wanted it to stay that way. The slightest upset, or change in routine, could trigger a relapse in her mum's health and Poppy wouldn't risk that for anyone. Her mum was her absolute priority.

June didn't wring her hands in agitation as much, now that some decisions had been taken out of her hands, and she spent her days gardening. She and Poppy had lived in a tower block, so June loved the huge heavenly garden she now had access to and smiled more often, which was promising. She still had dark episodes, so she couldn't return home to the flat. Poppy did hold some happy memories of her parental home, even though it was on the fourth floor of a building that often had a broken lift.

Poppy had been forced to build a career for herself, but was glad of that now. As a teenager it was a miracle that she'd gained any qualifications, as she had barely been able to concentrate at school. It was a blessing things had gone well. She'd been able to move on with her life, though she still visited her mum every week. She also met her old school friends for lunch once a fortnight in the local café, but she had never confided in them about how bad her mother's long illness had been. She'd hidden it from them, even when they'd all been at school together. Now she hadn't dare tell them she was dating Dylan. They'd be furious at her for not confiding in them and for risking it all for a man who would leave her eventually. She wanted to break free of the expectations most locals had about The Taylor brothers. It was ok to date them, but anything serious, not a chance.

Dylan sighed, regaining her attention. 'How was your mum?'

'She's no better. She still can't move back to the flat, or come here either. Not that she would. She feels uneasy in new surroundings and doesn't like change. She'd say I'd taken on too much – and that's not true, but she'd start to worry, regardless,' she said sadly.

CHAPTER 2

Snuggled up in bed with Dylan a few hours later, Poppy thought back to her lunch with her friends. Was she being too harsh on them? Dylan began kissing his way along her collarbone and she sighed and let her mind go blank. It was a trick she'd taught herself whilst trying her best to care for her mum. Sometimes the pressure had been too much, so she'd learnt to empty her mind for a while as a coping mechanism. Now she put everything else aside and concentrated on the very hot man who was in her bed, and doing extremely interesting things with his hands.

She lost himself in his arms and wondered yet again how she'd got so lucky and snagged a man like him, especially when he'd been the high school crush she'd watched from afar. They'd attended different schools but she'd known exactly who he was, as had most of her friends. Dylan's dreamboat status was a hot topic. He'd swanned around town with his brothers and their group of sexy friends, leaving a trail of broken hearts. He was all grown up now and he didn't seem to want anyone else, which made her excited and confused at the same time. One reason she hadn't told her friends about him yet was that she knew they'd say he would smash her heart to smithereens. Particularly Sasha, who was always so dramatic. Poppy didn't think he would, though. The way his hand trailed lazily up her leg and gazed into her eyes made her mind turn to mush.

She moved around to face him fully and he tenderly brushed her hair out of her eyes. She smiled and her eyes sparkled with mischief. 'What did you do today? I forgot to ask, as I was otherwise engaged,' she grinned, picking the covers up and glancing at his glistening body. He grinned back wolfishly, before pulling her to him, kissing her thoroughly. When they resurfaced, he tucked her under his arm so that her head rested on his chest and he could run his fingertips across her skin. She could hear the beat of his heart and it comforted her. In his arms was her favourite place to be.

'I didn't do much today, to be honest,' he said, finally answering her question. 'I finished that big job yesterday, so I had the morning off. I left everything to my staff. They can handle it.'

Poppy gave him a tight-lipped smile and picked at her shell pink nail varnish. She moved forward in her career every day and his complacency confused her. The incredibly beautiful, bespoke bedside cabinets, in her bedroom, were made by Dylan. There was such high demand for his craftmanship, but he acted as though his small furniture factory could pretty much run itself. 'Why don't you reach out to that contact I gave you? Jared Wright is building ten houses and four stunning industrial barns, on the plot behind this house.' One of the barns was directly behind her garden, but you would only be able to see the apex of glass of the second floor, so she wasn't worried about it at all. The barns were already there, but were being updated, as it had been farmland before Jared acquired it. He was going to offer work-home solutions for local business people. Poppy had been thinking of how to use the land herself, when she heard it was being sold off for more housing, but the price was beyond her reach right now. 'Jared mentioned he was looking for contractors for the interior.'

Dylan, frowned and a warning tone came into his voice, 'I don't need more contracts. I'm happy as I am.'

She took a deep breath and smiled, but it didn't quite reach her eyes. 'Ok.' She kissed his nose, wishing she didn't have to get up so early the next morning. She had a meeting herself with the multi-million pound property developer. Dylan might not want Jared's business, but she'd agreed to go and talk to the man about making bespoke sensory panels for his houses, similar to those she'd designed for depression sufferers like her mum. Mr Wright had read about her ideas in a glossy magazine and wanted to incorporate them into some of his own building projects.

Poppy marvelled at the exciting changes in her business. She often caught herself staring out of the window of her office in Cherry Blossom Lane, at the seemingly endless fields of wildflowers beyond and smiling gormlessly. It was the perfect place to inspire creativity. She just wished that Dylan could see there were similar opportunities for his own work. Jared Wright could be a valuable contact and working with him might help Dylan's business grow very quickly. The problem was that Dylan was content just plodding along. He did well with minimal effort, and that was good enough for him. Poppy wasn't like that. Her persistent motivation was to succeed, to help others who, like her, were carers. She had the determination to grow her business and make it stand out and make a difference. She made a profit, but she also provided a service that eased stress for others. It was win-win in her eyes.

CHAPTER 3

Poppy glanced at the inexpensive wristwatch her mum had given her for her eighteenth birthday. It was her most treasured possession. It always made her think of her mother and feel close to her. She looked around her office, lined with bookcases, and at the large window with views over the hills laden with wild flowers, and she felt the tension leave her. Walking through the front door every day, seeing the cherry trees that lined the road, swaying in the breeze, taking in the sight of the little flowers, never failed to ease her mind. She'd read somewhere that cherry blossom symbolised love, hope and happiness. She didn't know if that was true, but she loved the thought of being surrounded by such delicately beautiful trees.

She already knew what to say in the meeting with Wright Enterprises later that day and had her figures in front of her. If Jared Wright couldn't see her product was worth the price, then she didn't want to be working for him as a consultant. She'd learnt very early on that creatives were frequently expected to work for free, and she'd had to fight her corner. It was such a competitive world. She'd had plenty of knockbacks, but since hitting on the idea of improving people's mental health through their homes, she'd never been so much in demand.

People usually only got to meet Poppy at the planning stage. She hated publicity, as it had made her quake with anxiety and spend nights tossing and turning in rumpled sheets, but it was essential for business growth. Then the fear of the worry created more worry. It affected her work, so not talking about her family was one of her quirks, and PR companies just had to deal with it. She didn't want strangers to judge her mum when they knew nothing about her history, or what she'd been through. They either focussed on Poppy's creative ideas and got on with it, or they didn't get the interview. When her company was in its infancy, no one had been interested in taking her picture anyway. It was only now that they scrambled to talk to her. She wasn't risking her mental health for anyone. Occasionally, she had to step out of her comfort zone and feature in a very high end magazine, but it wasn't often that her home life or relationship status were mentioned. Dylan wasn't famous, so they weren't interested in him. Someone press-worthy like Jared would be of interest, but she'd just be very clear about their working relationship if it was ever brought up.

Billy loved the limelight, which helped a lot. She'd found him by accident when he'd stumbled into her newly refurbished office, thinking it was a casting agency. She was still tripping over packing boxes and trying to alphabetise her bookcase at the time. She remembered the way Billy had burst through the doors, saying he had an appointment for a casting. After she'd explained the agency had moved on, he'd followed her back into her office, plonked his backside on her desk and proceeded to ask her twenty questions about why she was there. She'd been so taken aback that, for once, she'd spoken about what she was trying to achieve and he must have heard the passion in her voice about her hopes and dreams. He'd paused, misty eyed, for a moment, before his bottom had begun to wriggle in excitement. He hadn't been able to sit still.

When he'd asked where her receptionist or assistant was, she'd made the mistake of mentioning she didn't have one yet. He'd promptly asked for a tour of the premises. She'd been so surprised that she'd got up and explained that there had originally been four interlinked areas on the ground floor of the building. The rooms had layers of dust and mismatched wallcoverings until she'd tackled them, as the agency had left ages ago and moved to a smaller property down the road. Luckily, Poppy had seen the potential of the place. It was in a beautiful location on a long road, that led straight up to a picturesque little village, with views across rolling hills. The whole area was dotted with cherry blossom trees, but her road seemed to be the only one lined with them.

She'd walked him around the space and explained how she had opened up the whole back wall and replaced it with two floor to ceiling windows and a set of folding doors that she'd swung open to let the afternoon breeze drift through and the scent of wildflowers fill the air. Next she'd led him to her favourite area with wall to ceiling bookcases, where a round table was set up for creative meetings with clients. This room also led to a charming private outdoor patio that she'd screened off from the larger paved area, that ran along the back of the building. They trundled up the stairs, to the flat that she might convert at some stage, but she'd mostly left that for now. She'd picked some wild flowers from the fields behind the office that morning, and they sat prettily by the window and drew your eye to the stunning view beyond. Billy had selected the prettiest bloom and tucked it behind his ear, which had made her laugh.

The area was up and coming, so she'd bought at the right time. Everyone along this section of the road seemed friendly and a couple of people from neighbouring buildings had popped by to say hello to the new girl on the block. She'd tried to hide her nerves at being a fairly new business owner, but was determined to push through her insecurities and to wow them with the transformation of her beautiful office space.

When they'd returned to the ground floor, Billy sat at the front desk, tilting his head from side to side and straightening his shoulders, as if deciding whether he'd take her on or not. Then he'd disappeared for twenty minutes. She'd sighed with relief at getting her peace and quiet back, only for him to return with steaming takeaway coffees and two fat croissants, telling her graciously that he'd accept the job.

Thank goodness for Billy. She grinned as she listened to him singing off-key. He was one of the most important people in her life now, and she was so grateful to him. He kept her sane with his endless sunshine and streamlined her whole operation. He organised her world and had turned into her best friend. Billy thought it was hysterical that she hadn't told her old friendship group about her sexy new business acquaintance, or who her hot boyfriend was. He nudged her about it often, but didn't push it too far. He still loved theatrics and was the darling of the local amateur dramatics group, but his new passion was Poppy and her business.

She sat sipping a cool coffee and musing about the meeting with Jared Wright today, curious to find out more about the man behind the company she was visiting. She'd read about him and spoken to him on the phone. The articles she'd studied suggested a dynamic and driven man, whose business was flourishing. He caught on to growing trends and people like her, who created them, and nurtured talent via partnerships. She liked his style. Her business was growing, but there was always room for more. She wanted to employ extra staff and had big expansion plans. It was funny – as a child she hadn't even dreamt of running a business. She'd just wanted to help people like her mum, so other kids didn't have to go through what she'd experienced. She supposed that this was her way of achieving that.

At the moment her business was making a healthy profit and still giving her time to do her charitable works. But she was mindful of overloading herself. She was the chief – and only –designer, though she had a team of skilled artisans like Dylan backing her up, to bring together a beautiful product range. In the long term, she wanted to find ways of making her sensory panels more accessible to smaller households, but for now that would have to wait.

She scooped up the papers she would need for her meeting and tucked them away in a pretty folder, ready for later. She knew her presentation by heart anyway. Her business had seeped into her bones. She knew every inch of her designs and how they worked. The notes were more for her customers. A developer like Jared Wright taking interest was good news. Her usual work on corporate sites, or with small independent building contractors, was exciting, but this was a whole new ballgame for her.

Billy wandered in, looking sharp as usual. His blond hair was slicked back today and he was wearing fitted black jeans and a crisp white shirt, worn loose, with a scalloped edge. On top of that was a tailored waistcoat. It made her smile. Billy never failed to brighten her day, managing to look sharp and sexy at the same time. Poppy didn't have a dress code at work, but usually wore black skinny jeans and a fitted T-shirt with little splashes of colour. She wasn't into designer clothes, even though she could afford them now. Her wardrobe held one or two beautifully-made items, but they were from artists and designers that she'd met along her creative journey. One of her new friends, Verity, had her own tiny boutique down the road. Poppy's feet often took her there without conscious thought. Billy teased her that she needed friends she could be herself with, which was why she kept popping over to check out Verity's latest stock.

'Is that top one of Verity's designs?'

Poppy looked down at herself absentmindedly and nodded.

'You seem to be getting close to her.'

Poppy shrugged. 'She's just a friend. I'm surrounded by them...' she joked feebly.

'Only work ones. Apart from me and Dylan. Everyone else you keep at arm's length. You're as bad as you say your old school friends are. You don't like change! If anyone chats you up, you steer clear of them unless they're a client. They invite you to parties and you always decline. You're a hermit. I know you have a boyfriend, but that doesn't mean you can't socialise.'

Poppy's hand shook. She should have told Billy the real reason she hadn't confided in her friends. It was more about her mum having a relapse from stress if people started gossiping, than Dylan's reputation. Poppy was a strong woman and it would take more than a fractured relationship to destroy her. Causing her mum stress, on the other hand, made her stomach swirl in pain. Poppy had already lived through the consequences of that more than once and would do everything in her power to prevent any breaks in the glimpses of light they saw these days. She knew her mum spoke to one of her old neighbours regularly. Gossip on the estate was rife. 'I don't hide from people!'

'Why don't you mingle with them, then?'

'Why would they want me for a friend? You're right, I'm pretty unsociable.'

Billy perched his bottom on her desk and looked at her with wonder. 'You're an exciting new entrepreneur – and why wouldn't they like you?'

'I don't have time for parties. My work commitments are too demanding.'

He slapped his hand against his forehead. 'You need to learn to network.'

'My business isn't big enough for me to fit in just yet. It's not that I feel intimidated, just a bit... weird. Like I'm the hired help.' Poppy sipped her cold coffee and nibbled on her croissant, leaving a trail of crumbs across her desk. Billy tutted at the sight, then went on.

'People book you months, sometimes years, in advance, to help advise on their building projects. You're a business owner, with staff, keeping self-employed artisans in work by recommending them all the time. You make a fortune. And you still feel you're the hired help? Are you mad?'

She flinched. Billy got up and for a second she thought he was going to shake her, but he just shook his head and picked up her coffee cup to go and refill it for her.

Then he turned, smiling mischievously. 'Do you have a seedy past, something that I don't know about?'

Poppy's eyes glittered a warning, but she just stuck her tongue out at him. 'I do not have a seedy past, as you well know.'

'Then why hide yourself away?'

She sighed and looked out of the window to the soft green hills, watching the birds swoop low as they flew past in the sunlight. 'I'm not.'

Billy walked to the door and turned back to face her. 'You know you are. I'd shout from the top of one of those cherry trees outside if I had as much talent as you.'

'You are such a drama queen,' she said, throwing a pen from her desk at him. He ducked and went to get their coffee. She frowned for a moment, then pressed a couple of buttons. Soft music filled the air, while the daylight lighting hidden in the front of the bookshelves blazed a little more strongly, as though filling the room with sunshine. She took a calming breath and let her mind relax. She moved a file she needed so that she wouldn't forget it for her meeting and settled back to check her emails, all thoughts of troublesome friends and annoying assistants forgotten.

ALSO BY LIZZIE CHANTREE

Romantic Fiction

The Little Ice Cream Shop By The Sea

Book 1. Little Shop By The Sea

The Little Cupcake Shop By The Sea

Book 2. Little Shop By The Sea

My Perfect Ex

Book 1. Cherry Blossom Lane.

If You Love Me, I'm Yours

The Woman Who Felt Invisible

Ninja School Mum

Babe Driven

Love's Child

Finding Gina

Shh… It's Our Secret

Non-Fiction

Networking For Writers